CONSEQUENCES

John Huggins

New Generation Publishing

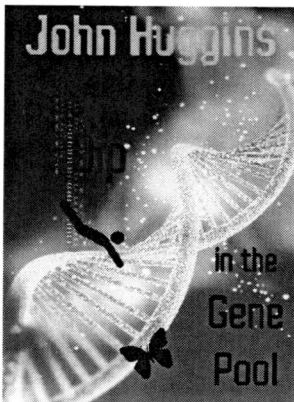

'A Dip in the Gene Pool' is a demonstration that you can attain anything you desire, so long as you crave it with sufficient avarice and are prepared to encourage other people to work hard enough to make it worth your while claiming the credit once your goal has been satisfactorily achieved.

Gabriel 'Angel' Smith is a gang leader returning to his old stomping ground after ten years pursuing his 'career' in foreign parts. His return coincides with the outbreak of a turf war between his old Eastgate gang and The Tyson Mob.
The city's Organised Crime Squad is in disarray and D.I. Daniel Loache is married to Smith's sister. One fears things can only get worse...

MOTHBALLED

J O H N   H U G G I N S

A team of 'experts' is appointed to assist with the logistics of establishing a training facility for competitors in the 2012 Olympic Games. However, difficulties soon arise, stoked by a variety of vested interests and compounded by the existence of a rare species; the elusive and highly endangered Carriage Clock Moth.

John Huggins is a member of Sheffield Authors Forum:

http://www.sheffieldauthors.co.uk/
john-huggins

John Huggins is originally from London, but has lived in Sheffield since the early 1970's. He started writing in 2010 following 36 years in the Cutting Tool industry and is currently working on his fifth novel. He claims all his books end up as black comedies, whether by accident or design.

Profuse thanks to Nick Garrett for his IT wizardry and much needed technical support; and to my wife Anne for her patience and editorial expertise.

The Countries of VOLGARIA & ASPADRIA

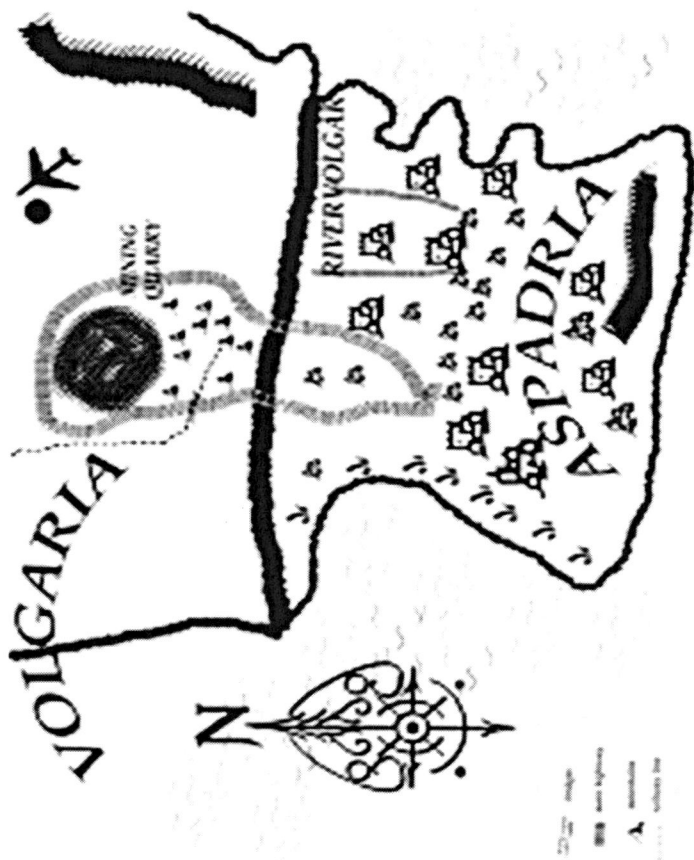

CONSEQUENCES (Synopsis)

The country of Volgaria, controlled by its formidable First Minister Stanislav Brastic, had long been dung on the boots of progress, the Bates motel on the road to nowhere and the accident that had already happened without any need to expend unnecessary energy working up anticipation.

Aborted, then isolated by its mother country Aspadria in the mid seventeenth century, Volgaria had endured a precarious survival as an independent state; impoverished, unloved and unwanted, with the worst climate in the hemisphere serving only to enhance its infinite undesirability.

In the fourth quarter of the twentieth century this situation drastically altered. A survey team from a large American conglomerate discovered that Volgaria, so long the ugly duckling, was instead a swan of unsuspected beauty. The unprepossessing tracts of land between its borders were to everyone's surprise found to contain vast mineral deposits. Overnight, the country's fortunes were transformed. Suddenly, Volgaria became the prodigal son for whom everyone vied for the honour of slaughtering a fatted calf.

Sadly, the American Government at this point elected to press their country's claim for development rights of the Volgarian mineral fields a little too vigorously and quickly found their representatives on the first plane home; but other suitors were close at hand to take up the slack, and lucrative partnership deals were struck without difficulty.

Meanwhile, over the border, Aspadrian Premier Troveski seethed at the unkind turn of fate; while the White House and C.I.A. conspired to come up with a means to regain their rights to a slice of the extremely lucrative pie.

Volgaria, meanwhile, accelerated its evolution from a primitive backwater into a twenty-first century, techno-powered, macro- Klondike; where mining engineers and industrial spies rubbed shoulders and everybody kept an eye on the door in case the next surprise was at their own expense.

Into this scenario stumbled Thomas Farlowe, an unstable, newly qualified engineer with a desire to escape the mundane and a thirst for adventure. He clearly couldn't have chosen a better place to launch an illustrious career.

MAIN CHARACTERS

In Volgaria

Past

Nervic Strumpi (1629-1653): Rebel leader, destined to become the founding father and initial First Minister of the independent country of Volgaria.

Present

Stanislav Brastic: Volgaria's illustrious First Minister.

Pasonak: Senior Volgarian Politician and Brastic's probable successor.

Kolat: } Politicians who support Pasonak's bid to

Sharma: } succeed Brastic as Volgaria's First Minister

Heinrich Schuster: German born spy, noted for his ability as a meticulous planner of covert operations.

Thomas Farlowe: Newly qualified English Engineer.

Kefira Haber: Senior member of First Minister Brastic's personal bodyguard; of Ukrainian birth.

Greta Fakhri: Senior member of First Minister Brastic's personal bodyguard; of Middle Eastern descent.

'Jock' Strachan: Experienced mining engineer, born in Scotland.

Desmond Palfrey: H.M.G.'s man from the British Embassy, Volgaria.

Yanni: Aspadrian criminal residing in Volgaria.

Masum: Middle Eastern undercover terrorist.

In Aspadria

Past

Count Otto Limburg (1611- 1668): Historic Ruler of Volgaria.

Kapinski (1627-1653): Advisor to Count Otto.

Present

Igor Troveski: Premier and guiding light of the Aspadrian Government.

Schtool: Leader of the Red Party and Cabinet Minister.

Spanzetti: Leader of the Blue Party and Cabinet Minister.

Hartz: Leader of the Yellow Party and Cabinet Minister.

Ezekiel: Transport Supremo, Cabinet Minister & Premier Troveski's Brother in Law.

Dick Crowshaw: American Ambassador to Aspadria.

Elsewhere

Kevin Cummings (England): A strangely dressed man of unknown occupation.

Frank White (America): U.S. Presidential Aide stationed at the White House in Washington.

Eugene Graveney (America): C.I.A. Director stationed at Langley, Washington State.

Comrade 'Monotone Voice' (Russia): Kremlin based K.G.B. Controller.

CHAPTER ONE

Schuster walked slowly down the steps in front of the old Council Chambers and entered the darkened underpass. In direct sunlight steam was starting to rise from the weathered paving slabs as the weather performed its annual transition from bitter cold to scorching heat and he was grateful for the brief respite. After all he had accomplished in this lifetime what a God forsaken place to finish his days. What sort of imbecile would choose to willingly remain in a country like this?

As he climbed the concrete ramp on the far side of the carriageway he considered whether it was worth the trouble to unfurl his ancient umbrella as a shield against the sun but concluded it would make little difference to his level of discomfort. His shirt was already plastered to his back and he could feel rivulets of perspiration beginning to cascade down the back of his legs.

This was only the start, he thought; in a matter of days the streets would transform into an even more hellish inferno. The tar on the road would melt and stick to the soles of his shoes and the air would become thick enough to slice with a blunt knife. The country's climate made no sense. Two months ago the ground underfoot would have been frozen too hard to pierce with a pickaxe; a month from now you would be able to cook an egg on a kerbstone without the necessity of removing the shell; yet it was this brief period in between that he had always despised the most; the rains having finally departed and the temperature slowly climbing day after day. It was the herald of things to come; the initial salvo in a brutal attack that would persist for a full six months. The first sting from the scorpion's tail; not fatal, merely intended to wound; with the promise of numerous more to follow. The endless malady from which there could never be even the briefest respite.

He shuffled on past the old brewery, muttering under his breath a curse at his discomfort; spat in the gutter as he caught the stink which still enveloped the block surrounding the disused tannery, despite the fact it had gone out of business more than a decade before; and glared at anybody who dared to meet his eye from the small crowd that had begun to form a huddled queue in front of the bakery.

Fifty yards on he paused outside a tobacconist's shop with grime streaked windows and an unreadable nameplate. He entered guardedly and purchased a small pack of black cheroots which he secreted in his inside jacket pocket. At that moment the pain started. It was not sharp; more of a fierce ache, but enough to make him screw his eyes and cast an imploring eye to the heavens. He staggered across the pavement to a twisted wire fence and leaned heavily against a wooden post as he rummaged in his pocket for his packet of pills and a handkerchief to mop the beads of sweat that had formed on his forehead and neck and were now beginning to form into a trickle that ran past his collar. Before he had even got the medication to his mouth, the pain subsided; the reaction to his telepathic prayer had been unexpectedly decisive and he was momentarily taken aback. Schuster raised his face to the heavens and with a wry smile forming on the corner of his lips waved his hand skyward in a mocking acknowledgement.

'I have no wish to meet with you either but we both know it will prove impossible to avoid one another's company for very much longer,' he derisively muttered under his breath.

A moment later he pulled himself upright and recommenced his slow trudge up the steep hill towards the wrought iron gates that marked the front entrance to the Volgarian Ministry.

CHAPTER TWO

Late in the month of September, in the far off year 1653, Count Otto Limburg paced the wooden floor of his study with a scowl on his sombre face that sent footmen and maids speedily scurrying to pursue their duties in the furthest reaches of his extensive bastion. Never a man noted for his ability to control an uneven temper he had lately offered succour to none and belligerence to anything on two or four legs that was unwise enough to cross his path. Limburg had a dilemma that refused to be resolved no matter how much attention he paid to it......and the one thing he could not abide was a problem without a solution.

He had originally speculated on summoning the best brains in the kingdom to help solve the conundrum; but on consideration had discounted this course of action on the basis that they were already present in the room. Now he was forced to think again. This prospect irritated him beyond belief.

To make matter worse his most logical confederate was Kapinski, and to put no finer point on it, Limburg hated Kapinski's guts. The man had the rare ability to be ingratiating, obsequious and smug at the same time and out of the three, smug irritated Limburg by far the most. The further annoyance was that for all his faults, Kapinski had an able and cunning mind; and, if anything, this would serve to make the man's presence even more insufferable.

Well, if it needed to be done, he concluded, Kapinski had best be summoned without delay. At least he could enjoy the pleasure of leaving the man to freeze in the glacial ante-chamber for an hour or more before allowing him admittance. Perhaps that would go some way towards knocking the supercilious smile from the oaf's impertinent face.

By late afternoon the scene was set. Kapinski, perched uneasily on the most uncomfortable chair it had been possible for the Count to procure at limited notice; while Limburg himself marched back and forth addressing himself to an invisible gallery of avid spectators; emphasising each point of impassioned oratory with an irrational thrash of an ebony walking stick that he clearly longed to bring down with a resounding crack onto the top of his guest's balding skull.

'*As you will have observed, Kapinski, Aspadria is currently a country incorporating both heaven and hell.*'

Kapinski nodded and smiled condescendingly before giving his full attention to a large bluebottle that, having paid insufficient heed to the impending change of climate, and was drowsily circling a discarded plate of bread and meat.

Limburg gripped the handle of his walking stick a little tighter and continued.

'*In the south, below the mighty river Volgar, this country boasts three magnificent harbours capable of mooring the largest maritime vessels any dockyards can produce; numerous creeks and coves which play host to our admirable fishing fleet; fertile soil that enables our farmers to grow a vast array of the finest vegetables; grassy plains to support our livestock and tree covered, rolling hills that supply more than enough timber for industrial and domestic usage. We have loyal soldiers, caring landowners, diligent serfs and pretty maids.....and most importantly of all, we have full coffers in our exchequer to grease the wheels of commerce, on the occasions when this course of action proves to our advantage.*'

Kapinski yawned, re-crossed his legs and sought a more comfortable position in the chair which appeared to be home to any number of skulking rodents.

'*Above the great gorge, however*', Limburg resumed, moving a hand to theatrically support what was apparently a heavy heart, '*we have desolate scrubland, bordering on bleak barren mountainsides, surrounded by a waterless desert. We have no industry, no farming......absolutely nothing that might prove of any benefit to this proud nation. However, what we do have up there is belligerence; belligerence, anarchy and insurrection! We have a population with a profound interest in smuggling, blackmail, rustling, murder, kidnapping and every other devil-spawned vice that might be conceived in the minds of evil men; and this combined with no desire whatever to countenance a full day's work no matter what the inducement. Added to which..........'*

Kapinski emerged from his reverie and without thought lunged ineffectively at the recalcitrant bluebottle, knocking a plate of food to the floor and bringing the Count's oratory to an abrupt halt. Ignoring the mayhem for which he had been responsible, he calmly enquired.

'Did you consider more rigorous law enforcement; the army?'

'Of course I considered the damned army, you idiot!' Limburg exploded. *'I've had detachments of troops up there three times this year already. The locals just retreat deeper and deeper into their God forsaken wasteland until my men are miles from anything that could remotely pass for civilisation; they then steal their horses, burst their water bags and if it is at all possible, slit their throats. I sent two thousand men over the Lobstock Bridge in summer; after a three month campaign less than half that number returned home alive.'*

Kapinski coughed delicately into a lace handkerchief, *'The bridges?'*

'What about the bridges?' roared Count Otto.

'A question, your eminence; how many structures link the northern territory to the south?'

'I don't know,' roared Limburg. *'Do I look like a man who has nothing better to occupy his time than counting bridges? There are the three major crossings at Lobstock, Grevelle and Chake.......and perhaps a further ten or*

twelve of lesser significance; possibly half of which could bear the weight of a loaded oxcart.'

The chair creaked ominously and came near to toppling as Kapinski leaned forward.

'And am I not correct in saying there is a Nationalist movement in operation advocating autonomy for the territory north of the mighty River Volgar?'

Limburg hesitated, partly because he wasn't sure which way the conversation was now leading; but more because Kapinski was starting to look extremely pleased with himself, which in itself Limburg found disquieting in the extreme.

'I think I might have heard something of the sort; little more than the usual idiot peasant spouting gibberish,' Limburg reluctantly conceded.

'Well, why not accede to their wishes; walk away and leave the rabble to stew in their own juices?' Kapinski enquired.

Limburg brought his walking stick down with a crack on the table top, dislodging more plates and upsetting a silver goblet.

'Do you understand nothing, man? That is exactly what I cannot do. The historical chains bind too tight. I dine with men who rule over vast empires. I would be held as a figure of ridicule if I was seen to be incapable of controlling a pack of mangy street dogs. I need to come up with an equitable solution to this problem; but it must leave no room for doubt as to who was wielding the corrective rod of iron and who was left whimpering in a darkened corner as they licked their wounds following a brief encounter with its remedial shaft. Things cannot be done that would not bear minute scrutiny in a harsh light; in this matter perception is all. I cannot be seen to be weak. It is a matter of our country's honour; and honour can only be truly satisfied when it culminates with a well polished boot coming to rest on the nape of an unwashed neck.'

Kapinski considered for a moment, then leaned back and exhaled.

'If that is the case then I believe I might have an equitable solution.'

The pain those words bought to Limburg was mitigated only slightly by the fact that within seconds of their utterance, Kapinski leapt to his feet massaging his buttock; showing every evidence his nether regions had just been gnawed upon by a rat.

Over the next hours the scheme was divulged, discussed and dissected in minute detail. Limburg was forced to reluctantly acknowledge its simplicity and brilliance. As the clock struck midnight Kapinski departed with his Master's praises ringing in his ears. He had requested no reward for his endeavours, but was more than aware of the fame that would undoubtedly come his way in the fullness of time as the originator of the *Kapinski Resolution*. The guard that Limburg insisted accompany him to his dwelling served to reassure Kapinski that his place in high society was now assured; and that full recognition of his undoubted genius would not be slow to follow.

CHAPTER THREE

The next morning at six o'clock sharp a gleaming carriage accompanied by an honour guard of twelve men mounted on thoroughbred steeds departed Count Otto Limburg's palatial castle and took the main highway heading north. At almost the same moment a farm labourer, walking early to the fields, came across a decapitated, naked corpse on a side road leading from the Limburg estate. He immediately raised the alarm and summoned the local Watchmen from his bed. After a brief examination of the corpse it was confirmed that the cause of death was attributable to a slit throat; and that they were either witness to a murder most foul or the worst case of suicide that had taken place in the region in recent times.

Three days later a resident of northern Aspadria was summoned from his bed and informed that eminent persons had arrived from the south and were requesting he immediately attend an audience at the local inn. Being of a naturally cautious disposition the man alerted half the village before complying with the request and in consequence The Dead Pheasant hostelry enjoyed its best day's trade since the repeal of the banning order pertaining to the attendance of unmarried women at heretic hangings.

'*Are you the famous Nervic Strumpi?*' inquired the liveried yeoman with a courtesy that bordered on sarcasm.

'*What if I am?*' replied Strumpi, wiping sleep from his eyes and tucking his tattered shirt into the waistband of a badly torn pair of trousers.

'*Well if you are that man,*' continued the messenger haughtily, '*I carry a letter of the highest importance from my master, Count Otto Limburg, which is strictly for your eyes only.*'

'*Suppose I am the man you are seeking but I don't take full understanding from the written word?*' said Strumpi with due emphasis on the hypothetical nature of the reply.

'*Then we are both in the shit,*' countered the Yeoman, '*because I can't do the difficult words either.*'

Several hours passed before the Landlord of the Inn was disappointed to witness the arrival of a fat monk in black garb, who reluctantly declared himself willing to act as translator. After a further hour the carriage and escort took the road south carrying both Strumpi and the protesting monk, who couldn't be left behind for fear he would divulge the contents of the royal missive. By nightfall they clanked across the Chake Bridge and in a further forty eight hours arrived at Castle Limburg to be greeted on the forecourt by Count Otto dressed in his finest livery.

Over the next few days Nervic Strumpi was obliged to reappraise his true worth as a political visionary and an Aspadrian citizen of undenied brilliance. He had never perceived himself as a natural orator and in consequence had tended to rely on his six foot frame and broad shoulders as ultimate validation of the strength of any argument he chose to put forward. Yet the Count and his retinue listened to each of his pronouncements with open mouths and clutched at each word as if it were a nugget of pure gold.

Neither had he perceived himself as particularly charismatic; but it soon became evident he had been underselling himself on this count as well. Ladies of the court fought tooth and nail for his attentions and dissolved into bouts of hysteria as soon as he made even the smallest humorous remark.

For a week Stumpi was fed the best dishes the kingdom could provide, accompanied by wines the like of which he had never known existed. Before meals there were exquisite aperitifs, after the plates were cleared there were rich ports and smooth brandies; even when he staggered off to bed not five minutes would elapse before a gentle knocking at his door would announce some vision of loveliness who would coyly enquire if he was feeling lonely and would like some company to help while away the long and lonely hours of the night.

When seven days were completed Strumpi met with The Count in his private quarters and was astounded to see that the great man had taken the trouble to record his opinions in writing. Limburg even read back parts of Strumpi's arguments that had made a particular impression and freely admitted to being stunned by their insight and humbled by their perceptiveness. He further stated that on the basis of what he had heard over the last week he felt compelled to re-evaluate his standpoint. Thanks to Strumpi he no longer regarded northern Aspadria as part of his extended fiefdom but rather as an integral part of a large and diverse family that it was his duty to care for in the best manner possible. Learning from Strumpi's teachings, he now fully appreciated the error of his ways and proposed to make immediate amends for his unfortunate mistakes of the past by giving the northern reaches of the kingdom the freedom they required in order to blossom and prosper. He even proposed a name for this new realm; Volgaria, after the mighty river that flowed aside its southernmost border, he solemnly informed a rapt assembly, quietly chortling into their lace handkerchiefs.

In conclusion, he regally bowed from the waist; and with a tear trickling down his freshly powdered cheek, clutched Strumpi to his bosom in the manner of a much loved son, before presenting him with a document upon which he had signed his name.

Strumpi was taken aback by the Count's kindness. He couldn't actually remember saying a lot of the things attributed to him; nor, for obvious reasons, was he able to read them back to confirm their veracity; but after all, the brandy had been very good and they sounded like the sort of thing he would have wanted to say, so probably he was once again undervaluing his contribution to the proceedings. His elation that his true worth was finally being recognised overwhelmed him to such an extent that without further ado he snatched the quill the Count proffered and with as much of a flourish as he could manage, scrawled a large X in the area indicated.

As Strumpi prepared to depart to bring the glad tidings to his fellow countrymen, messengers were already taking to horse, armed with copies of the 'The Limburg Resolve', and within a week there was not a man, woman or child in the kingdom who was not aware of what had transpired and taken a view on its possible merits.

Within that same week a sizeable contingent of masons could be observed on the main Chake and Lobstock highways, marching north. They were immediately followed by architects, engineers and labourers; all in the company of a large detachment of infantry which were in turn followed by an artillery unit, towing heavy cannon and accompanied by wagons bearing large barrels of gunpowder.

Strumpi's arrival home was a quiet affair. He knew he had much to accomplish and so wasted no time in summoning a meeting of the elders of the largest villages, situated north of the Volgar River. The assembly took place five days later and set out a rough constitution for their embryonic state. The vote on the name for the country was less successful, but after a lengthy debate, Volgaria was confirmed in deference to the Count's wishes. From this point things went somewhat downhill as Strumpi struggled to articulate the specific advantages of the new order; while, at the same time, taking open criticism for not persuading Aspadria to decriminalise rustling and reduce the sentence for kidnapping to a stern lecture and a negotiable fine.

Nevertheless, it was suspected that he might still have carried the day if a perspiring messenger had not at this point ridden his horse into the main hall with news that large scale construction work was underway on the south bank of the river. The hall fell silent and all eyes turned in one direction.

'*Just as I told you,*' Strumpi pointed out triumphantly. '*They are upgrading the bridges in preparation for an increase in trade between our two mighty nations.*'

One year later a vote taken amongst the elders of the country of Volgaria showed them to be massively in favour of reunification with their Aspadrian neighbours. They had little option but to go cap in hand with this request as their precarious economy lay in tatters and their citizens now found themselves reduced to eating whatever they could scavenge from the desolate countryside. All bridges over the River Volgar with the exception of those at Lobstock and Chake had been destroyed and the two remaining crossings were protected by newly constructed garrisons, manned by Aspadrian troops, many of whom had suffered the loss of comrades in earlier campaigns against their sister nation, and had little sympathy with its current predicament.

No access across the two remaining bridges was permitted to Volgarian citizens without a special warrant signed personally by Count Otto Limburg, and these were observed in common parlance to be rarer than rocking horse shit.

The ministry of Nervic Strumpi had proved mercifully concise, encompassing barely fourteen days before he was slashed to death with a scythe by one of many who favoured an immediate return to disenfranchisement.

Count Otto Limburg rejected the Volgarian reunification appeal out of hand, with the haughty proclamation, *'what is done can never be undone.'* There is a rumour passed down from generation to generation that he then crossed himself, looked skyward and added, *'praise the good Lord in his high heaven.'*

For more than three centuries Aspadria progressed in comparative harmony, while Volgaria lurched from crisis to crisis. For all of that time Count Limburg was revered by his people and regularly referenced in worthy epistles as 'Otto the Cunning.'

It was not until modern times that this sobriquet to the Limburg name was shortened and coarsened to one of disparagement; and sad to relate, in recent days the Count's name has rarely been referenced in the land south of the River Volgar, without the accompaniment of a severe scowl and an ejection of spittle in the direction of the nearest gutter.

CHAPTER FOUR

Schuster approached the Ministry building with caution; deftly manipulated the thick metal ring that released the heavy locking mechanism and heaved open the massive Iron Gate. While doing so he pointedly ignored the guard with the automatic rifle, stationed to the right of the broad driveway, screened by a bank of thick foliage from the view of by-passers on the roadway outside.

He proceeded slowly towards the forbidding concrete building paying no heed to the dust from the granite chippings underfoot which was slowly masking the shine of his well polished boots. As he neared the set of steps that led to the entrance to the central foyer he hesitated for a second to compose himself. It had been a long time and he wanted to be certain he conveyed the right impression. After a moment's deliberation he appeared satisfied and prodded the glass door firmly with the handle of his furled umbrella; watching with fascination as it swung soundlessly open to reveal the grand entrance hall that he remembered so well from years gone by. He adopted a slight swagger as he approached the reception desk, glancing confidently to right and left as if he owned the building and had reluctantly deigned to undertake a tour of inspection.

'Schuster,' he stated without qualification or expression, aware the time of his appointment and the person he was to meet would already be well known to anyone entrusted to staff the front desk.

The receptionist immediately met his eye, smiled a cool acknowledgement and reached for the phone; at the same time indicating with an outstretched palm a leather armchair offering a view of the well tended gardens.

'A coffee, Herr Schuster? I'm sure the First Minister will not be many minutes,' she added as an afterthought.

Schuster realised things hadn't changed very much with the passing of the years. Regardless of circumstances you were always obliged to wait; it was just a question of how long they would choose to keep you dangling.

'*No coffee,*' he said without preamble, as he retraced his steps and settled himself in a padded chair near to a large window that overlooked the elegant driveway. The wait would be at least ten minutes, he thought; then a further fifteen in the ante-room upstairs; long enough to consider the unpleasant possibilities that could be awaiting a new arrival but not enough to appear obviously ungracious or openly hostile. He settled back in his seat, crossed his legs and closed his eyes while he listened intently for any sound emanating from the building. There was nothing; it was as silent as a graveyard.

Suddenly the spell was broken. '*Was it him?*' whispered a young female voice from the direction of the Reception area.

'*No, his father you fool; keep your voice down,*' came the muffled reply.

They will never forget, he thought; but then again, why should they?

Exactly ten minutes had elapsed when the Receptionist appeared at his side, he noted with a degree of satisfaction.

'*Herr Schuster, would you be kind enough to follow Greta up to the second floor?*'

Schuster turned as a stunningly attractive girl with long slender legs and shimmering blonde hair materialised at his side. She was dressed in a stiff white blouse and a black skirt as big as a pocket handkerchief and smelled alluringly of expensive perfume. She graced him with a warm smile and wiggled becomingly three steps in front as they slowly ascended the broad stairway to the upper floor.

'*Anything you need please press the bell on the wall,*' she informed him courteously, as they entered a wood panelled room that could comfortably have accommodated a thirty piece orchestra; before immediately turning on her heels and leaving him alone to contemplate the departing bat from her heavily mascaraed eyelashes and the waft of imported perfume which remained in the air for some minutes after she had completed her stylish exit.

Somebody's mistress, perhaps, thought Schuster; or perhaps they take her in turns.

He refocused his mind and selected a straight backed chair fashioned from highly polished rosewood before casting an expert eye over the elegant decor. Mandatory paintings of Strumpi and Limburg adorned the walls; the former with a tasteless, almost comical, look of bewilderment; the latter more classical, with the great man looking slightly liverish; as if he had just received a premonition of what might be forthcoming few centuries down the line. An array of First Ministers, some projecting an air of confidence, discreetly garlanded with the vague suggestion of a watery smile; some with ruffled brows and lined foreheads, so absorbed in the troubles of their time that they had barely remembered to turn their good side to the man wielding the horsehair brush.

Now it starts, he thought. Ten long years and suddenly they need me again. What could be the nature of the problem that would make him solicit my help after all this time? Brastic always loathed me so it will undoubtedly be something extremely unpleasant.

'*Heindrich, what a pleasure.*' Schuster flinched and allowed the glasses case he was clutching in his left hand to fall a few inches onto the tabletop as he was caught completely unawares. Brastic had chosen to enter soundlessly from a side door and arrive at his side twelve minutes in advance of his perceived schedule. The First Minister was smiling broadly which was always a bad sign. '*Let us enjoy a glass of sherry before we get down to business; have you already eaten?*'

Schuster struggled to his feet, regained his composure and allowed his hand to make a brief contact with Brastic's dry palm. He hated sherry and his host was well aware of the fact. At least the esteemed First Minister had not attempted to kiss him on both cheeks. He had never come to terms with receiving that greeting from someone who despised the very ground on which he walked.

The blonde girl immediately reappeared at Brastic's side laden with a crystal decanter and two cut glass goblets; before proceeding to dispense vintage alcohol and radiant smiles in both directions with equal generosity. One of Brastic's special girls thought Schuster, revising his earlier prognosis. Dressed like a whore but with a look in her eye that alluded to an entirely different calling.

'So Volgaria prospers under your astute leadership,' said Schuster, with an affability that did little to dilute the three parts irony in the mix.

The First Minister was far too experienced to be tempted by such poor bait. 'Too kind Heindrich; yes, of late things have developed better than many would have anticipated.'

Not that much better, thought Schuster, or I'd be comfortably seated in my study with Mahler on the turntable and a novel in my hand; rather than sitting here waiting for you to tell me why I've been dragged half way across the city in response to what you choose to define as a matter of some urgency.

As if in receipt of a telepathic communication Brastic's smile disappeared from his lips; and with it any feeling of intimacy that had previously existed was instantly gone. Even the temperature of the room appeared a good deal colder.

The First Minister took a sip of his drink and calmly stared across the table straight skewering his guest with his eyes. 'I have a little problem that I thought might prove of interest to you, Heindrich,' he began.

Schuster sighed, rose from his chair and walked to the window, swirling his drink slowly around the glass as he looked out across the elegantly manicured lawns. He gave the impression he was grasping for delicate words, yet no matter how vigilantly he sought them out, they succeeded in consistently evading him; that he was in search of the succinct explanation that would be instantly recognisable to all, and straightway render a plethora of inexplicit babble totally unnecessary. And yet, to his supreme embarrassment, he was failing in this undertaking and in consequence would be obliged to present a blunt but painful confession that he was fully aware would cause embarrassment to all who were obliged to listen.

'I'm afraid it is all too late, Minister; to my great shame I found myself no longer competent and was obliged to retire. These days I pass my time reading books and occasionally making a futile attempt to grow roses, which, despite my sensitive ministrations, proceed to quickly die in your country's unusual climate. Sadly, I know nothing of anything anymore. Old age crept up and robbed me of my wits before I had the good sense to anticipate its arrival. My health is also not as robust as it once was; these days the most strenuous activity my Doctor allows is a short walk in the fields bordering my home; and the only problems that seem capable of holding my attention for longer than a fleeting second are those brought about by the movements of wooden figures on a chequered board.'

Brastic listened patiently; then placed his glass on the table and formed a pyramid using the fingers of both hands.

'I think perhaps you are a little more active than you are prepared to admit, Heindrich. Despite my busy schedule I make a point of keeping abreast of the latest developments in your line of business; and some of the whispers circulating give me great cause for concern. You are still in touch with a number of your old friends; is that not the case?'

'All my friends are long dead, Minister; many of them brutally murdered in their beds. I would be of no help to you. I am totally out of touch and have no understanding of the politics that play out in the modern world.'

Brastic pursed his lips and permitted a small scowl.

'Be very careful, Heindrich. It is no secret the Israelis are still showing an interest and even for a man of your advanced years there would be severe repercussions. They won't forget you know and they certainly have no intention of forgiving. When you answer my questions, please keep in mind that the last ship set sail for Argentina a very long time ago.'

Schuster snorted indignantly.

'It was nothing to do with me, as you are well aware. It is not possible to visit the sins of the father upon the son no matter how much they will insist on trying.'

Brastic laughed loudly and clapped his hands as if acknowledging the conclusion to a pleasing theatre performance.

'Heindrich, Heindrich, why do we have to once again play out this silly charade? It is my eyesight that is failing not my memory. Do you imagine the photographs that I had in my library were mislaid; or perhaps you suspect they decomposed with age? I know what you did; you also know what you did though you persist in pleading ignorance despite a mountain of clear evidence to the contrary. In the end you know you will be obliged to accommodate my request, because a refusal to do so would very quickly see you lying dead in the gutter. In my view you would very probably say yes to what I am about to ask even if that wasn't the case. The reason being; I believe my proposal cannot fail to intrigue you. So, please don't let us go through all this unpleasantness for no good cause. Just accept my little commission and in a week you will be back sitting in the study of your nice little house and this will all be over and forgotten. The only difference you will notice is that the bank manager will rush to hold the door for you the next time you choose to grace his premises.'

Schuster settled back in his chair. The pain in his chest was returning but it had to be worth one last throw of the dice before he was obliged to capitulate. He sensed he would need to make it a good. Brastic was smiling again. He gave an involuntary shudder.

'I think it has escaped your memory, First Minister, that I know too much for you to blackmail me.'

The smile for a second left Brastic's face and he stared sternly across the table from behind hooded eyes; then without warning he relaxed and broke into a broad smile.

'On the contrary, Heindrich, you know exactly the right amount; which is the precise reason I selected you to play a part in this little enterprise.'

CHAPTER FIVE

It was so out of character there had to have been some sort of catalyst to initiate the chain reaction. Granted, the loss of both parents in a car crash could be seen as part of the explanation; as could missing a First Class degree by a couple of marks when it had at one time seemed a nailed on certainty. However, anybody believing either of those was the real reason would most definitely have been barking up the wrong tree.

What started the avalanche that would have such far reaching consequences was a clap of the hands from Kevin Cummings. Kevin Cummings, who would go to his grave still sporting a downturned moustache and a pair of wispy sideburns which succinctly demonstrated why taste had chosen to wipe the 1970's from its memory banks. The same Kevin Cummings, who confided without embarrassment, that he had a fully operational model train set in his loft; and still remained an avid collector of the inappropriate enamel brooches which had once been obtainable by the surrender of stickers from a suitable marmalade jar. Kevin Cummings, who maintained the unreserved right to have a crisp crease ironed into his stonewashed blue denim jeans; and held his head high while walking the streets in thick platform soled boots, years after the dictates of fashion demanded the practice should be discontinued. Kevin Cummings, so bereft of taste it was amazing a queue of unfortunates did not gather at his side in an effort to demonstrate that whilst they might also get it wrong, they would never get it as badly wrong as this man; or at least not without a good deal more application and practise.

There should of course have been some sort of law prohibiting the likes of Cummings from any form of international travel. It was nothing short of immoral to inflict such a person on countries that had already been obliged to cope with despotic leaders, starvation, drought, natural disasters, outbreaks of foul wasting diseases and a variety of new strains of debilitating plague. Had these lands not already suffered enough without adding to their burden?

Yet it came to pass a sun bronzed and clearly affluent Kevin Cummings could be found sprawled indecorously on an imitation leather armchair in the plush reception area of the hotel that had that year been chosen to play host to the annual University Leavers' Dinner for engineering students; and unperturbed by the fact he was neither a student nor a master, and in fact lacked even the most tenuous connection to the University's engineering faculty, Cummings remained regally ensconced, showing a supreme willingness to tip back a glass of anything on offer and regale any poor sod who could not get out of his way fast enough with tales of his travels to faraway lands.

Why exactly he was there in the first place nobody seemed fully aware; but he exuded such supreme confidence that it was difficult to imagine it was by an error of his own making and much more likely it was due to an oversight which at this late hour it was impossible to correct. And for that reason alone Cummings remained unmolested by the forces of officialdom; allowing his planet to freely revolve on its axis and patiently wait for Thomas Farlowe to be attracted by his gravitational pull.

Yes, it should be admitted Farlowe was slightly the worse for wear after front loading three parts of a bottle of Polish vodka before leaving his home; and choosing, bravely if unwisely, to chase that down with several glasses of warm and extremely indifferent Chardonnay, provided at no extra charge by the dinner's organisers, in order to set the evening off on the right foot. This, however, still fails to fully explain why Farlowe chose to abandon a hot date with alcoholic oblivion in order to stop and listen to Cummings' honeyed words; but listen he did; and at that unlikely moment a seed of destiny was first sown, fertilised, and if we are to remain completely objective on this subject, scandalously over watered.

Scarcely seven days had elapsed following his rendezvous with fate when the Farlowe residence sprouted a wooden board, proclaiming to the world its availability for immediate purchase; two more sunrises passed and a barely comprehensible note was scribbled and posted to the Rolls Royce Company in Derby, explaining that due to unforeseen circumstances he would be unable to join their labour force the following month, or for that matter for the foreseeable future; and seven days further down the line a Norton motor cycle of considerable age and indifferent pedigree materialised from a Breakers yard near Luton, and could be freely observed in a semi-horizontal position, freely belching oil onto the flagstones of Chez Farlowe's ravaged front patio.

It was slightly more than nine months later, when confined to a hospital bed in the unlovely country of Volgaria, that Farlowe finally had the opportunity to sit back and dispassionately review the misfortunes that had recently befallen him.

Sprawled on a blood splattered, lumpy mattress in this miserable corner of the world, hundreds of miles from any vestige of civilisation and with barely a brass farthing to his name, he first began to consider how this situation had ever been allowed to come about; and with sweat trickling languidly from his careworn brow as he laboured to hold rigid a broken collar bone that seemed resolutely disinclined to heal he pondered the matter yet further; and despite quite understandably feeling somewhat less than overflowing with the milk of human kindness, the cogs of his mind proceeded to grind slowly but remorselessly forward in pursuit of a satisfactory resolution.

It was then, and only then, after he had finally been able to cogitate to his heart's content and view each minute of the preceding months with a clarity and perspective that had hitherto been denied, that he felt able to unreservedly apportion the requisite blame for the sorry entanglement in which he now found himself inescapably enmeshed.

All right, he would be the first to concede he had been a little hasty in his actions and even possibly a teensy bit thoughtless; though, in his defence, he had at the time been emotionally vulnerable and seeking solace in the bottom of a glass. However, taking all the relevant factors into account; prejudging nothing; dispassionately weighing each individual issue without a hint of partiality, bias or prejudice, he had come to the conclusion there was no alternative other than to lay the blame squarely at the door of Kevin Cummings; for had he not been beguiled by the conjured images portrayed so vividly on that warm summer's evening a few short months ago, it was clear his life might have taken an altogether different direction; and it was equally obvious that no matter what the alternative might have offered, it could only have played out more to his personal advantage.

Farlowe lay on his bed wishing he had a cigarette and a decent novel so he had an excuse to delay confronting reality. It was fair to say, the place where he had ended up was unlikely to feature on a calendar depicting exotic resorts that it was essential to visit before they became overexploited due to cheapening air fares. It certainly didn't spring to mind as any of the locations described with such eloquence by the sartorially challenged Mr Cummings either. Granted, it could legitimately be tagged as unusual; some might have gone so far as to say, weird; strange enough in fact that anyone in possession of their full faculties might well have considered it wise to venture back across the country's porous borders with the minimum of delay. There were however logistical problems to address before he could consider making a less than dignified exit. His injury was at last on the mend but his motor cycle was a write off and his remaining traveller's cheques had mysteriously disappeared when the emergency services had conveyed him from the scene of the crash to his hospital bed.

He wasn't totally naive. He had always realised it would be necessary to seek some form of employment once he had stumbled across a suitably desirable location to lay down some temporary roots, but those lofty ambitions had in no way been directed at this miserable corner of the earth. This country was positively unpleasant. This was the sort of place you left in an attempt to better yourself, not one you considered entering in search of job satisfaction. He had only chosen to pass through its territory in the first place when an unfortunate misunderstanding with a police constable over a small quantity of marijuana had made it expedient for him to evacuate altogether more convivial surroundings with the minimum possible delay; and that had been as a final resort when his map refused to provide any other reasonable alternative. The only facts he could state about the country of Volgaria with any degree of certainty were that the food was foul, the infrastructure primitive and the climate positively unpleasant.

However, now the gods of fortune had chosen not to smile on his plans for a gap year he was forced to entertain thoughts that under different circumstances would be classified as unthinkable. Namely, that perhaps it was possible this could be just the sort of God-forsaken backwater that might be prepared to offer employment to an engineer with a second class degree, limited practical experience and no work permit.

He casually broached the subject with a nurse who had mysteriously found her way here from some far flung corner of North Africa. She could offer no practical advice but located a dog eared copy of a quarterly periodical, written in English, and apparently aimed at stock market investors. The magazine spoke volumes about the country's development possibilities, though a

25

good deal of the language that was used proved totally incomprehensible to someone who filed their bank statements in the waste paper basket. It transpired that the Country of Volgaria had until the last quarter of the twentieth century been the sort of place you avoided like the plague; in fact you would be wise to avoid it even if you had the plague because you could certainly guarantee the hospital facilities would do little to set you on the road to a full recovery. The country had no assets, no resources and as far as anybody could detect no hope of changing that status any time between now and the final run down to Armageddon. Volgaria was an overnight stop on the road to nowhere. It was a country that was liked by nobody; it didn't even seem to like itself. It was so badly regarded that following the Second World War, the Soviet Union had purposely ensured Volgaria was positioned on the western side of the Iron Curtain.

Then, out of the blue, an American-owned Mining Company with regional offices in Switzerland had entered into negotiations with the Volgarian Government to undertake a survey to search for mineral deposits. (There was a heavy handed editorial allusion to the fact that the permission would probably have been granted on the basis of a suitable bribe rather than a business initiative.) Surprisingly, the venture had proved a massive success. The survey found evidence of coal, natural gas and oil on the Volgarian plains and small deposits of silver in the range of hills running to the east of the country.

Eureka! The surveyors were at this point about to retire home more than satisfied with the outcome of their endeavours. However, while their luck was good and their plant was not desperately required elsewhere they took a gamble and extended exploration for a further week........and as a consequence of this entrepreneurial gamble they struck pay dirt in such proportions that it dwarfed their earlier findings to the periphery of significance. They found iron ore; they found it in such vast quantities that they radioed to their district office to report an equipment malfunction. When the initial euphoria had been controlled, analysts confirmed it to be one of the largest deposits ever discovered in the history of the planet; and the quality of the rock to far surpass anything currently being mined at any other location in the world.

Farlowe paused, skip read several pages which appeared to cover a lot of boring detail about joint ventures to build a railway line and an airport, and then started taking interest again when the paper took great relish in raking over an unresolved dispute between the American surveyors, who at their Government's behest had demanded exclusive drilling rights, and the Volgarian authorities, who clearly weren't intent on giving them.

The negotiations on the subject started badly and quickly deteriorated; culminating in the Americans being unceremoniously shepherded to the Volgarian border by armed militia. That must have really angered the US interests after the work they had put in on the initial survey, Farlowe surmised. He skimmed further down the page; Volgaria was now estimated to have the second largest deposit of iron ore in the entire world!

The article branched into a very enthusiastic précis by the editor, culminating in the suggestion that its readers, 'get into Volgaria without delay'..........and offering a sister company's services to assist them in doing exactly that. Farlowe turned back to the front page; the magazine was dated two years previously and from the quality of the journalism was probably already out of business.

Now his interest was aroused he decided it was only sensible to get a current analysis. He employed all his charm to persuade a young Doctor to loan him her laptop and set about reading all the snippets of information the article hadn't chosen to touch upon. When he had finished the picture was a good deal less rosy. Volgaria came across as the point on the planet where East European repression met the California gold rush. It didn't sound like the sort of place where health and safety had been heard of, let alone regarded as a major issue; but on the other hand it also didn't sound like the sort of place where anybody would be overly concerned about the lack of a work permit or a disappointing showing in his final paper. It didn't in fact sound like the sort of place where paperwork would count for anything at all.

CHAPTER SIX

The Aspadrian Parliament convened daily, Monday to Friday, but Thursdays were always regarded as something special. On Thursdays there was a meeting of the inner Cabinet, so in theory at least this was the day when big decisions were taken and fresh initiatives presented for consideration and debate.

Aspadria had come a long way since the days when it religiously followed the dictates of Count Limburg and over the years had chosen to embrace most forms of Government. In the intervening years it had experienced several bloodless coups that had resulted in large swathes of the population being horrifically butchered; two popular uprisings, that proved so unpopular that anyone found to be in any way involved had been put up against a wall and summarily executed; and a cunningly orchestrated revolution that expended so much energy on its planning and implementation that it somehow lost sight of what it had intended to achieve when it eventually took power, and in consequence imploded immediately after seizing control.

Over the years Aspadria had flirted with Fascism, Anarchism, Communism and any number of varieties of Radicalism, all with similarly unhappy outcomes; in the end settling upon, a convoluted form of Democracy that in practise amounted to little more than a benign Dictatorship. The inner workings of the Aspadrian government system were fully understood by very few people; least of all the Aspadrian voter who regarded the requirement to make their way to the polling station every few years as an unnecessary imposition when it was clear to anyone with half a brain that no matter which way they cast their ballot their lot in life would invariably remain unchanged. The populous were however, prepared to stand in the streets and wave flags in support of virtually anyone who was prepared to offer a day's holiday and unlimited access to supplies of free alcohol.

The actual power house of the current administration was an inner sanctum consisting of appointed representatives from the three major Political parties. These august personages broadly agreed on everything of importance, but were prepared to bicker incessantly over issues of minor relevance, so that nobody could accuse them of not taking their responsibilities seriously. Their ranks were supplemented by a sprinkling of senior military figures who paid little heed to anything other than initiatives that might in some way affect their careers. Added to the mix were an assortment of luminaries appointed to represent diverse factions whose interests might, it was suspected, have been otherwise overlooked. The actual make up of the delegation was interesting but largely irrelevant. Nothing ever passed into law in the country of Aspadria unless its need was assessed and personally approved by the country's Premier, and he made a point of putting his signature to very little. However, this in no way deterred the cabinet officials from examining every issue put before them with the vigilance you would expect from men whose salaries and commodious accommodation was dependent upon being seen to do their duty to the best of their abilities; as aptly demonstrated by the attention now being lavished upon the weighty matters that were currently under scrutiny.

'If you had listened to me in the first place we wouldn't be in this mess,' said Schtool of the Red Party.

'We listened to you over the American Fleet,' said Spranzetti of the Blue Party,' *and look where that got us.'*

'There is no point in dredging all that up again,' said Hartz of the Yellow Party, immediately regretting his unfortunate choice of words. It still rankled with Hartz that he had somehow been goaded into supporting Schtool on that fateful day and he had been ruing his impetuosity ever since.

'Regardless of what you say, it is plain the Americans will remain firmly behind us,' said Schtool.

'So far behind us that they sold us a consignment of faulty armaments and then chose to harbour their fleet in Turkish waters,' countered Spanzetti bitterly. *'Despite what you say, Schtool, it's abundantly obvious to anybody who can see further than the end of their nose that the Americans don't like us at all; they just dislike us a little less than the Volgarians.'*

'They dislike everybody less than the Volgarians, since their mining surveyors got chucked out of the country,' said Hartz who had once enjoyed a camping holiday on the Italian Adriatic coast and had thereafter been able to successfully impose his views on the governing body as an authority on international affairs.

'Do you really think it wise to consider allowing the Americans to set up camps in this country? To get intoxicated in our bars and rampage unhindered through our streets urinating in the gutters and propositioning our virtuous womenfolk?' said a Bishop, appointed specifically to consider all matters under debate from an ecclesiastical prospective. The Bishop, for reasons best known to himself, rarely left the confines of a nearby hostelry; however, he read a good deal of sensationalist literature and was firmly of the impression that debauchery of this sort was entirely feasible unless he remained vigilant.

'They would have to find them first,' mumbled an anonymous Major General from the far end of the room.

'Bear in mind the fact that a quarter of our population are practising Muslims,' said a fat man dressed entirely in white robes and an Arabic headdress who had a title which included the words ethnic and diversity.

'So you regularly insist on informing us though you never explain why that is in any way relevant,' said a short man with an inhaler who chain smoked and was always keen to sit near an open window.

'Gentlemen, gentlemen,' said Premier Troveski, deciding he had heard enough and it was time to take

matters in hand. *'I would be grateful if you could give me your full attention while I underline the progress we have made on the subject of defence procurement. On today's order of business it is listed under the subheading of 'Diplomacy and International Affairs'.'*

The room fell silent. Troveski was the supreme power in the room and nobody had cause to doubt it. Not least because he personally sanctioned all appointments to Government posts, allocated car parking spaces and signed off expenses claims. Nobody in their right mind ever chose to rub Troveski up the wrong way unless they were very brave or extremely masochistic. There were a lot of back alleys in Aspadria and the Premier was reputed to know each one intimately; he also had the final say on late night restrictions to street lighting.

'The situation is as such,' he continued, casting a frown at the Minister for Education who was folding his agenda document into a paper aeroplane. *'I have once again approached the Volgarian Government on the thorny subject of reunification but sadly my overtures were rejected out of hand. Added to which I understand there are a number of bed sheets currently hanging from scaffold poles on the North side on the river, which read,* **'What is done cannot be undone; Up Yours Troveski!'**, *from which I deduce that, for the moment at least, the furtherment of diplomatic negotiations with our nearest neighbour can be regarded as having run its course.'*

'It's all that idiot's fault,' said the Transport Supremo, waving an arm in the direction of a painting of Count Limburg surrounded by a multitude of adoring angels that had hung at the head of the room for as long as anyone could remember.

'I think it's a little harsh to condemn a man three centuries after his death, Minister,' rejoined the Premier; possibly in the hope that posterity would prove a little kinder to his political initiatives. *'It was a decent enough idea but the Gods of fortune can be cruel. Let us move on.'*

He hesitated, wondering how much he should tell them.......as little as possible might work best in case things didn't work out precisely as he had envisaged.

'*You will be pleased to know we have now taken delivery of the final consignment of American tanks,*' he continued guardedly.

'*These would be the American tanks that don't work?*' said the token independent radical who had been invited to attend the meetings in an observational capacity, in a flawed attempt at injecting a feeling of inclusivity into Government proceedings.

'*They do work!*' barked the Premier testily. '*They just require a few minor modifications to enhance performance.*'

'*Like fitting them with tracks that would enable them to travel successfully across the countryside, instead of gouging great lumps out of our roads,*' the same voice continued.

'*The tanks have been purchased with a specific objective in mind,*' continued the Premier, pointedly ignoring the interruption, while at the same time giving careful consideration to the heckler's probable route home.

'*I have already put a plan into being that I am confident will bring this whole matter to a satisfactory conclusion. At this time I cannot speak further. All I require is your trust.*'

After a small hesitation the entire Aspadrian Cabinet dissolved into a fit of unbecoming giggles. It was his use of the '*trust*' word; it happened every time. The Premier sighed loudly, before concluding it might be best to cut his losses and resume his seat, leaving his audience still wanting more.

CHAPTER SEVEN

Thomas Farlowe stood outside the hospital and flexed his shoulder. It wasn't yet fully mended but at least the sharp pain had reduced sufficiently to enable him to lift his arm to head height without wincing. He loosened a further button of his shirt collar and surveyed his surroundings. He had been warned about the Volgarian climate but after weeks in a hospital bed nothing could have prepared him for the searing heat he now encountered. The ground was cracked and dry, the air felt thick, gritty and listless; nothing moved in the sweltering heat. He glanced upwards seeking signs of relief but the sky was completely cloudless; there was not the slightest hint of a breeze. According to his research it was like this for six months of the year and then as cold as fridge for another five. In the period in between it sluiced down rain like you were standing underneath a waterfall. Was it possible people actually lived here by choice?

He caught a bus, then another, and after a short hike which left him soaked in perspiration and gasping for air, he reached his destination. He looked through the perimeter fence at a sight which was beyond the bounds of his imagination. This was excavation on a scale he would never have thought possible. As far as the eye could see massive machines were ripping into the surface and filling enormous dumper trucks with load after load of dull brown rubble.

'Sightseeing or looking for work?' said a heavily accented voice at his elbow. *'They're setting on labourers at gate three if you get your arse in gear.'*

'I'm an Engineer,' said Farlowe, wishing there was a greater element of truth to that statement.

'Then you've come to the right place, Sonny. We've never enough of them,' said six foot six of bronzed muscle

hiding behind a red beard and mirrored sunglasses. *'The name's Strachan by the way. Don't call me Jock unless you're sure I'm out of hearing; I've been known to take offence.'*

The interview proved brief, mainly because the Hungarian conducting it didn't speak much English. As soon as he had untruthfully announced that he had work experience with Rolls Royce he was accepted on the spot. He was then pointed to a derelict wooden shed containing an aged bunk bed and a primitive metal sink and advised these were his living quarters; before being reminded that it might be advisable to get a good night's rest as his first shift started at six the following morning.

The first few months were painful beyond belief and he quickly got to appreciate the wide gap that existed between theory and practice. However, he was a quick learner and soon picked up the necessary skills to survive. After six months he felt fairly competent; after a year he was a fully fledged member of the team and people paid attention when he spoke.

It turned out he had struck lucky; in Volgaria labourers were relatively plentiful but Engineers were a scarce commodity. The work was gruelling but the money was terrific if you could steel yourself to put up with the terrible working conditions. The main problem, however, was the climate; no matter how long you worked in it you never got used to the weather; you froze, you boiled, you were soaked to the skin. Every task took longer than usual to complete because of the atrocious climate and everything had to be fixed and back in service with the minimum delay as bonuses were geared to quotas and down time was never adequately factored in.

The site was truly enormous, covering a good deal of the land mass between the two bridges and working north for the best part of fifty miles. The productive areas could best be described as scrubland, and were bordered to the east by a mountain range and to the west by waterless desert. The main highways ran from the Chake and Lobstock bridges along the periphery of the gigantic excavation and joined in the north of the country to complete an enormous loop. The bridges across the river Volgar to the south represented the country's only link with its Aspadrian neighbour.

The work force was truly multi-national. He was working for a German consortium; if he had managed to avoid bumping into the abrasive Mr Strachan he could have walked a couple of miles further and ended up being employed by Norwegians, Danes, French, Spanish, Canadians, English, Russians or any of another dozen nationalities that were overseeing projects to rip rock out of the ground. There were no American Companies on site but despite this there were plenty of American nationals working in the various teams. Each company was engaged in what was referred to as a 'Partnership Agreement' with the host nation; he didn't have the slightest idea how the system worked but as far as he could see everybody seemed to come out of it reasonably happy.

After eighteen months he was viewed as an experienced hand and transferred to Procurement, which meant for a lot of the day he was tied to a desk in the main site office. This had its advantages because at least you were out of the sun, rain or God knows whatever else, but it was bad because you lost some degree of contact with your work colleagues. It did serve to slightly improve his linguistic skills though, which were in truth pretty awful and he began finally to get some sort of a rudimentary understanding of the Volgarian language. (Rule one; you spoke Volgarian; you never referred to it Aspadrian even though the languages were pretty much the same in every respect including pronunciation and spelling.)

A key moment in his new life occurred on a Saturday afternoon shortly after he had completed his second year of service. It was a weekend and he was sitting alone in the site hut trying to figure out what parts he would need to fix a piling rig that had been brought in to provide foundations for a small on-site smelting plant. The first thing he heard was an almighty crash; followed by total silence. It was the rainy season and as usual at this time of year water was streaming from the skies. He opened the cabin door but couldn't see much further than a couple of metres in any direction. For no good reason he grabbed a waterproof and headed to the back of the hut; it was a lucky decision. Perched in the middle of a slurry pit was a yellow bus which was slowly being swallowed by a lake of liquid mud. At the windows were contorted faces screaming soundlessly. It seemed the track running down the hill had collapsed in the incessant rain and the bus had slid sideways off the roadway, taken out the perimeter fence and toppled down a thirty yard bank before skidding wheels first into the morass.

He never clearly remembered what happened next. He could vaguely recall cutting his hand while dragging the empty oil drums and finding it difficult to properly secure the scaffold boards once he had wrenched them into position. He certainly remembered smashing out the back window of the coach with a block hammer and the difficulty in squeezing bodies through the narrow gap without cutting them to ribbons. He didn't recollect actually going inside the vehicle; which was strange as the exact layout remained indelibly printed on his memory for years to come.

The only immediate fatality was the driver who had broken his neck colliding with the window screen; an old lady died in hospital a couple of days later of injuries sustained in the accident, though probably that was as much due to shock as anything else. There were numerous minor injuries, a couple that were fairly severe, but mercifully no more fatalities. The bus had sunk from sight within minutes of him dragging the last passenger clear.

He was commended for saving the lives of fourteen people. He was a hero; for a complete week he was a Volgarian national hero; he did a stuttering television interview, had his picture in the newspapers and even gave his autograph to a group of girls he met in the street who recognised his face and thought he might be a pop star. Then just as he was getting used to it, the adulation ceased and life went back to what passed for normal in this very strange country.

It was at this point that he came to a couple of realisations. Firstly he had adored the excitement and adulation much more than he had thought was possible and secondly he had for the time being abandoned any intention of returning home.

CHAPTER EIGHT

'Let me tell you of my intentions,' began First Minister Brastic calmly. *'In a matter of weeks I will retire and I intend to leave a legacy that will long be remembered.'*

Schuster adjusted his seating position and waited for Brastic to resume. You already have the best legacy any man could wish for, he thought. You ousted the Americans when they got greedy and you set up contracts with half the Countries in the world to rape the countryside of whatever small charm it once possessed. Volgaria has risen from the ashes. Your name will be revered, or at the very least derided, in history books from this day forward. Either way, you will certainly not be forgotten.

'I might have been persuaded to continue in office, added Brastic thoughtfully. *'It would have been necessary to amend the constitution but these things are always possible. However, the younger men want their hour at the helm. That is the way with younger men; much ambition and little patience.'*

So, it's not a question of walking away at your own volition; you are being pushed, thought Schuster; or at least firmly eased out of the door earlier than you intended. They don't want you around anymore and yet because of your record they are powerless to force you off the stage before you have taken one final encore; and you are the sort of person who desperately craves to hear the applause ringing in your ears for one last time.

How typical of the type of man you have always been; defined by your work and nothing else. What will you ever find in retirement that will act as adequate compensation for being denied the very thing that gives your life any degree of meaning? You will be dead inside a year; then they will be at liberty to rewrite the history books to suit your successor's requirements; and you are fully aware there is little you can do to stop this from happening. So you want a last hurrah; one that maybe your successors will find less easy to edit from the records. An epitaph to stand for all time and be revered by generations to come.

'I have considered the matter carefully and decided I would like a purge on criminality,' said the First Minister in a gentle voice.

Schuster threw his hands in the air; it seemed unworthy; vaguely pathetic. Was this really the best the old war horse could come up with?

'This is an insult. What do you need me for? You have enough thugs out there in different coloured uniforms to purge a nation three times the size of this one.'

Brastic had obviously anticipated the reaction. 'Calm down Heindrich and listen; it is not quite as simple as I have made it sound. I have decided to specifically target criminals hailing from our unloved neighbour across the southern border.'

Schuster sank back in his chair.

'Why Aspadria? This country is overflowing with miscreants from the four corners of the earth. There are enough Sicilians, Bulgarians, Georgians, Ukrainians and Serbians to keep you busy for two lifetimes, and that's without taking account of the Jews, the Arabs and the blacks.'

'Heindrich, you were not born here so you can never fully understand. The citizens of this country were treated like effluent by that scum from south of the river for century upon century. We carry a hurt that wracks our souls from birth. The time is now ripe for us to repay a little of the debt. Every dead Aspadrian counts for ten from any other nation in the eyes of a true Volgarian. A man who arranged for twenty high-powered Aspadrian criminals to be strung from gibbets on the north bank of the River Volgar for all to see would live on in my people's memory as a national hero for all time. There is no doubt *about this; the act would be viewed as an unprecedented national triumph.'*

'*To this enterprise I can contribute nothing,'* said Schuster calmly. It was not hard to see why the new order wanted Brastic bundled into a hurried retirement. The old dog had clearly lost all sense of reason.

'*Guile, Heindrich; your contribution will be guile. I want no loose ends. The International Criminal Tribunal in the Hague has been kept extremely busy of late and I have no wish to travel so far north at my advanced age. Don't misunderstand me; I want people to be clearly aware of my involvement in the enterprise.....that is of course the entire point.....but none of my finger prints must be found at the scene of the crime. I want a mist to form, through which I can first be clearly observed, and then into which I can totally disappear. I want to rub noses deep into the dirt without getting the smallest blemish on my lily white gloves.'*

Schuster leaned forward and stared across the table.

'*Minister, I fail to understand your reasoning; the people already know you for what you are. Is this is a personal vendetta?'*

'*The 'reason' is mine; the 'how' is yours, Heindrich. You devise the plan. I pat your back, offer my congratulations and arrange for a shiny limousine to drive you home the minute you construct a strategy that I find acceptable. You have a blank sheet of paper on which to compose your masterpiece. I look forward to rising to my feet to applaud its undoubted brilliance.'*

'*But if you target Aspadria there will be repercussions; surely you see that. Their Government is hand in glove with the Americans. They have modern artillery and tanks. I really don't understand why.....'*

'*But you will Heindrich; in the end you always do. Your clever little mind will think up a plan which will overcome all of these problems. In the meantime I have taken the liberty of informing your housekeeper that you are staying with me for a short vacation. She has packed a case which you will find at your bedside. This room is now your office; you have my assurance you will not be disturbed.'*

'I see little has changed; you want everything to your own dictates while you explain nothing,' said Schuster coldly.

'I think we both appreciate there can be no other way. Oh, I think I omitted to mention; I have a small surprise for you. I have provided you with a personal assistant.'

'I don't need one of your tarts, Brastic. I am competent to take care of myself.'

'How age affects us, Heindrich; you would have done much to have the lovely Greta obeying your every whim once upon a time. In the archives we still have a record of some of your favourite games. You were always so imaginative even in your formative years.

No, it is not Greta, I'm afraid. I have provided you with a thinker; not as accomplished at waggling her arse but deeply gifted in a number of other ways. I feel you will grow to like her; just be careful you only look and don't touch. I am told that on occasions she can become hard to control.'

'I need nobody. I am happy to work alone,' said Schuster with an air of finality.

'Unfortunately, Heindrich, like so much in life, this is not a matter of choice. If you need me pick up the phone and I will be found. Good luck; I have every confidence that you will arrive at a satisfactory solution to my little problem. After all, I'm sure you will be keen to get home as soon as possible; is that not the case?'

CHAPTER NINE

Thomas Farlowe was uncomfortable in Desmond Palfrey's company from the day they first met; from his, *'name's Desmond but call me Des; everybody round here does'* to his russet coloured corduroy trousers straining to hold together over a large beer belly. From his rugby club blazer which appeared to depict a unicorn looking lasciviously at a damsel in distress, to his old school tie in shades of purple and orange that always made Farlowe feel vaguely bilious. From his insistence that tea didn't taste right unless the milk was added last, to his laugh that was always slightly grating and invariably several decibels too loud. Palfrey appeared to be a throwback to a bygone age when you put the idiot son into the church and if they wouldn't take him, phoned up an old friend in the Foreign Office and enquired about the availability of overseas postings. In these circumstances it was therefore extremely annoying that not only did Palfrey make Farlowe feel strangely uneasy, but also vaguely inadequate.

Palfrey announced proudly he was from the Embassy; Farlowe had made every possible effort never to darken its doors.

'Spotted your name in the newspaper; well done old man with that coach crash business. Our stock went up with Johnny Foreigner that day I can tell you; had the Minister for the Interior eating out of my hand for the best part of the entire week.'

And one thing quickly led to another.

'No Work Permit, Thomas; well that's rather naughty of you; what would your mother say if she knew you were working illegally in a shithole like this place? Didn't they ask you to show your Visa at the bridge when you arrived? Slip the guard a crumpled fiver to look the other way, did

you? Don't worry; it's the usual procedure in this part of the world. Can't understand how the place manages to hold together; no administration to speak of; classic example of a country that will finish up going to the dogs.'

Underpinning this, however, was the helpful civil servant.

'I'll try to sort some papers out on the quiet; know a couple of coves on the inside who can make documents that blend in seamlessly with the background.....they also are pretty adept at adjusting the filing to suit. I'll front up any necessary lucre; we can settle up at a later date. Nothing untoward that I should know about, is there? You've not bumped anybody off since you've been north of the river, I suppose?'

But there was no such thing as a free lunch.

'Now we've got all that sorted out I wonder if you could see your way to doing me a tiny favour in return?'

Eventually Farlowe got the picture.

'Forget it! No way am I spying on my colleagues!'

But sometimes you start the engine just to demonstrate it will still turn over.

'Of course not, Thomas; wouldn't dream of asking. What interest could I possibly have in that hairy arsed Glaswegian thug you hang around with? Just wondered if you could let me know anything interesting that crops up on neighbouring sites; new machines, that sort of stuff. I know you grease monkeys live in each other's pockets. H.M.G. would be extremely grateful.'

Then before you know it the bloody thing is in gear and roaring down the hill while you are still trying to remember which pedal you need to stamp on to bring it to a halt.

'So you reckon the Eyeties have acquired a twenty ton four seven fifty and the South of Calais Wogs are expecting to take delivery of an improved multi-excavator before the April thaw. Well done old bean. King and Country are in your debt good and proper for this lot; just the ticket.'

And when you do eventually get your feet sorted out and put your weight on the brake, you find it goes right to the floor.

'Any chance you could ask Van the Man if he's heard anything new? Little bird said the Cloggies are pushing for a contract extension in the western sector which might indicate the spoils over there have turned out better than anyone surmised.'

Farlowe never sold anybody down the river but whenever 'Jock' Strachan shouted, *'Eh Thomas, your poofy mate's just pulled into the car park,'* he felt guilty by implication.

How Palfrey succeeded in plying his trade remained a total mystery. He sometimes entered the site canteen blowing an imaginary trumpet and yelling *'Stand by your beds, Her Majesty's Secret Service on the premises.'* Nobody ever took a blind bit of notice outside the odd disparaging remark, which Palfrey batted off with his personal brand of acerbic wit.

'If you had been in my house at school you Australasian shit digger, I would have taken pleasure in having you buggered.'

He appeared to live the bluff that beat all bluffs; nobody seemed entirely sure where the buffoon ended and the Foreign Office emissary was meant to begin.

There was, also, a different side to the man. One day when they met for a delivery of information in a strip club in the centre of the Red Light district, a drunken Russian took exception to a chance remark and lunged at Palfrey with a broken bottle. In one move he swayed and swivelled until his assailant was safely out of reach before appearing to over balance and trip. There was a sharp crack as Palfrey stamped down hard in a seeming effort to regain his equilibrium. The drunk emerged from the fracas with a badly cut eye and three broken fingers. Palfrey apologised for his clumsiness and offered to call the Russian a taxi to take him to the local hospital. You needed to be quite close to realise the pantomime ballet had been very well choreographed, and the Russian's injuries had not been inflicted by accident.

CHAPTER TEN

Schuster laid out his case notes carefully on the long polished table. Listings of potential targets and locations were no great help at this stage; he needed inspiration of a different kind. The indigestion pain returned and he stepped out onto the balcony overlooking the Ministry's palatial gardens. Searching in his pocket he located the packet of cheroots, selected one and lit it, striking the match on a brass 'No Smoking' sign attached to the outer wall. Small victories were all he could hope for these days.

His concentration was disturbed by a light tap on the door to his newly acquired office. A young woman entered, walking unsteadily with a bulky satchel weighing heavily on one shoulder. She was small and trim with big eyes and wore a hijab, a tunic style top and neat skirt which stretched to the floor. She lowered her eyes and stood directly in front of him obediently awaiting instructions.

'I don't need you. Get out. I made it clear to Brastic I work alone,' Schuster yelled.

'But nevertheless I am here,' replied the girl serenely.

Another of Brastic's whores, thought Schuster; but this time he chooses to present me with the other face of the coin. A Muslim of some kind, presumably; whatever that faith is meant to currently represent with mindless clerical butchers appearing to direct their every action.

'Don't you understand my words? Go away,' he snarled.

'Perhaps I could fetch you a drink?' she said ignoring his rebuke.

'I am in need of nothing; if you must stay sit in the corner; do not speak and do not move.'

For the rest of the day Schuster paced the floor smoking, muttering, sometimes cursing. A couple of times his eyes came alight but the spark went out again as fast as it was ignited; the pain in his chest came back but he chose to suck on a mint and ignore it.

All the time he could feel her presence and smell her perfume; it served to disturb his concentration, though she never spoke a word or moved a muscle. When he realised he was making little progress he retired to his sleeping quarters without saying a word.

The next day he washed, shaved and ate a light breakfast before returning to his task. When he entered the room she had already arrived and was seated in the same chair as yesterday; neither acknowledged the other's presence. For all he knew she could have been patiently sitting there all night.

In the cold hours of dark he had conceived the small glimmer of an idea; nothing of substance, but possibly something that could be nurtured and encouraged to grow in the bright light of day. He noticed that a new packet of Cheroots and a tube of his favourite mints had materialised on the table next to the case notes. The work of one of Brastic's flunkies or the unwanted interloper sitting motionless by the window, he wondered?

By midday he knew he was on to something that could possibly work; the only question was did it work in his interests? He decided to put together a broad plan that could be adapted to fit requirements and set about constructing an outline. When he had finished he sat back reasonably satisfied.

He despised using the telephone and reluctantly decided to put his unwanted assistant to some use.

'*You.*' He addressed the chair rather than the person seated in it,

'*I need data; tell Brastic I want the personnel records of all the foreign workers currently employed at the mining plant; tell him to pay special attention to Americans, Canadians.....and the British.'*

She arose, picked up her satchel, walked slowly across the room and extracted a large manila folder which she placed within his reach.

'You can call me Kefira,' she said calmly, returning to her seat.

'Don't you hear me? I have no interest in your name; just do as I have instructed,' Schuster shouted.

For the first time she fully raised her head and stared straight into his eyes. Schuster took a pace back. This one had a raging fire burning inside.

'I suggest you examine the folder, Herr Schuster,' she said, forcing her voice to remain calm.

It was all there, records on anybody and everybody, neatly filed in alphabetical order. To add insult to injury, English speakers were logged on the front pages.

'How did you know this was what I would require?' he asked, suspiciously.

'It was logical, Herr Schuster; I merely anticipated your request.' she replied.

He pushed the existing paperwork to one side and spread the new folders across the table.

'Come here, woman; let me see you do some work for a change. Fetch a large sheet of paper, the bigger the better.'

She immediately produced paper from her satchel which when unfolded covered half the desk. He considered what else she might have in that bag; a horse, a steam engine........

'Scissors!' he shouted.

Like a miracle they also materialised in the palm of her hand.

'Now we set everything out as a detailed plan, in such a way that even an idiot could understand.'

She noticed the 'we' with deep satisfaction, no trace of which she allowed to register on her face.

The next morning First Minister Brastic was summoned. She used a direct number to make contact, Schuster noted. She must truly be one of the chosen few. He talked; Brastic listened; the enigmatic Kefira stood meekly in the background and barely seemed to draw breath.

Brastic considered the proposal for no more than a minute before treating the room to a rare smile. *'Proceed'* he said, as he walked out through the door without a backward glance.

Schuster waited ten minutes then dismissed Kefira on an errand, dragged a chair out onto the balcony and positioned himself in such a way that the door could not be opened. He made a number of long phone calls, each in a different language and was mentally exhausted by the time he eventually returned to the desk. Nonetheless he was pleased with the overall outcome. These people were not so very hard to out think as long as you understood the way their minds worked. Any fool could have constructed a scheme that would serve the purposes of the accursed First Minister Brastic but it took a greater degree of proficiency to come up with a plan that would also benefit its originator. The next problem was staying alive while it was being executed; he suspected that might prove a considerably more difficult proposition.

CHAPTER ELEVEN

'We are conducting a review,' said the man in the light blue uniform with grey piping at the collar, in fluent but heavily accented English. Everybody listened intently because the two officers standing directly behind them were carrying automatic rifles and looked as though they wouldn't be averse to confirming they were in good working order.

'We have been remiss with our paperwork for many years and now we intend to do better. Please have no concerns; this is merely a matter of routine.'

Thomas Farlowe yawned. It was hot in this damned open air car park and he had better things to do with his day than fill out forms to accommodate a Volgarian bureaucracy that had never previously shown the slightest interest in any form of documentation.

'We will address each nationality in alphabetical order. The first will be America, Britain and Canada.'

'It's U.S.A. so it starts with a U, which should make us Yanks somewhere towards the back of the queue,' shouted Tosh Koslowski in a drawl that was instantly recognisable, from somewhere near the centre of the pack of sweating site workers.

'Not in Volgarian,' replied the blue uniform with a cold smile. *'The names of people I require to attend an interview will be posted on the board in your dining area. I believe yours is likely to be one of them Mr.....Mr Koslowski.....so please try to be on time. There will be penalties for late arrivals as a failure in punctuality will be interpreted as a direct insult to the authority of the Volgarian Government.'*

Jock Strachan elbowed Farlowe in the ribs as the meeting broke up.

'They are getting too bloody civilised out here for my liking, Thomas. Nobody I met could write their name when I first arrived; now look at them getting all high and mighty with their 'correct documentation'. You watch, they'll be holding bloody fire drills next. First sign of a country falling apart is when they start to hold fire drills. You have my word for it.'

Farlowe had never seen the Volgarian Ministry building up close and was deeply impressed. So impressed he nearly turned about face and joined the queue to catch the next bus back to camp. The building was massive and appeared to be constructed exclusively from horizontally laid grey concrete slabs. In order not to overtax the visitor's imagination, grey concrete pillars had been subtly positioned on either side of the front entrance to support grey concrete arches, with the extensive facade being broken only by a number of grey concrete window sills; each one of which appeared to be crying out in desperation for a window box containing a geranium. He couldn't get a clear view of the roof but felt it unreasonable to expect it to be anything other than grey, and in all probability constructed from concrete.

The windows of the building were tinted black and winked ominously in the blazing sunshine; any view they afforded to the main road and surrounding industrial wasteland was obscured by sets of drawn venetian blinds, grey in colour. The grounds were forbiddingly surrounded by a fence of featureless black wrought iron railings approximately ten feet in height. It was an Orwellian fantasy writ large. Brutalist architecture raised to its unimaginative zenith.

In the past week and a half there had been a good deal of shuffling back and forth between the Site and the Ministry building but nobody who had attended an interview had shown any inclination to discuss the details of their interrogation in any depth. Farlowe took his seat in the specially cordoned off waiting room and tried to anticipate what was most likely to go wrong.

...... *'Are you happy in Volgaria, Mr Farlowe?'* asked the old man with cold eyes and a strong German accent, who was seated behind the large desk puffing irritably on a pungent miniature cigar. He didn't look like he would be particularly interested in getting a reply so Farlowe smiled benignly and waited for the follow up line.

If it's a German emigration survey, he thought, hopefully the conversation will centre around the quality of the local sausage and the best places to meet girls with blonde hair, blue eyes and large chests encased in low cut, frilly white blouses.

'.......because your method of entry into the Country appears to have been somewhat unusual,' his inquisitor continued after a protracted pause.

Well, perhaps not a survey as such but more an attempt to dredge up a few details to fill in the blank boxes on a routine form that would immediately be filed and forgotten about.

'......and it seems since you were released from the local hospital you have been employed in this country despite possessing neither a Work Permit nor a Visa.'

Where's that coming from, Farlowe asked himself? Palfrey was meant to have straightened those details out months ago. Was it worth speaking up and trying to wrong foot the miserable devil old devil? Probably not; he looked a vindictive old swine and twice already he had winced and leaned forward a little as if he was in some degree of pain.

'......Do you like money, Mr Farlowe? That question is not a stupid as it sounds. Several nations in the South Pacific find no use for it whatever.'

This would presumably be a German Joke to put him at his ease. He felt pleased to have noticed it. They weren't always so easy to spot.

'......*Because we would appreciate some help in a small matter that would be of great mutual benefit.*'

Not again, please! Mind you, at least the old German was at this stage asking politely. In most of the books he had read covering this subject, the offer was usually accompanied by a string of threats and an unwarranted degree of brutality.

'......*And you would of course be generously compensated for your time and trouble. We realise it would be unrealistic to expect you to work for nothing; and as you are not a Volgarian citizen we cannot appeal to your sense of patriotism.*'

Now, what the hell was this about? If the German wanted him to spy the answer would have to be a resounding no. God, he had only just squared his conscience after accepting Palfrey's job offer; and he had only agreed to that because the man from the Ministry had insisted he was providing information that was vital to the British Government. But hang on a minute; perhaps he should at least listen to the proposition before turning it down. It was coming from the host country, after all, and he didn't want to be slung out on his ear if there was any possible alternative. He would of course report the approach to Palfrey and give him all the details so his conscience would be clear. And, after all, there was absolutely nothing to stop him saying *no* once he was made aware of what exactly the Volgarians wanted him to do.

'......*And quite naturally the Volgarian Government would include with that payment retrospective documentation which would make your immediate deportation totally unnecessary.*'

Ah, a little poke from the stick at the conclusion. He might have a set of papers already gathering dust in his bottom drawer but he had a strong feeling that unless he was judged by the German to be cooperating fully they were unlikely to prove to be the right set of papers. Anyway, how confident did he feel about gambling his job on documentation that had been provided by Desmond bloody Palfrey? Clearly, there was nothing to be lost by listening to what the man had to say. After all, what exactly had he got to lose?

CHAPTER TWELVE

Schuster opened his eyes and peered both ways, while at the same time taking care to keep his head completely motionless. She was at the periphery of his vision over by the window; curled up like a cat in an armchair on a winter's day. Even in here he could not escape the attentions of that accursed woman. Despite his best efforts she noticed his eyes had opened and leaned forward.

'You are in hospital, Herr Schuster; you had a small heart attack. The First Minister insisted you were provided with the best private room and were attended by his personal physician.'

He knew this of course; you didn't have to be a genius to work it out from the elegant surroundings. He was still important; at least for the next couple of weeks. After that his life expectancy would be considerably less assured.

He thought back; he had just finalised the details of the outline to his satisfaction when Brastic had informed him that he wanted each pairing to be accompanied by one of his Iron Maidens. He had begun to revise his plan to accommodate the latest instruction, not in the best of humour he was forced to concede, when suddenly the pain had returned; this time worse than ever........then; then everything had gone blank.

He decided he needed a diversion while he gathered his thoughts. He glanced at the front of the newspaper she appeared to have been reading while he lay unconscious. *'So you think you can you read?'*

'Yes, I can read, Herr Schuster. I am fully conversant with the Volgarian language. I also speak English, Russian and German fluently and have a broad understanding of French......plus a little Spanish.' She was good, he was forced to admit; not a sign of the rage that must be prickling her from the inside. It was a pity.

He took great pleasure in getting under people's skin and it was a disappointment when they failed to rise to the bait. He must try harder.

'*Not the words, idiot; can you read the picture?*'

She turned the paper round in her hand and examined the front page. '*It is the Government, Herr Schuster. It is the ten men who are most prominent in governing this country.*'

But at this time only one actually counts, thought Schuster; the other nine are merely there as window dressing. Why did people imagine Volgarian politicians scrambled so hard to get to the top? Anywhere but the very apex of the slippery slope counted for nothing.

'*I know what it is; what I am asking you is, can you read what it says?*'

'*It doesn't say anything,*' she replied calmly, meeting his stare. '*It is just a reproduction of a photograph taken outside the ministry building yesterday or perhaps the day before.*'

'*Of course it says something, you fool; it's there right before your eyes if you just take the trouble to understand what it clearly conveys. Allow me to translate as you are obviously incapable. In the front at the centre is Brastic who is the First Minister and currently all powerful; he will, in due course, be succeeded by Pasonak who is standing directly behind him on his right hand side; Pasonak has the support of Kolat and Sharma, who are grouped behind him on either side. The three standing to Brastic's left are young hopefuls coming through the ranks; can you not see the glint of ambition, burning in their eyes? The three at the back count for nothing; notice the dullness of their expressions. Their day has come and gone. They are merely marking time while they wait to retire to a log cabin situated near a distant lake where they will fish in the daytime before slowly drinking themselves to death; each one still dreaming of what might have been if the roll of the dice had been a little kinder. Learn to read a photograph like a balance sheet or you*' *will always remain ignorant of information that is right before your eyes.'*

'I have never been taught to read like that,' Kefira replied with mild indignation.

'Then I suggest you would be wise to learn very quickly. This sort of detail is vitally important if you have a grain of ambition. Volgaria is a dangerous country for those who walk its streets ill prepared. Now, where did you put the planning documents?' Schuster adjusted his pillow and pulled himself into a sitting position. That felt better; now he had reasserted his authority he felt ready to resume.

Kefira reached to the side of her chair and located her ever present satchel.

'I have them here. When you.....when your health failed the First Minister commanded me to place them in a sealed envelope. I have it here in my satchel.'

'Get it out. I wish to refresh my thinking,' commanded Schuster impatiently.

Kefira hesitated. *'It is too soon for you to be working. We should postpone further discussion until the morning, by which time you will undoubtedly feel a good deal stronger.'*

She has concerns for my wellbeing, thought Schuster. I treat her like a soiled dishrag and still she allows her maternal instincts to override cold logic. No wonder her sex have been subjugated for eternity. They deserve nothing better.

'I have no energy to debate the matter with you. Get the plans out immediately.'

She obeyed without further argument; her cheeks reddening slightly as she reached for her bag.

'Did you read them?' accused Schuster, in an attempt at a further provocation.

'There was no opportunity. I only know full details of the part of the plan we worked on together; do you wish to update me on any later amendments?

'There is no need. The changes are minor and will become apparent as we proceed.'

She pointed to a section on the paperwork with a puzzled expression.

'I still consider the Englishmen a mistake. In my opinion their accents are too obvious and this alone makes them unsuitable for their role in the subterfuge.'

Schuster once again reached for the rubber coated iron bar suspended from the ceiling above his bed and used it to pull himself into a higher position.

'I have already submitted the details to the First Minister and everything is agreed. America is a very large country. They speak with such a variety of accents that your concerns will undoubtedly prove groundless. Don't lose sight of the fact that each of the Englishmen is paired with an American who can conduct the majority of the conversation. If you wish to act like a mother hen I will allow you to personally oversee the distribution of the personnel we have at our disposal but I consider any deviation from the agreed plan as totally unnecessary.'

She nodded a reluctant assent.

'Can I clarify the exact role of the English speakers in the enterprise? I presume the intention is to make it appear that the Americans have ultimate responsibility for any arrests?'

She was bright enough he had to admit. Just as well he had made certain she knew no more than was necessary.

'You do not need to know the reasoning,' he hissed impatiently. 'It is time we moved on to more important details.'

Then he paused and reconsidered. It would help if her report back to the First Minister indicated that they were working closely as a team and that she was fully conversant with all details of the operation. That might prove a benefit as the plan developed, especially if it helped to mask the truth.

He turned and looked into her large brown eyes. He was forced to admit she had an exceptionally beautiful face for a member of such an ill blessed race. He remembered a time when young girls like her were only too eager for his friendship; word had soon circulated around the camp that his special friends got to live a lot longer than those he found in any way disagreeable. He could afford to indulge her a little. Perhaps she might even be persuaded to spend the evening with him when he felt a little stronger; maybe, even join him in one of his little games. It wasn't as if she had the power to influence the outcome in any way; she knew nothing of several points of important detail; what harm could it do?

'Alright, yes......the appearance will be that the arrest of Aspadrian citizens is being coordinated by the American military, possibly in liaison with the C.I.A.; at the very least it will seem that the United States is working hand in glove with the Government of Volgaria in an advisory capacity. We will ensure word reaches the street almost immediately and assume that it will have found its way across the border to Aspadria in a matter of hours.'

'Are you not concerned by the risks?' she questioned.

'Trust my words; with American involvement in the operation appearing an absolute certainty, Premier Troveski will not feel able to lift a finger.'

She moved her chair a little nearer the bed and glanced in Schuster's direction with something approaching respect.

'It is not difficult to understand why First Minister Brastic holds you in such high regard, Herr Schuster. The plan is both simple and effective.'

He knew it was true but it was still good to hear the sentiment put into words. He felt a warm flush come to his cheeks; it was just like the days of old.

'It may need a little fine tuning but the basic concept is sound. I hope it will not become boring. I thought it might be best to put a small surprise at the very end in order to be certain no one had drifted off to sleep.'

She smiled sweetly at his joke, showing a set of even, white teeth. He was forced to admit he was beginning to enjoy the woman's company. It was good to have an intelligent audience after spending so many years alone, wrapped only in a cocoon of distant memories and bitter regrets. It was a pity he could not tell her more. She was bright enough to appreciate the complexity of the manipulations that it had been necessary to introduce in order to ensure his survival and safeguard his future.

What a foul world this was. The things you had to endure just to survive. It all could have been so very different if life had taken a slightly different course. He had been born with the necessary vision to achieve greatness; to be the one who gave the orders rather than the lackey obliged to bite hard on his tongue and merely appear to obey them. He knew he also possessed the inner steel to ensure his commands would be carried out implicitly. Things had looked very promising for a few short years but then life had changed completely. It was Russia that proved the beginning of the end; the failure to take Russia that ultimately caused his father to be torn from the bosom of his family, put up against a wall and summarily beaten to death; and as a consequence for him to feel obliged to seek shelter anywhere that would be prepared to take him; to be grateful for sanctuary even in a backwater as foul as this. It was always Russia that proved one step too far for the men of vision; too big a country with too large a population and the climate........the climate was nearly as bad as this infernal hellhole.

Penetrating the mists of time her voice interrupted his thoughts.

'May I query one point?' I don't understand the need for the task force to reassemble? Once their part in the mission is completed surely it would be better for the operatives to be conveyed straight back to their base?'

This was the problem with involving intelligent people; they tended to ask intelligent questions. Which was the precise reason why he had always insisted on working totally unaided. It avoided unnecessary explanations; explanations that would require a degree of invention which could prove an annoying distraction from the bigger picture on which he wished to concentrate his mind.

'I want to conduct a short debriefing before we part company; I am led to believe there is a possibility of future strategies that will be based on the same model,' he improvised.

'But is it not the......'

Schuster's patience quickly ran short. *'Enough questions now. Let us check the teams one final time; pass me the working list.'*

'Herr Schuster, are you sure there is nothing more you wish me to know?' she enquired meekly.

Schuster laughed; a rare occurrence but one that had happened more frequently in the last forty eight hours than for a very long time.

'What more could there be for me to tell? You know everything of importance. I think it would now be possible for you to complete the project without me even being present.'

He closed his eyes and cleared his mind. The important thing was to remain completely calm. The heart attack had been an inconvenience but ultimately it would not affect the strategy. Brastic was working against a deadline and there was no way for him to see the full picture until it was too late. For the time being he was still holding all the key cards.

This thought made him feel mildly elated. Warm inside, like he had just swallowed a large gulp from a bottle of top quality schnapps. He had stayed alive for so much longer than many would have considered possible by relying on his wits; with luck he would once again have the last laugh. The important thing was to miss nothing and trust nobody; to always remain one step ahead of the pack of baying hounds.

'That's also what I thought, Herr Schuster; tell me, did it never occur to you to consider my name?' Kefira asked softly, as she slowly uncoiled herself from the chair, gently massaging her fingers, one against the other as she pulled

herself into an upright position. She lowered her feet to the floor, steadied herself, stretched skyward and took half a pace forward, sneaking a surreptitious glance in the direction of the porthole window in the solid oak door that led onto the outside corridor.

'What about your name?' asked Schuster, slightly startled; his mind quickly returning to the present on hearing a small alteration in the tone of the woman's voice.

Kefira paused to kick off her shoes, bending down to tidy them neatly under the chair she had just vacated. She reached behind her and purposefully picked up the pillow on which she had been resting her head. She plumped it lovingly between her fingers, held it to her lips, sniffed it, buried her face in its softness; encircled it with her arms as if she was cradling an infant to her breast.

She took a decisive step forward, lifting her foot high above the ground as if mimicking a stealthy approach; then gazing deep into Schuster's eyes she pursed her lips before breaking into a gentle smile. In an instant she had become transformed into a very young and mischievous girl who had discovered the other person she needed to complete the cast in an elaborate charade she had long been planning in her mind; and this discovery seemed to fill her with infinite joy. It was as if a wearisome restraint had suddenly been removed permitting her to indulge in a fantasy she had been desperate to act out; and the release to do so caused her to experience immeasurable pleasure; pure ecstasy; it bathed her in a constant stream of genuine unbridled delight.

She now seemed totally mesmerised as smiling coyly she stooped and lowered her free hand to the hem of her long dress and slowly raised it an inch at a time, wiggling seductively to aid its gliding passage high over her thighs and buttocks. Liberated, she edged forward lifting one leg into the air and then the other, until she was kneeling on the very bottom of the bed. She again stared deep into

Schuster's eyes a mere body length away, playfully stuck out her tongue, licked her lips and pouted mischievously.

'It's Jewish, Herr Schuster. Did you not know?'

Although the room was silent her voice could barely be heard, sounding like a hushed whisper from a small child in a large and darkened room.

She smiled again, wider this time, before starting to gradually ease herself along the length of the bed a little at a time; her eyes losing focus as she entered deeper into some strange personal trance, her knees sinking deep into the soft mattress without her seeming to be in any way aware of the fact.

'It translates as lioness,' she added in a husky undertone, making a small demonic snarl in demonstration; then laughing softly at some private joke she was reluctant to share as she raised one hand in the air in the shape of a small raised claw.

'I'm surprised you didn't know this. I was led to believe you took a deep interest in the people of my race when you were a much younger man.'

In the other hand she still firmly gripped the pillow. She slackened her hold very slightly, flipped it over and balanced it carefully on her outstretched palm; then gripping it by the corner of the cover she shook it playfully like a dead rat suspended in midair only by its tail, teasing Schuster's eyes to be drawn in its direction.

Then suddenly it seemed the dream was broken and she reluctantly allowed herself to be returned to full consciousness; appearing slightly bemused and possibly a little embarrassed by her erstwhile frivolous behaviour. As if she had been spied upon enjoying herself at some form of unseemly recreation when she should really have been attending to matters of far greater importance. She shook her head slightly in reproof, possibly as a form of chastisement, maybe just to assist in fully focussing her mind; before deftly transferring the pillow to both hands, pushing it out in front of her and tightening her grip.

She looked up to the ceiling, sighed deeply in contentment and swallowed a big gulp of air as if she was summoning her full concentration for a major effort. Then digging her bare toes deep into the bedding to gain a firm purchase she sprang forward; allowing the pillow to precede her as it sailed high into the air, before gracefully descending in a smooth arc and settling in its resting place.

The utterly horrified Heindrich Schuster seemed mesmerised by what was happening as the weight of the human form settled gently onto his chest and the warm cloth began to block the apertures to his mouth and nose; and in consequence was able to let out only the smallest squeal of terror as he desperately struggled desperately to draw breath for one final time.

CHAPTER THIRTEEN

'So what we have experienced is a minor inconvenience, not a major disaster. An untimely exit but I suspected Schuster's health might prove a cause for concern.' First Minister Brastic walked to the window and contemplated the view, seemingly unconcerned.

'Tell me, did he suffer much at the end?'

'It was far from pleasant. He regained consciousness briefly but struggled to draw breath. He cried out only once,' said Kefira without undue emotion.

'Good' said Brastic, clapping his hands enthusiastically. *'I hoped it would not be entirely without pain. I detested the man. He deserves to rot in hell.......So; do you feel you are fully prepared?'*

'Yes Minister, everything is in hand,' she replied calmly. *'Herr Schuster had already briefed his chosen operatives on the ground and finalised the details of the transport requirements. I would however like to make some minor adjustments to his final plan.'*

'No, Kefira. Brastic sounded adamant. *'Leave things exactly as Schuster arranged them. He did everything with a specific purpose though he would never have chosen to share his full intentions with anyone, least of all you. You do well to ask the question but I will be satisfied to implement the plan exactly to his design. Change nothing in case it affects the balance of his scheme.'*

'If you say so Minister,' said Kefira with resignation.

'Do you suspect Schuster was anticipating his death?' Brastic enquired, seeming reluctant to entirely abandon a topic which obviously gave him some degree of pleasure.

'No. It seemed to take him totally by surprise,' she replied shortly.

Brastic was once again on his feet pacing; appearing to consider how best to approach a delicate subject.

'The Doctor reported a degree of bruising to his chest and throat. His mouth was also cut. Apparently he had bitten through his tongue,' he stated, without any great show of emotion; more in the form of a question than a statement.

'My clumsy attempt at resuscitation proved totally inadequate, Minister. I should have called the doctor immediately instead of first trying to revive him myself,' she replied.

'No matter, Kefira; at least the old swine did not die alone. I think Herr Schuster would have appreciated you being close at hand in his final moments. He was a shrewd man. I'm certain he appreciated his days on this earth were likely to be somewhat limited.'

Brastic was uniquely qualified to make a pronouncement on this subject as he had already decided that Schuster would be assassinated once his usefulness was over. Over the years Brastic had gained a well earned reputation for never leaving unnecessary loose ends when other alternatives were readily available.

The Doctor had seemed perturbed by the bruising on Schuster's body and the cut to his face but Brastic had paid scant attention to his concerns. Like many men with important responsibilities the First Minister was a pragmatist and on occasions like this found it better to survey the big picture rather than get bogged down with unnecessary hypothesis. Schuster's use to him had been very nearly over. Providing his death in no way jeopardized the coming operation, he had saved on the price of an assassin's bullet.

There had been a lot of minor detail for Kefira to finalise but most matters were quickly reconciled. The men from the mining plant would be collected by coach at a number of prearranged pick up points. They would be paired off with suitable partners and ferried to the locale of their specific operation, where each team would receive a final briefing from a local field officer. The raids would take place the same night. The local Constabularies had been made aware of the level of manpower that would be required and that side arms only would be required unless they were otherwise instructed. They had also been told that standard interrogation techniques could be deployed to gain full written confessions from their prisoners once the men from the mining plant had been safely withdrawn from the area. The miners had been made aware that their part in the exercise consisted merely of shouting loudly in authorative American accented English.........and that they were not permitted to enter the zone of activity until any firing had completely ceased. When the operations were complete a short debriefing would take place at a prearranged central point; after which the men would once again be deposited on a coach which would conduct them to a series of strip clubs, karaoke bars and brothels as a thank you for their cooperation; after that they would be paid in full and returned to their base. It would be a long and busy day for all concerned.

Kefira supposed that with Schuster's absence from the proceedings now assured it would fall upon her to make a brief speech of thanks; but she still failed to see what this was likely to achieve. However, Brastic's directive was in no way ambiguous, so she would need to give the appearance it was being religiously observed regardless of her personal feelings on the matter.

There had been a late worry when the leader of an Aspadrian drug smuggling gang had temporarily disappeared off the radar but he was now satisfactorily accounted for; an attempt by a market competitor to firebomb the premises of a gaming club with an Aspadrian owner who specialised in currency laundering had also been tidily resolved and a number of bodies were even now floating in a southerly direction in the river Volgar as testimony to the fact.

Despite this, Kefira was still not entirely happy. Schuster had alluded to a possible surprise. Even as a small child she had never enjoyed unexpected disclosures.

CHAPTER FOURTEEN

It had the atmosphere of a Stag party, thought Farlowe. Put twenty fully grown men on a coach with the prospect of a night away from home, a brief acting role, followed by a lengthy pub crawl with women thrown in for good measure.......and all paid for by the host nation; well, what else could you expect?

Each pairing from the mining camps had been allocated a lithe looking female companion to accompany them on the raids. This was viewed as an extra bonus. The two Canadians who were designated to team up with Greta were especially pleased with the possibilities offered by the night ahead; they had been heard quietly discussing the possibility of drugging her and smuggling her back to the site dormitory once the operation was safely concluded.

The more Farlowe thought it over the less sense it made. If all they wanted was a chorus of American voices why didn't they hire a company of actors? How convincing were this lot likely to be, even in the unlikely event they were forced to remain reasonably sober for the duration of the exercise?

The party consisted of three Brits, seven Americans and ten Canadians. The breakdown was apparently determined by the fact the Canadians had proved easier to bribe, and not, as suggested by a shaven headed numbskull from Toronto called Hutchinson, that it was because men from the north of the continent were more proficient at speaking in a credible American accents!

Farlowe had reported the course of events to Des Palfrey as a matter of course but the man from the Embassy had seemed strangely uninterested. *'Sounds like a decent night out to me. I only wish they had asked me along. Keep half an ear open; you never know what you might hear. Enjoy the knees up; make the most of the free booze. Just relax and be yourself.'* This seemed strange advice to pass on to a man who had presumably only been hired in the first place for his ability to appear to be somebody he wasn't.

The fleet of cars left at ten in the morning so that the teams would be safely tucked away in their specific locations by early evening. He had been partnered with an American called Browler, who alternated short spurts of gibberish with long periods of monastic silence. His Volgarian liaison was a tiny girl called Kefira, who wore a Muslim headdress and full length dress that only served to accentuate her beauty rather than disguise it. She had eyes the size of saucers, a smooth complexion and a trim figure, and appeared to assert some degree of authority within the task force, as, before they set off, a number of the other girls could be seen shuttling back and forth, asking questions and receiving specific instructions.

The journey was totally uneventful; Browler sat in the front with the monosyllabic driver so Farlowe got to try out his Volgarian on his radiant companion; however, it seemed to bemuse her rather than help to break the ice. She seemed totally distracted throughout the entire trip and when he sneaked a sideways glance she was either frowning into deep space or retrieving notes from a satchel that was always balanced on her knees.

On arrival they checked into a seedy boarding house and ate a sparse and unappetising meal before temporarily retiring to their rooms for a brief rest. Browler had been given a leave of absence; while he had been detailed to accompany the girl to a meeting with their local contact.

They left the lodgings at six sharp and walked up a main thoroughfare towards town. The early evening was warm without being oppressively hot, a rarity in this unusual country, and he found himself enjoying the leisurely stroll. His enigmatic companion led him past workshops and churches, shops and bars, some of which were disused and some enjoying a thriving trade. She made no effort to talk so he resigned himself to a companionable silence; after several hundred yards she poked her arm through the crook of his elbow and they continued the rest of their journey like a young courting couple. Eventually they stopped at a rather shambolic corner café which looked like a haunt for locals rather than somewhere that relied too heavily on passing trade. They located an empty table and Kefira ordered a bottle of the rough local red wine.

'*Bad Muslim,*' Farlowe said, pulling a face in mock horror.

'*Bad assumption, Mr Farlowe,*' Kefira muttered, under her breath.

Five minutes passed before a large man with a Latino moustache and a broad smile appeared out of nowhere and joined their table. He was casually dressed in a sports shirt and jeans and seemed totally at ease.

'*I am Yanni; pleased to make your acquaintance,*' said the new arrival, offering Farlowe a large hairy hand. '*I picked you up as soon as you left the hotel. There were no tails. Who booked you into that dump? You could have done a lot better at my cousin's place and I could have negotiated you a special price.*'

'*It wasn't easy to miss you; I saw you and your female companion in the doorway; you stuck out like sore thumbs,*' said Kefira, ignoring the offer of accommodation. '*Where's the girl now?*'

'*She's covering the street. We can't afford to get complacent. Anouk has many friends both sides of the border.*'

Yanni clicked his fingers, drew a shape in the air with his finger and the waiter was immediately at his side with a glass and a large bottle of cold beer. It was evident he was a man who commanded respect in this part of the world. The waiter looked extremely anxious to be of service.

'*Do you want me to start?*' he enquired.

Kefira ignored the question and stared blankly ahead. Yanni took this as a 'yes', downed half the glass in a single swallow and began talking.

'Anouk Tibor is an Aspadrian national but has been based north of the river for the best part of ten years. He dabbles in gambling, drugs and prostitution but is not shy about getting involved in anything that turns a profit. In recent years, however, his main focus has been centred on cars. For some time he ran a hijacking operation that was very successful and highly lucrative but this has now been moved to the back burner. He is now giving his full attention to the airport.' Yanni paused for another swallow.

'Over a period of six months he got a number of his men recruited as security guards at the multi story car park opposite the main airport building where foreign nationals garage their motors when they are travelling abroad. His men have been provided with sophisticated adjustable broad band transmitters that will open pretty much anything that comes off a standard production line without triggering the alarm. Anouk brought a kid over from Korea who handled the development and production of the units. By now he will either be very rich or several feet underground; I cannot tell you which, but I have my suspicions. The units are very simple to operate; you turn the handle one way and every door lock within a five metre radius pops open; you turn it the other way and they close. The car alarms remain totally unaffected,'

'It would take the authorities about ten minutes to pick up on a scam like that; why haven't there been arrests?' interrupted Farlowe, in an attempt to sound like he knew what he was talking about.

'Because, my friend, nothing is stolen,' replied Yanni with a broad grin. *'In fact I would suggest if so much as a packet of peanuts was ever lifted from one of those cars the security guard with the sticky fingers would be dragging his feet along the bottom on the River Volgar before he was many days older.'*

Kefira scowled and continued to stare straight ahead so Farlowe thought it best to followed her cue.

'You are wondering where the profit is?' urged Yanni, with a look of disappointment that the interruptions had ceased as quickly as they had began. *'It's easy; all the nice big motors are fitted with satellite navigation. So you push the 'home' button on the machine and you know immediately where the owner lives; you know he's rich because of the car he's driving and you know he's out of the country because his vehicle is parked at the Airport terminal.'*

Yanni paused awaiting a comment; when nothing was forthcoming he quickly gave up and waved for another bottle of beer.

'When you get to the mark's house half the time it will be empty and the other half it will be occupied by a wife or employees who aren't going to risk getting their heads blown off without a much better reason than protecting a few trinkets. Nobody has made a connection between the cars and the house raids so.......'

'Where do we make the arrest?' interrupted Kefira, who appeared to either dislike Yanni or had become quickly bored with his story.

'Anouk's house; I've written down the address. He'll be home tonight from eight o'clock because he's entertaining. There will be plenty of stuff on the premises that you can link back to recent thefts. Some of it has been lifted within the last seven days.'

'You seem very well informed,' said Farlowe, choosing to break his silence.

Yanni's smile got even broader.

'I am close to Anouk; he trusts me implicitly. I am in fact the guest who is joining him for dinner later tonight. I must remember to eat quickly. Please don't come early; I don't want to get indigestion.'

'Did I omit to mention?' said Kefira contemptuously. *'This is Yanni Tibor, Mr Farlowe, Anouk's younger brother.'*

'*You trust him?*' asked Farlowe, as they retraced their steps in the direction of the lodgings.

Kefira shrugged; '*It's in his interest to cooperate. He wants to take over control of the family's involvement in the airport scam and in order to do that he needs Anouk out of the way. Yanni's assistance is bought and paid for; that part's not a concern.*'

When they entered the hallway Farlowe bent to kiss her cheek but she ducked and prodded him in the chest.

'*Good Muslims don't do that until they are married, Mr Farlowe. Didn't you know?*'

He though he detected a faint smile as she disappeared from sight. A moment later a door banged and a bolt could be heard sliding firmly into place. They had thirty minutes to kill before they were collected and obviously the woman had every intention of spending them alone.

CHAPTER FIFTEEN

'You've done what?' queried Hartz of the Yellow Party incredulously.

'I have ordered them out on manoeuvres.' repeated Premier Troveski of Aspadria, petulantly, *'It's what you do with tanks when you want to make sure they work to your complete satisfaction,'* he added with withering sarcasm.

'But how can you have allowed this to happen when they are incapable of being driven across the countryside?' questioned Schtool of the Red Party.

'They are currently involved in sophisticated arterial manoeuvres and reported to be performing admirably,' replied the Premier calmly.

'Do we assume from that reply that they are being driven on my roads?' countered the Transport Supremo.

'They are not 'your roads', Ezekiel; you always take these matters too personally,' replied the Premier to his Brother in Law, in an understanding manner.

'They are always 'my roads' when anything bad happens on them; they are only returned to the jurisdiction of the Aspadrian Government when there is a chance they might be viewed in a positive light,' returned the Transport Supremo with resentment.

'No harm will come to 'your roads', Ezekiel; the vehicles have been specially modified to fulfil their purpose,' said Premier Troveski soothingly.

'Modified in what way?' enquired Hartz of the Yellow Party.

Premier Troveski sighed. *'They have been fitted with specially developed, high technology, vulcanised protective's; sophisticated, urban prophylactics might be an accurate description,'* Troveski announced quietly.

'*So in summary,*' interjected Spanzetti of the Blue Party, with his face adopting a martyred expression, '*we purchased from the United States of America fifty tanks which were to all intents and purposes useless because they couldn't be driven across open country due to a design fault. However, we have now modified their method of construction so they can be fitted with wheels and tyres which enable them to be driven on the country's roads......and currently they are out there somewhere,*' he waved a languid arm in the general direction of the window, '*on manoeuvres*'.

'*Wouldn't it have been more cost effective to have purchased open backed trucks like the Somali militia uses and fitted machine guns on the back?*' questioned Hartz of the Yellow party, scornfully. '*At least that way we would have had the advantage of having wheels on the vehicle from the outset.*'

'*One good thing,*' interjected Schtool of the Red Party, '*at least we won't have difficulty in finding them. It will just be necessary to locate the biggest traffic jams on our road network and look for them at the front.*'

Before the criticism could gather pace Troveski rapped the table loudly with his knuckles.

'*I know exactly where they are, my dear Schtool. Even while we speak twenty five of them are entering the main approach corridor to the Lobstock Bridge; while the other twenty five are parked in lay-bys a couple of miles short of the water crossing at Chake.*'

'*Why?*' said the Radical who was always obliged to sit at the far end of the room and only got to speak when the people seated in more advantageous positions were too slow in chiming in with the next question.

'*At this stage as a precautionary measure only;*' answered Troveski, with statesman like untruthfulness, '*foresight is rarely rewarded, my friends, but the lack of it can prove a supreme embarrassment in these troubled times. Shall we just say that in the last few days some very interesting information has come into my possession which*

I will endeavour to make work to this country's advantage.'

The unexpected telephone call from the German, Schuster, had changed everything. Troveski now felt destiny was on his side. It had been well worth trading the promise of a comfortable sanctuary for the obnoxious German, for what amounted to an open invitation to invade the territory of his unloved northern neighbour. His military might could now be used to the country's advantage, rather than existing only as an idle threat. He closed his eyes and contemplated the future. He would become a national hero if he pulled this off; a demigod. They would build a column at the Chake crossing with his statue at the very top; he might even volunteer to design it himself; something tasteful, combining mild triumphalism with great dignity. The figure would be casting a resolute eye to the north and pointing high over the mighty river Volgar in the direction he was confident his army would soon be seen to march.

That would be the least of it. He would institute a national holiday. His effigy would be paraded round the streets on Saints Days and people would cross themselves with reverence when they spoke his name. He had always known in his heart the Aspadrian people would never countenance a reunification with Volgaria, no matter how tempting the terms; but an occupation; that was a different matter entirely. The ultimate joy would be that the old fox Brastic would have brought it all on himself. He looked around the table at the eager faces but realised it would be a mistake to say anything more; better they live in hope than expectation. He first needed to shore up a little ground on the home front. The next communication from Schuster was due in a matter of hours and after that things were likely to become a good deal more interesting.

CHAPTER SIXTEEN

It was pitch black and they were a long way behind schedule. They had been sitting in a car with no lights and no air conditioning for the best part of an hour and Farlowe was both hot and bored. They were parked half way up a hill on a tree lined street in an affluent suburb, but all he could see through the side window were occasional movements at the window of the house opposite, and that wasn't the one which was home to the target.

Kefira was totally absorbed; she took frequent messages on a two way radio and her mobile phone went off every thirty seconds. Balanced on her lap was a foolscap file which must have been written in Braille; this she meticulously updated after each conversation. Whenever he spoke she frowned and put a finger to her lips in a request for silence.

To make matters worse, the American, Browler, was fidgeting in the front seat, periodically letting off steam about whatever had gained his attention in the preceding ten seconds. Farlowe made a mental note to keep as far away from him as possible once they got back on the coach. He was extremely annoying even for an American and had the concentration span of a goldfish.

Suddenly it was all action. An open backed Mitsubishi pick-up truck sped up the hill and screeched to a halt blocking half the road. Policemen in a variety of different coloured uniforms immediately materialised from behind every bush. There was a mad charge to see who could get to the door first, and then a crash as someone smashed a window, followed immediately by two shots, then complete silence. Kefira slipped out of the car door and was gone. After a thirty second pause a lone figure appeared at the gate and beckoned. Browler cleared his throat in anticipation of his opening line. In perfect synchronicity they threw open the doors of the car and stumbled across the road yelling unheeded and totally incoherent commands in different dialects. Browler took the lead and disappeared through the main doorway. Farlowe followed and was immediately aware of a muffled crash; it seemed like someone had been hit. As things went black and he slipped out of consciousness he just had time to work out it was quite possibly him.

The sun streamed through the half raised window blind. It was now evidently morning. He wrestled back the bed covers and pulled himself into a vertical position, took a sip from a glass of tepid water positioned at his bedside, retched into a conveniently placed flower vase and tried to remember what exactly had happened. He felt his head; it was swathed in what felt like an extremely large bandage; he tentatively examined his body which was covered in an array of abrasions and purple bruises. It looked like he had once again found his way to a bed in some sort of hospital.

Just as he thought things couldn't get any worse Kefira barged through the door looking pensive. He managed a weak smile.

'Am I insured?'

She frowned and offered no sympathy; *'You look terrible. Are you well enough to listen?'*

'Well there's nothing wrong with my hearing,' Farlowe replied, feeling confident something fairly major was wrong with just about everything else.

She passed him a newspaper.

'How well do you understand the language? Not brilliantly, if I remember our last conversation.'

He struggled with the words; trying to make sense of the front page article while his head continued to throb to the beat of a drum; something about a crash.

'I'm better when it's spoken,' he lied. Then he slowly began to realise what he was reading. *'What, all of them?'*

She nodded and pulled a chair closer to the bed.

'The coach conducting the pick-up went over a cliff; no survivors except the driver. The local Police have taken him in for questioning.'

Farlowe tried to get his mind in gear which involved ignoring the pain.

'How long have I been unconscious?'

'Forever; something like thirty six hours,' she replied without referring to her watch.

Farlowe wanted to ask how his injuries had been sustained but somehow he couldn't find the right words. When you considered the outcome, he decided the sensible course of action was to sit quietly and mutter the odd prayer of thanks.

CHAPTER SEVENTEEN

'You are through to the White House and my name is Frank White; how can I be of help?' the voice on the telephone was authorative, crisp and cultured.

'Mr White, it's Dick Crowshaw, U.S. Ambassador to the country of Aspadria. Listen, I've been trying to file a report for over an hour and I've been transferred four times already. The last guy told me you might be the best man to speak to.'

'Sorry for your trouble, Dick; what can I do to help?'

'I guess I'll need to start the story again. Frank, without wishing to sound rude, can you tell me who you are? I am assuming this is a secure line, right?'

'The line's fine, Dick; I'm a Presidential Aide. My job is to help resolve problems. Just tell me what it is that's bothering you and I'll try to sort it out.' The voice sounded like it had said those words a thousand times before; polite but unquestionably bored by the regular repetition.

'I'm sorry, no offence to you, Mr White, but I think I should be filing this report with someone from the CIA; it might be better if you could just redirect my call through to Langley. Have you got a contact over there who specialises in security matters?'

'Calm down, Dick. If you have any doubts I will be happy to get an Under Secretary out of bed to confirm my position......but I have to confess, it might not prove a great career move on your part.'

'Well, you might be right. Perhaps it isn't strictly necessary for me to disturb anybody ....errr, it's difficult to know where to start, Frank......is it alright if I call you Frank? It's just, I think there's a war about to break out down here.'

'Start at the very beginning, Dick; take your time. Just give me the facts as you see them and I'll tell you what needs to happen.'

'Right....well everything's kicking off, Mr......Frank. You know about Volgaria, right; the country with the minerals just north of here? Well, the word came down the line three days back that the Volgarian police were setting up some sort of housekeeping operation; cleaning up a bunch of no-goods; smugglers, drug pedlars and racketeers working out of the border towns on the north side of the river. Under normal circumstances this would have been no big deal but it turned out the police units had chosen to specifically target Aspadrian citizens. Well, you can guess how that news was received down this way. After show trials the Volgarian authorities would have organised public hangings and God knows what else. They would have gone for it big time. It's still quite barbaric up there. They kill people who step out of line at the drop of a hat.

The next news we got was about the deaths of those poor boys from the mining development in the coach crash. Are you following this o.k., Frank? Volgaria is just over the border from Aspadria; directly north across the river. You know about the coach crash already, right? Eh, sorry, it's been a difficult day; of course you know about the crash; that was a stupid thing to say, it's on the front page of every newspaper ....err, well, the guy who calls the shots down here in Aspadria is called Troveski; Premier Troveski. He's a bit of a meathead to be honest but of course I get to work with whatever I am given. Frank, this Country is a political mess; it's meant to be a democracy and at the moment it's supposed to be governed by a coalition of several parties and err........look, to cut to the chase, the truth of the matter is, Troveski is pretty much in total control and does what the hell he likes. Are you getting this, Frank? Am I making any kind of sense?'

Frank White rolled his eyes and then yawned silently before casting a despairing look towards the ceiling.

'Perfect sense, Dick; I think you've making a first class job of giving me the big picture.'

'Well, Premier Troveski, the guy in charge down here, recently bought a bunch of tanks from our Government and I've just been told he's had them positioned along the border with Volgaria......Volgaria, the Country with the minerals, directly north of here.......and it looks like he is going to invade at any moment!'

'Yes, Dick,' said Frank White, concentrating hard on trying flick a paper clip into a plastic beaker.

'And err....Frank, I need some advice. I want to know what I should do about it?'

'Dick, I'm really glad you took the time to call me on this but there is absolutely no need for you to be concerned. We are fully aware of the situation down there and it is being carefully monitored on a minute by minute basis by our top surveillance personnel. We are constantly getting updated pictures from our drones and we have satellites passing overhead that can pick out a cockroach crossing the sidewalk. In addition we have rapid deployment troops standing by to take decisive action the instant we determine the best possible option.'

'Frank err....Do you people in Washington understand the history of this place? Aspadria has been looking for an excuse like this for years. They hate Volgaria, Frank; they put out the word they are intending to help the Volgarian Government put down civil unrest and re-establish law and order but believe me it will end up being a bloodbath.'

'What civil unrest would that be, Dick?'

'Well it's kind of complicated....err, when the Volgarian Police arrested the bunch of Aspadrian Hoods, word slipped out that the police operation was being directed by some arm of the American Government. It's now been leaked to the Aspadrian media down here that Volgaria is experiencing some sort of coup aiming to *unseat their democratically elected government and that the insurrection is being backed by the C.I.A! Right now, everything is crazy, Frank. We don't even have an Embassy in Volgaria these days so there's nobody north of the river I can talk to who could help me get a handle on what is really going on.'*

'Where would they get the idea the C.I.A. is involved, Dick?'

'American Nationals were heard giving the orders when the arrests took place.....and errr.....Frank, believe me, I'm struggling to make sense of this myself. I would guess the Aspadrian Government thinks there has been some sort of agreement reached between the U.S. and the government of Volgaria over the mineral rights and........ Look, Frank, I honestly don't know. Maybe the Aspadrians think it's in their best interests to get their military involved quickly before any of the major powers take an interest. Christ, Frank, believe me; the Aspadrians down here have been looking for this sort of opportunity for years.'

'Well, as you correctly pointed out Dick, we don't have anybody at all in Volgaria at this time, let alone the C.I.A. Listen, leave this with me for an hour or so and stay by your phone until you get a return call. Thank you for the heads up but please be assured, this is not a matter of great concern. Have a tall drink, sit back, put your feet on the desk and relax. I can assure you we reconcile this sort of problem every day of the week and we'll have this one put to bed long before it has any chance to develop into anything bigger. Have a good day, Dick.......and feel assured, you have no cause to worry.'

Frank White dropped the phone with a look of relief and leaned back in his chair. He then cupped his hands to his mouth and hollered across the room.

'Jarvis! Get that idiot Winslow out of bed and tell him to call a guy called Dick Crowshaw at our Embassy in Aspadria and instruct him to sit on his ass and keep his lip buttoned or his next posting will be to Outer

Mongolia........then, get hold of Eugene Graveney at Langley and tell him I'll be calling in thirty minutes for an update on the situation in Volgaria. Oh, and Jarvis, make sure Winslow is made fully aware his man Crowshaw never made a call to Washington this evening and that he has never heard of anybody called Frank White.

No wonder that set of retards were passing him down the line. It's the messenger that always gets shot when the news is bad. It's the first rule of politics. I wonder which one of those bastards is trying to set me up?'

'Right, now, back to business guys; jacks over fours. I think the dollar bills are coming home with Uncle Frank tonight; read 'em and weep, my friends; read 'em and weep.'

CHAPTER EIGHTEEN

'Good to see you old boy; tell me, is everyone wearing them like that this year?'

When you were laid flat on a hospital bed a couple of steps from death's door, swathed in a bandage that made you look like a woman who was auditioning for the shower scene in *Psycho*, your first choice of visitor wouldn't be Her Majesty's man in Volgaria, Desmond Palfrey. Palfrey used up too much oxygen, blotted out too much light and fulfilled none of the requirements of a man lying in bed with an aching body and a splitting headache, one step from death's door.

'Just stuck our deceased comrades on the plane home to Blighty,' he confided, as if reporting back on a drinks party he had been obliged to leave a little early.

'I saw the Yanks and the Celine Dion appreciation society down there doing the same thing. Everyone's looking for answers, Thomas.' Palfrey somehow succeeded in making even this sound like positive news.

'Is it safe to talk in here?' Farlowe enquired.

'I would think so, old chap; doubt if you could hear an elephant fart over the noise that air conditioning unit is making. I'll turn on a tap, though, if it makes you feel more comfortable; but I warn you, I'll be back and forth to the lavatory between every sentence. I'm a martyr to my bladder; runs in the family apparently.'

'Well, I should be out sometime tomorrow,' said Farlowe hastily changing the subject. *'Then at some stage I need to come back for another scan; apparently my brain might be swollen.'*

'That sounds to me like positive news,' said Palfrey with a merry twinkle in his eye that confirmed that he at least was enjoying the conversation. *'Wearing a thing like that on your head would lead a lot of people to doubt that*

you ever had one. Did you have any luck in finding out how it came about?'

'No, I did ask the woman who was doing the organising but I drew a blank; she claimed she had more important things to worry about at the time, which I suppose is understandable. All I remember is walking through the front door of the house we were raiding and running into a lot of bright lights, a few stars and lot of black. Next thing, I woke up here a day and a half later, looking like an Arabian sheik. I was told the Volgarian Police found me on the floor in a pool of blood. They claimed they didn't touch me but I was told they were smiling a lot when they said it.'

'How did the operation go? Not yours, Thomas, the police one,' enquired Palfrey, still in jocular mood.

'A total success apparently; if putting twenty odd men from your own side in the morgue can be looked upon as any sort of success.'

'So a dream campaign.........up until the crash, that is?'

'Yes, to the best of my knowledge everything was running like clockwork; until suddenly it wasn't.'

'I don't like to be the bearer of bad news but there are further ill tidings on the wind, I'm afraid. I've just been told the Coach driver has also cashed in his chips. The official version is he committed suicide while in custody.........but the word on the wire has it, he caught a nasty.'

'He died while being questioned?' asked Farlowe.

'Not exactly; it is whispered in darkened corners he was picked off in his cell by some miscreant with a high powered rifle and a steady trigger finger. The worrying part being, the nearest vantage point was a hundred and fifty metres away and the space the bullet needed to pass through was the size of an ice cream tub. All the hallmarks of a professional hit by a top grade marksman. Someone, it appears, wanted to be sure the driver didn't suddenly develop a dose of verbal diarrhoea.........um,

different question entirely; tell me about the little missy who was giving the orders.'

'They call her Kefira; age mid twenties, small, slight build, very pretty, dark hair I think, big brown eyes. Dresses like a city Muslim; head scarf, long tunic dress; quiet manner that oozes competence.'

'Kefira what?' asked Palfrey.

'No idea; never heard anyone call her anything else. She seemed to be respected though. Nobody argued when she told them what needed to happen.'

'How's she running an operation like this when she's just out of gymslips?' enquired Palfrey, in a manner that suggested Farlowe might in some way be responsible for her rapid rise to a position of authority in the Volgarian militia.

'You are asking the wrong man, Palfrey. I'm the Engineer, you're the spy. You work it out.'

CHAPTER NINETEEN

The next morning Farlowe was discharged. He still wore the head bandage but apart from that looked relatively normal which in no way reflected how he felt. He gathered together his meagre possessions and prepared to depart when a firm tap at the door announced Kefira's arrival.

'Are you decent? At least you look a little better; come here, that bandage is already coming loose.'

She retrieved a safety pin from her shoulder bag, pushed him back onto the bed and efficiently reapplied the dressing.

'Now we are going for a short drive,' she said, looking critically at her handiwork and continuing to sharply prod sections of his skull with her finger.

She walked him to the car, helped him into the passenger seat and had the vehicle in gear before she confided, *'First Minister Brastic wishes to see you immediately.'*

'I'm meant to be resting with no excitement. What does he want?'

'He gave me no indication. I was just ordered to act as your chauffeur. You can sit in the back and pretend you are a person of great importance if it will make you feel happy.'

Farlowe decided to sit back and enjoy the journey; not from the back seat though, in case the driver took offence and decided to drive him off the edge of a cliff. He wasn't convinced that lightning never struck twice and the fatality count for this operation was already beginning to mount up. The trouble with the journey was Kefira didn't seem in anyway inclined to make casual conversation; and there was nothing much to see out of the window except the usual desolate scrubland and the occasional impoverished hamlet. The sun beat down relentlessly and after a short while he felt his eyes grow heavy.

He woke with a start. They were now in some sort of town and there was noise all around; a lot of noise. Someone was trying to climb on the bonnet of the car while someone else was banging on the window on which he had been resting his head with a lump of brick. Everyone was shouting; a lot of people were waving sticks; some had placards but Farlowe couldn't understand what they said.

'Ignore them,' said Kefira without any show of emotion, and a moment later she accelerated sharply; in the process dislodging the man from the bonnet and propelling him unceremoniously in the direction of the gutter.

They drove on for a further fifteen minutes before they encountered a considerably larger crowd demonstrating outside the front of the Ministry building. They parted like the Red Sea when Kefira showed no signs of slowing down and the gates leading to the parking compound swung welcomingly open a matter of seconds before they would have been reduced to matchwood.

'He wants to see me first,' said Kefira. *'Sit down here; I will probably not be very long.'*

Farlowe selected a corner seat on one of the wooden pews that lined the corridor and thumbed through a five year old motoring magazine, written in a language he failed to recognise.

'Kefira, things were going so well, then in an instant everything fell apart,' said the First Minister. He indicated a window five metres from his desk, *'Are the streets still restless?'*

She nodded.

'It's Troveski,' he sighed. *'He sits the other side of the river stirring the pot with a long stick and awaiting his moment to strike.'*

Brastic stood and paced the carpet.

'The toad has rabble-rousers on every street corner and some of our idiot countrymen listen to the poison words spilling from their mouths. I could put the military on the street and clear them in an hour but that would make it too easy for our enemies to pretend we are engaged in a civil war.'

'First Minister, why don't we dynamite the bridges so we deprive the Aspadrian forces of a crossing point?' Kefira ventured.

'You think I have remained locked in this room for two days without taking that into consideration? Sadly, it is impossible. The original bridges crossing the Volgar River were constructed by Aspadrian labour and have always been considered as part of that country's territory. Why do you think they have check points all across the waterway but our passport control is on home soil? Believe me I still considered this as an option but Troveski has troops covering every inch of the crossing. If we had planes at our disposal it might be different; but even then it would be extremely difficult as anti aircraft guns are mounted all along the Aspadrian river bank; and this is without taking into account the fact that any attack by Volgarian forces would be regarded as the instigation of hostilities by the outside world.'

Brastic paused for a moment, as if lost in thought; then with a sigh resumed his monologue.

'Send in the Englishman and wait in the corridor outside. When he comes out stay close to him and report back anything he says and anything he does. It's possible he may choose to trust you; men in his situation usually find it necessary to voice their thoughts. He may be useful, this one, or he may be another curse sent from on high. We can only hope and pray.'

CHAPTER TWENTY

'Mr Farlowe, welcome; my name is Brastic and I am First Minister of this glorious Country. I wanted to see your face and take the opportunity to extend my profuse apologies for the misfortunes that have recently befallen you. However, Mr Farlowe......perhaps you wish me to call you, Thomas?.......I must be honest and confess that is not my only reason for asking you here today. Can you speculate on my motives for welcoming you to join me for this conversation?'

'I have no idea, Sir,' replied Farlowe, ignoring the initial question,

'Was it, perhaps, to enquire about my injuries.'

'No, I'm afraid that isn't the reason, Mr Farlowe. I am not really very interested in the state of your health and to be brutally honest under normal circumstances I wouldn't have cared very much if your head had been ripped from your shoulders and used as a football.'

Farlowe endeavoured to remain expressionless as Brastic continued.

'I understand from my informers, Mr Farlowe, that you have close connections with your Embassy; that you have a special friend working there with whom you frequently have meetings in back street cafés and bars. I allow nothing that happens in this country to escape my notice, no matter how seemingly insignificant. It is the way I have managed to remain in power for so long.'

Farlowe attempted to look untroubled though he could feel his heart beating a little faster.

'The man from the Embassy is just an acquaintance, Mr Brastic; nothing more. To be honest he is something of an embarrassment but I can't seem to shake him off.'

'Mr Farlowe, I will speak frankly as it is the only way that you will know that what I am about to tell you is the

complete truth. Even when you hear it you may not believe a word....but I must assume that will not be the case. Please concentrate on what I am about to say because the outcome will quite probably have a profound impact on both our futures.'

Brastic hesitated and composed himself.

'As a Government representative I have always served my country faithfully. I am first and foremost a patriot. I have now risen to an exalted position but my dedication to achieving what is best for this country has never for one minute wavered. I don't claim I have not benefitted in a small way from the many changes that have recently occurred in this country; but whatever I have gained, has been earned ten times over. Brastic has been good for Volgaria, so why should Volgaria not be good to Brastic? A fair question, I am sure you will agree.'

The First Minister again paused and appeared to take special care with his choice of words.

'Politics is not an easy profession, Mr Farlowe; there is an expression in this country that I think translates well; 'Men who dig coal find it difficult to keep their hands clean'. This is of course especially true if you have directed your nation's affairs through a period of major transition. It is, of course, far easier if you have the opportunity to hang on the coat tails of others and only walk the streets after the gutters have first been sluiced with water and swept clean.'

It dawned on Farlowe, Brastic was slowly starting to lose his initial composure and beginning to become more agitated. It also became apparent he appeared to have been drinking.

'As you may be aware my term as First Minister of the country will very soon be at an end. I am not entirely happy with this situation as I do not feel it is in this nation's best interests for my power to be curtailed at this point in time. I did propose a constitutional reform that would have served to delay my departure..........but sadly certain parties were happier to address their own

concerns, rather than those that might best benefit their country, and my suggestions were ignored. In these circumstances I was obliged to withdraw and consider the situation in a completely different light.........and in the end I came to a quite startling conclusion.'

Brastic now appeared to be rationalising a chain of thought largely for his own benefit. Farlowe had temporarily ceased to exist. The words he spoke were delivered with calm assurance but each one was being retrieved from the bottom of a lake of molten lava. His eyes were alight; he was now connected to the outside world by only the finest of threads. He summoned an inner strength and continued.

'To face the facts, I will be succeeded as head of Government by a mental cripple. In a sane society Kolat and Sharma would not be trusted to run a kebab house; and Pasonak; ah, Pasonak, my illustrious successor; unguided he will take only months to bring this country to its knees.'

The First Minister paused to mop his brow.

'With this unsatisfactory situation looming I thus concluded that I needed to think the unthinkable; namely, that the interests of this country would be best served by the greatest heresy any Volgarian citizen could ever contemplate; I speak of an attempt to reunify with our closest neighbour and oldest enemy, the country of Aspadria.'

Brastic seemed now to want his words of sacrilege to be uttered so there was no possibility they could ever be retracted. He fixed his eye on a point a thousand miles away and fired off sentences like bursts of machine gun fire.

'I contacted Premier Troveski, a man who, like me, has spent so much of his life weighing and balancing expedients that he can identify the exact straw that will break any camel's back. I suggested that the interests of both our countries could be best served by a degree of *mutual co-operation that would prove as convenient to mutual betterment as it would be unthinkable to propose.'*

'I sketched the outlines on a canvas and once Troveski realised that he could believe what was set before his eyes he grew to share my vision that we had before us a once in a lifetime opportunity to achieve great things; but that to reach such a goal it would be necessary for us to trust one another and have the courage to see that what we were doing was not just for today or tomorrow, but for the very future of both our nations.'

'Don't misunderstand me, Mr Farlowe. I am not a fool. I was careful to establish firm ground rules. It was agreed for the foreseeable future a Volgarian national would remain in control north of the river and Troveski would exercise power only in the south. Aspadria would provide the necessary finance that would enable this country to gradually draw itself away from our current reliance on foreign powers for the efficient extraction of our mineral wealth. Aspadria would throw open her borders and allow free access to her ports so we were no longer solely reliant on the overworked northern rail link and the foreign airport. It would also underwrite further exploration, as well as assisting in the development of existing projects and would be rewarded with a generous industrial partnership agreement in compensation. Aspadria would also throw open the door to its centuries of cultural heritage so Volgarian citizens could start a programme of educational development that would in time enable them to take a more prominent place on the world stage. The advantages were colossal for both nations and once the initial hurdles had been overcome we might even find ourselves in a position to commit the ultimate heresy and consider if we could put together a workable plan for reuniting the two countries into a single entity.'

Brastic now looked like a man who had crossed an arid desert only to discover a dead sheep floating in his water hole. There was no light in his eyes. He subconsciously licked his lips and continued in little more than a whisper.

'But there are some people who never learn to share; greed is so prevalent in their makeup it is engrained in their very souls. After all my hard work, my months of rigorous planning, Premier Troveski decided on an alternative course of action. He mislead his Parliament as to my intentions and laid the foundations for insurrection. You have doubtless seen the unrest on the streets; Troveski's doing without the slightest shadow of a doubt. Two weeks ago I was officially advised by word of mouth that the deal was off. Even while we speak Aspadrian tanks are massing on the far bank of the river Volgar. My friend from the south has clearly evaluated the situation and concluded he can achieve more with force than with diplomacy.'

Brastic again paused and took stock.

'You will be wondering, Mr Farlowe, what any of this has to do with you? Allow me to explain. After Troveski's withdrawal from our agreement I felt that the least I could do was to leave him with a timely reminder that while I still draw breath deviousness will never go unpunished. A plan was devised under my direct supervision to sweep away a portion of the Aspadrian scum that pollute our border towns, while at the same time make retaliatory action from the south a complete impossibility. As you will no doubt appreciate, Aspadria might have considered some form of retribution against a small nation like this one, but it would most certainly never contemplate a show of arms if an American involvement was evident.'

The two men sat in total silence for several minutes. The sound of the wall clock was suddenly very loud. Farlowe tried to think of something to say that wouldn't sound entirely facile.

'But it seems they did.'

'They did indeed, Mr Farlowe, and the only explanation is that Premier Troveski was somehow made aware that our plan was in fact nothing but a subtle ruse. Who perpetrated the deceit I was not entirely sure. Possibly a German with a guilty conscience; or even the

young man currently seated in a chair at the other side of this desk, if he had been clever enough to evaluate the information that had come into his possession and work out the path down which his little acting role was likely to lead.'

Farlowe swallowed and tried to get his brain working, hoping his life did not depend on his next sentence.

'I can only give you my assurance, First Minister, that I am not that clever. Anyway, I've been in hospital. I haven't even had access to a phone. I also don't know anybody in Aspadria and I have only had two visitors, one of whom works for you.'

'Which, after careful consideration, is exactly what I concluded, Mr Farlowe. In fact it occurred to me that rather than possibly being a spy, you were in fact the one person on this planet I could definitely trust. Let me put this plainly; what you see before you is a man with no hope........as I sit here and watch the hours tick by I put a signature to my own death warrant; it is only a question of whether it is the idiot Pasonak or the devious Troveski who gets the honour of carrying out the sentence.'

Brastic again paused so he could carefully choose his words.

'Mr Farlowe, I trust you still maintain your close ties with the British Embassy because I now need you to put them to good use. I require a safe passage out of this country and the easiest way to achieve that is to utilise the tools that I currently have at my disposal. Mr Farlowe, advise your people I wish to immediately lodge an application to become a citizen of the United Kingdom.'

CHAPTER TWENTY ONE

'Eugene Graveney? It's Frank White here; how's the weather in Langley, Eugene?'

'The same as yours, Frank. I'm only eight miles up the road unless they moved The White House without telling me. If you shout loud enough I will probably hear you without needing the telephone. Anyway, I haven't seen the outside of this room for two days so the weather hasn't featured high on my priority list. We are only just coming up for air on this one. It's been pretty tense round here but I think we've just about got our ducks in a row.'

'Sorry Eugene; it's force of habit. I spend my life talking to people half way round the world so these days it just slips out as a natural introduction. Anyway, how's the family?'

'Mary Beth divorced me last year and she's now shacked up with a Life Guard half her age somewhere near Santa Barbara. She got a face lift, her tits pumped full of silicone and bought a little villa on the cliff edge where she grows grapes while she figures out how to spend the rest of the divorce settlement. Never hump your secretary, Frank; in the long run it works out far too expensive. The eldest boy's got a crack habit and the only time I hear from him is when he needs a bail bond. I haven't heard from the youngest since his mother packed her bags. He says I ruined his life by never being there for him and he was going to join a commune in Nevada that does yoga and smokes dope while they await the second coming. Families, Frank, I hate everything about families; give me a nice friendly dog any day of the week. At least they wag their tails and look pleased to see you when you get home from work.'

'Well, sorry to hear that, Eugene,' said Frank White, now reluctant to enquire if The Washington Redskins were

having a good season in case it served to make matters worse. Instead, he hastily changed the subject. *'Any repercussions from the assignment?'*

'Nope. No thanks to that crazy Kraut though. He did his level best to screw things up.'

'How long had he been on our books?'

'Way back; nineteen fifties I think. Schuster was the longest running double, treble or God knows what in the history of the species; not that he had been a lot of use in recent times.'

'Why did he do it, Eugene? What was the sense?'

'No logic Frank; just an old man wagging a central digit in our direction after all the years of misery we must have caused him. His health was shot. He knew this was his swan song and he decided to go out big. He was on a three way loser; it was just a question of whether God, the Israelis or our boys got to him first.'

'What's happening down there?'

'Nothing significant in the last twelve hours; the Aspadrian tanks are still lined up at the border crossing. A few minor riots in the larger Volgarian cities; nothing we didn't anticipate.'

'Are we in a position to go?'

'Yep.'

'Remember, Eugene, you don't move a muscle without my personal O.K. We have got to be whiter than white on this one or the President will have my hide nailed to the wall of a shed. He only approved the deal because I convinced him the tanks we sold to Aspadria were a heap of junk. If he finds out we turned a blind eye to American Companies assisting with their modification he will go ballistic.'

'No problem, Frank.'

'Between you and me I'm having nightmares over this, Eugene. Just picture what could happen if the wrong people started adding up the numbers and came to the right answer; can you picture yourself standing up in front of a congregational committee and trying to explain how

an ex Nazi, who had been on our books for over fifty years, masterminded the death of twenty of our boys?'

'Only seven were ours, Frank. The others were Canucks and Limeys.'

'Excuse me if that doesn't make me feel an awful lot better, Eugene. If anything, I think it just serves to raise the stakes a little higher. Just make sure everything goes through me personally O.K? I want 'justified intervention' written in letters ten feet high before we lift a finger. I want atrocities so bad the liberals are pleading with us to go in and clean up the mess. If there isn't the necessary carnage we need to make some bad stuff happen; understand? Oh, and I want to see Aspadrian tanks at least ten miles into Volgarian territory before we shoot hell out of them; make sure everybody is totally clear on that.'

'Not a problem Frank; don't lose sleep over it. You are the man calling the shots. Nobody from this side of the fence goes to the can without checking with you first. Listen, how are you intending to justify us selling the Aspadrians the tanks in the first place?'

'Let me worry about that. It wasn't my signature on the bill of sale and I've already got a couple of candidates lined up to take the fall. O.K. Eugene. We'll speak again tomorrow. Love to the family.'

It was a full ten minutes before it dawned on Frank White that he would have had difficulty in closing the conversation with a less tactful exit line.

'Sam, it's Eugene. I just came off the phone with Frank White. He doesn't seem to have any more idea what's going on down there than we do. If there was an ISIS or Al Qaeda involvement then Frank sure as hell doesn't know anything about it. Let's keep it that way. Washington has totally bought into Schuster being responsible for the coach crash so bury anything that might paint a different picture. Burn any files that might cast doubt on that assumption; then think about burning anyone who might have read the files. Make sure there is no paper trail; be certain nothing was committed to paper that doesn't point directly at that bastard Kraut. Thank God we popped the damned driver when we did. God knows what he might have said. Who would have thought the crazy Nazi would end up proving useful after all these years? Who knows; he might even have been the guy who set up the whole shooting match. I certainly wouldn't have put it past him.

Anyway, just keep it neat and tidy. The Oval Office is always happier with certainties when it comes to an issue like this so let's not give them any reason to speculate. We might even end up with a pat on the head when the dust settles. As far as I can see that leaves everything pretty much straight. I'm beginning to believe the Good Lord just might be a Republican voter after all. Just make sure everything is one hundred percent watertight, Sam. Frank White is as nervous as hell, and when Frank's nervous, I'm nervous. He's got a damned good nose so make absolutely sure there's nothing left outside the freezer for him to smell.

And Sam, as soon as that's done start talking to your people on the ground. Once we've got the White House off our backs we can start to think about who might really have been pulling the strings. If it wasn't Schuster then I want a list of other possibilities. Keep it quiet but start putting things together. If it was those Muslim bastards it won't be long before they come out of the woodwork and go public; and by the time they do I want to be one pace behind them with a baseball bat in one hand and a rocket launcher in the other.'

CHAPTER TWENTY TWO

'.........*not to mention phone hacking,*' said Premier
Troveski sorrowfully; giving the clear impression he was
genuinely loathe to discuss a subject so contemptible with
a group of people who were clearly capable of condoning
that sort of heinous activity.

The party of newspaper proprietors, Editors, Sub
Editors, Senior Reporters and other luminaries from the
trade wriggled uncomfortably in their seats for the
umpteenth time in the thirty minutes since the Aspadrian
Premier had began to address them.

*'I have also received no fewer that twelve reports of
trespass, which as you will be aware is a crime punishable
in our law courts with a sentence of two to five years hard
labour.'* He paused to cast a glare at a fat man with a
floral tie sitting with his eyes half closed in the very front
row, in case anyone in the auditorium was in any doubt
that the perpetrators of this crime were indeed close at
hand.

*'And a further twenty three alleging an invasion of
privacy which, you might be unsurprised to learn, the
Aspadrian courts view with no less seriousness,'* Troveski
continued, taking the opportunity to wave an arm in the
general direction of a group of shirt sleeved men checking
the early racing results on their mobile phones, who had
strategically positioned themselves to left of the dais on
which he was currently standing.

A number of pointed looks were exchanged across the
hall and there was little doubt that these would have been
accompanied by a shuffling of feet were it not for the fact
the majority of the audience had been obliged to remain
seated by the presence of two large security guards with
wooden truncheons who had been designated to patrol the
auditorium's central aisles.

'So, I have no alternative but to ask myself the perplexing question; what precise action is now required to reassure the public their rights are being protected by their appointed Government?' continued the First Minister, taking the opportunity to single out a bald man in a pin striped suit with a piercing scowl.

'Because I'm sure you will agree, this situation clearly cannot be allowed to continue.' His eyes circled the room before settling on his secondary target; a young man with a deep suntan, dressed in a sports shirt and light blue cardigan who looked like he should be out for a stroll on a windswept promenade rather than suffering the menacing atmosphere that currently prevailed in the badly lit room.

The bald man was simultaneously elbowed sharply in the ribs by his neighbours on both sides and after some prevarication reluctantly rose to his feet. Immediately a huge sense of relief was evident; so evident it could have been mounted on a plinth and exhibited as a work of modern art that would probably have won prizes. Finally a scapegoat had felt obliged to poke its above the parapet and provide the sniper with a clear target. This considerably lessened the chance of any of the other guilty parties being singled out for verbal castigation.

'If you leave this in my hands, Premier, I am confident that I can construct a robust, self regulating judiciary that will be able to bring any transgressions of the type you have highlighted to an immediate conclusion.' The bald pin stripe submitted in a voice that appeared to offer more hope than conviction.

'That address would be a good deal more convincing if it wasn't exactly the same one you gave last time we found ourselves in this unhappy situation,' countered Troveski pointedly.

'Allow me to prompt your memory, my friend. One week ago did one of your titles not publish a centre page spread of a young actress naked in her bath, which upon examination, Troveski paused to examine a sheet of paper in his hand to confirm the precise detail of the dereliction, *'proved to have been obtained by a photographer who had scaled a telegraph pole opposite her home with the aid of a step ladder! I'm sure even you will agree the 'robust regulation' you assured me you would construct the last time we were obliged to have this troubling conversation seems to have fallen somewhat short of the mark. I am at a loss to think of an alternative course of action; direct Government intervention now looks the only possible means by which these outrages can be bought to a halt.'*

The bald headed, pin stripe mopped his brow and looked to right and left for support. None came, so he was obliged to battle on single handed.

'I beg you to reconsider, Premier Troveski. I promise that this time I will give the Committee more teeth; robust self regulation with swingeing fines for any transgression is undoubtedly the correct solution to this problem. I am totally convinced the matter can be satisfactorily addressed without the need for Governmental involvement.'

There was a pause while Troveski slowly looked around the room, before he wearily sighed and turned his attention to a separate wodge of papers.

'While I consider the matter, gentlemen, let us turn our attention in an altogether different direction. As you are doubtless aware our Volgarian brothers to the north are currently suffering untold horrors at the hands of unspecified renegade forces and......'

Troveski was interrupted as the hall descended into chaos. A tall thin man seated at the extreme left of the second row leapt nimbly to his feet, shook his fist in the direction of the compass point he judged to be north, and screamed; *'light the fires and let us watch the bastards fry!'* This comment elicited a standing ovation and repeated cheers from the entire assembly, which proved impossible to bring under control until they had crossed hands and sung the first three verses of the Aspadrian national anthem.

Eventually armed officers with riot clubs moved into the hall and the pandemonium was contained; but the room was now alight with expectation and the atmosphere remained electric.

'If you will allow me to continue,' hissed Troveski in a menacing growl that insinuated it would be the worst for anybody who doubted the wisdom of resuming their seat and remaining completely silent. He adjusted his collar and slowly glared around the room, staring down any one who made any attempt to meet his burning glare.

'As a staunch ally of Volgaria and a close personal friend of First Minister Brastic, I would not sleep easy in my bed if I stood idly by and allowed the ugly situation in the Volgarian border towns and beyond to develop. In consequence I propose to swiftly despatch a peace keeping force across the River Volgar by means of the Chake and Lobstock bridges to help subdue the subversive elements that are currently running riot in a number of our neighbour's major cities..... and to duly return our sister nation to its previous state of happy equanimity.'

This statement was met with looks of total incomprehension. A small man in a bow tie groaned loudly and collapsed into the aisle, where he remained completely ignored by his fellows as he writhed dramatically on the polished wooden floor boards. Nobody spoke, nobody moved; nobody dared to breathe. People looked at each other but found it impossible to make words that could adequately express their feeling of utter distaste. Their brains, seemingly incapable of efficiently processing the information with which they were being presented, chose a last ditch defence mechanism and completely shut down; thereby rendering each member of the audience effectively transfixed and totally speechless. The room was now like the epicentre of a monstrous typhoon. There was perfect silence, complete stillness in the air; while at the same time there remained a frightening awareness that a terrible danger lurked very close at hand.

The Premier surveyed the scene with clinical detachment, withdrew from his pocket a white linen handkerchief, loudly blew his nose and proceeded with his oratory as if he was of the impression there was nothing amiss.

'Because of a certain unwarranted and ill advised animosity towards our northern neighbour, which I cannot avoid pointing out has largely been fanned into flame by some of the more short sighted editorial comment printed in the very newspapers over which you are meant to exercise direct control, it is conceivable that my laudable intentions could be open to.....how shall we say.....misinterpretation. In consequence I have taken the liberty of producing a small hand out, the salient points of which you might see fit to print on the front pages of your first editions in large bold type..........quite naturally, using words of your own choosing.'

Helpers materialised from the wings and scurried between the rows of seats, swiftly pushing pamphlets into the hands of dumbstruck figures. The audience remained open mouthed, appearing too shell shocked to fully understand what was happening around them, let alone comprehending the content of the notes with which they were now being presented.

All this time Troveski stood rigid and unmoved, meeting nobody's eye but studiously watching for a reaction. None was forthcoming so he decided to raise the stakes.

'You will perhaps have already taken note that the salient points are in bold capitals,' he continued. *'I am of the impression it would be a grave mistake to underemphasise the phrases* RESCUE MISSION *and* PEACE KEEPING FORCE *when you construct your finished article.'*

As the Premier straightened his papers to leave a wall of sound arose from the audience as they awoke from their stupor, their minds kicked into gear and everybody tried to speak at once.   Troveski immediately returned to his previous position and clapped his hands for silence.

'I omitted to mention.....while this worrying situation continues I will be unable to devote the necessary time to consider the vexing press complaints issue.   In the circumstances, please carry on with current procedures until I summon you back here for further discussions at a later date.'

Troveski strode from the stage to complete silence and immediately beckoned an Aide from the wings.

'Get rid of this bunch of tossers as quickly as possible; the television and radio people are due to arrive at three and I don't want them getting any idea of our agenda before I've had a chance to lick them into shape.'

He paused for a moment, as if wishing to ask a question to which he might not like the answer.

'Tell me, are the next lot likely to be any more adept at reading between the lines? I've been on that stage for half the morning and it's been like drawing teeth.'

The Aide ran his finger quickly down a list of names, grimaced, and sadly shook his head.

'Looks like it's going to be a long night then,' said the Premier, glancing down at a sheet of paper. *'Just refresh my memory, what exactly have we got on the next bunch that will make certain they don't get any silly ideas?'*

CHAPTER TWENTY THREE

Farlowe stepped out into the blazing heat with Kefira at his elbow. He looked up at the Ministry building and pictured Brastic peering down on him from one of the darkened windows above. His head wound was starting to feel uncomfortable now he was once again in direct sunlight but he was under strict instructions that the dressing was not to be removed under any circumstances.

'Are you coming with me?' he asked the girl. She nodded, looking no happier with the situation than he was.

'I need to go to the British Embassy; do we take your car or use the bus?'

They travelled in silence both buried in their own thoughts. She drove with her usual degree of efficient detachment; the car almost appeared to steer itself. In some streets there was evidence of earlier rioting; windows had been broken and half hearted attempts had been made to construct primitive barricades. They encountered several burnt out cars and odd bits of displaced furniture. At one intersection a mannequin in formal dress had been positioned in the centre of the road to direct traffic. Occasionally loud noises could be heard from nearby but they saw very few people on the streets. The vast majority of the population seemed to be keeping their heads down and waiting to see what happened next.

'Why did you try to kill me?' Farlowe asked, as casually as he could manage.

He momentarily caught her off guard, but in an instant the expression of surprise had vanished.

'What makes you think that?' she replied without emotion.

He smiled but didn't speak; let her work it out for herself; she was a good deal brighter than him after all.

Kefira parked in the road outside the Embassy building; Farlowe quickly jumped out of the car and headed through the gates before she could ask him questions he didn't want to answer. The Receptionist looked cool and efficient, closeted in a long wooden booth fronted by a Perspex screen. He was very conscious that the ragged bandage made him look like a third world refugee and that a large man who had been loitering near the door had quickly taken a interest in his arrival.

'I'm a British citizen,' Farlowe blurted out. It sounded more like an apology than a statement.

'I haven't got an appointment but I need to speak with Des Palfrey urgently.' Why hadn't he thought to phone ahead? That wouldn't have required too much imagination, would it?

The Receptionist offered a regulation smile that played on her lips for a little longer than was strictly necessary. *'I'm afraid he's not around at the moment Mr........?'*

Farlowe panicked. *'Look I know what he does. I'm one of his contacts. If you could just tell him I'm here I'm sure he will..........'*

She interrupted before he could get into full flow.

'Try the Lazy Lion; out of the front gates and two blocks left. They say it's his local these days.'

Either it was his imagination or she had smirked and exchanged a knowing look with the large man who was now standing very close behind him. The ten strides to the door took an age to complete.

Farlowe heard Palfrey before he saw him. He was sitting on a high stool at the far end of the bar telling a ribald joke to a middle aged waitress dressed in a grubby black dress and laddered stockings. While never allowing her attention to waver from his story she occasionally engaged herself in lethargically lifting ash trays and rubbing a dirty dish cloth along the top of the counter. As he approached she casually threw her cleaning rag high across the bar and into a sink with a display of surprising athleticism; before breaking into a wheezy chuckle, squeezing Palfrey playfully on the arm and unsteadily clomping off down the bar.

'Just look at the thighs on that. I think I'm in there,' said Palfrey, ignoring an introduction in favour of leaning forward to better follow the line of his paramour's erratic exit.

Farlowe ordered them both a beer and spent the next ten minutes recounting an abbreviated version of his meeting with First Minister Brastic. When he had finished Palfrey looked thoughtful. He turned to the bar, ordered another drink and swallowed a large mouthful as he deliberated.

'Interesting, that; I wonder what exactly we should do about it?'

'That's what I was hoping you would tell me.' replied Farlowe.

'Well, you see, it's not my precise area of specialisation,' continued Palfrey, picking up a beer mat and casually flicking it into the air with his thumb.

'It's exactly your area of specialisation, Palfrey,' said Farlowe testily. *'It's a simple enough question; do you want him or don't you?'*

'Wouldn't think so,' Palfrey replied in an offhand manner. *'Sounds like a total shit to me. Give me a bit of time to think it through; I'll talk to a chap I know who...........'*

'What do you mean 'you'll talk to a chap you know'?' interrupted Farlowe. *'The First Minister of Volgaria is sat in that bloody Ministry building waiting for an immediate answer. How long will it take 'this chap' to get back with a reply; an hour, a day, a week?'*

Palfrey quickly raised his index to pursed lips.

'Keep the voice down, old boy; this is a regular watering hole. No point in getting over excited and upsetting the natives. These things are a lot more delicate than they appear on the surface; difficult to rush this sort

of situation.' He glanced at his watch, then leaned a little forward looking slightly uncomfortable.

'Look, it's possible you might have got the wrong end of the stick as to my part in the grand scheme of things.'

'I don't follow. What 'grand scheme of things'; it's a simple enough decision, Palfrey; either you want him or you don't want him. Don't you have the authority to make this sort of call?'

'Not exactly old chap; I'm more into liaison; I try to steer clear of the hands on stuff as far as I can; now if Johnny Spindler were here we could put this to bed in no time at all........Johnny's in Switzerland at the moment; loves his skiing, does Johnny. It reminds me of the time Eddie Hughton and I met up in St Tropez......... .'

'Palfrey, what exactly is your job?' interrupted Farlowe, sorry that he had asked the question the minute the words had left his mouth.

'You are well aware of the answer to that old boy, a cog in the wheel at Her Majesty's Embassy, Volgaria.' answered Palfrey sharply.

'Precisely, which cog in the wheel?'

'Well I have a myriad of diverse responsibilities. One day I might be......'

'Specifically, Palfrey......today for instance!'

'Keep the voice down old boy. Nothing to be gained by drawing attention to ourselves. It isn't just walls that have ears.'

'Palfrey, in words of one syllable, what is your ordinary day to day function at the British Embassy in Volgaria?'

'I'm a Records Clerk.'

'A what?'

'I'm a Records Clerk......and don't turn your nose up like that; it's an important placement in any Embassy. The wheels of diplomacy run smooth in the political world thanks almost exclusively to the production of accurate paperwork.'

Farlowe banged his bandaged forehead theatrically with his fist and immediately regretted it.

'In that case what has been happening to all the stuff from the site I've been feeding back to you for the past months?'

'Ah, I see your concern. Don't worry it's not been going to waste. I've been passing it on to our brothers in arms.'

'What brothers in arms?' enquired Farlowe, feeling increasingly lost.

'Our allies; hands across the water; the special relationship; the Yanks you ninny, who else?'

'I must be simple; I really don't understand,' said Farlowe, feeling he must have missed something important that was key to making sense of the conversation.

'Look, I'll explain. It was a simple matter of expediency, Thomas my boy. Our lot never showed the slightest interest in anything I brought them.....and God knows I tried them enough times; and then a year or so back I bumped into this Yank in a bar, and well; one thing led to another.'

'What thing led to what other thing?'

'You really aren't keeping up are you, Thomas? The Yanks; they haven't got an Embassy over here so they find it hard to keep their finger on the pulse........and on the odd occasion I just lend them a bit of a helping hand.'

'But you are a United Kingdom citizen and you work at the British Embassy!' exclaimed Farlowe in exasperation.

'What's that got to do with the price of fish? I render a slight assistance to our closest ally and receive minimal compensation for my time and effort. I do it in my own time, not H.M.G's.......well most of it, anyway. It's not like it's the Russians, is it? I'm helping the good guys; our friends and allies,' replied Palfrey sounding aggrieved.

'Don't you realise they could chuck you in prison for spying, you idiot; come to that they could probably chuck me in prison for spying as well!'

'That's plain ridiculous, Thomas. The Yanks are on our side. We work hand in glove with them to hold back the scourge of Communism. And don't think for one minute I didn't give our lot first offer. You know what? They just laughed in my face! They said 'who did I think I was, James Bond!!' It's always the same; unless you wear the right tie or have membership to one of those snotty clubs in Mayfair, nobody listens to a word you say.'

'But you do wear the right tie, don't you?' asked Farlowe, already dreading the answer that might be forthcoming.

'Afraid not, old boy; born on the wrong side of the tracks, you see. I cover it well, I know, but it's all writ large in the personnel files back at base; and you would be amazed at how quickly word gets around when you are posted to a God forsaken backwater like this one. I'll never make anything of myself while those stuck up bastards stymie my every move; probably would have been better off taking up acting. I've been told I display a certain talent in that direction on more than one occasion.'

'But I saw you handle that drunk in the Strip Club.....'

'The Lewisham Estates teach a harsh lesson, old chap; but that isn't what they are looking for at the F.O. I'm afraid. Men of action are not their stock in trade. They are only interested in Jeremy's from Cambridge with a lisp and a First in Political Science,' said Palfrey with rancour.

Farlowe paused to consider. 'Alright, well assuming that is the case, surely the Americans will want him even if the U.K Government don't.'

'That might very well be true but it would be for entirely the wrong reasons. It was your friend Brastic who was instrumental in getting them kicked out of Volgaria after they had spent a small fortune financing the mob who conducted the initial mineral survey. No love lost there, old boy, I can assure you. America is the last place Brastic would want to end up. Why do you think he's talking to you? You don't imagine for one minute dear old *blighty would have been top of his shopping list when he was forced to consider packing his case and sliding quietly out of the back door.'*

'Well, isn't there anybody at the Embassy that you could ask?' enquired Farlowe, a note of desperation creeping into his voice.

'Take it from me, there would be absolutely no interest in the blighter from our side of the fence; and the Ambassador wouldn't thank me for posing the question. If anything it would best suit King and Country if Mr Brastic were to remain in situ and await his fate. Ironic really, because he never did us any harm. Granted, he took back handers whenever they were on offer but so would anyone else in his position. He also did everybody a big favour by keeping the Yanks out of play and there were a lot who were extremely grateful for that at the time.'

'Try to look at it from H.M.G.'s viewpoint, Thomas; old Brastic's not really got a lot going for him, has he? The person they definitely don't want to rub up the wrong way at this point in time is that new bloke, Pasonak. Think about it rationally; how would Pasonak be likely to react if H.M.G. jumped in and spirited away his old boss and mentor just when he at last had the opportunity to settle a few old scores? And there will be some to settle I can assure you. Mr Brastic's nobody's favourite Uncle these days, I'm afraid.'

Farlowe buried his head in his hands, remembering to do it as gently as possible.

'Anyway, must make a move,' said Palfrey, checking his watch for the second time and jumping to his feet as if he didn't have a care in the world, *'the devil makes work for idle hands you know. Listen, as you've asked nicely, I'll take my life in my hands and check with the Ambassador if there is any chance we can take him.....but don't hold your breath for a reply. I hope you realise this will doubtless damage my diplomatic career for all time, but there's no lengths I won't go to for a close friend.'*

As Palfrey headed for the door Farlowe had a final thought.

'If all that's true, then how did you manage to get my Visa and Work Permit straightened out?'

'Forgeries, Thomas my boy, courtesy of Uncle Sam; don't worry about it, they'll be fine. Down here nobody ever checks into paperwork; not unless you do something illegal, that is.'

CHAPTER TWENTY FOUR

Greta Fakhri exited by the front entrance of the Ministry building, decorously sashayed her way down the gravel drive and took the main road heading towards the centre of town. The guard at the main gate whistled softly under his breath and dabbed at his forehead with the sleeve of his uniform as she wiggled past, dressed in an extremely short skirt, high heels and a light plunging blouse that left little to the imagination. She was clearly undaunted by the vicious heat, wearing a pair of oversized sunglasses, with a wide brimmed hat perched jauntily on her voluminous golden curls; to all eyes a beautiful young girl enjoying a leisurely stroll in the summer sunshine as she unashamedly flaunted her stunning figure for all to see.

After several hundred yards she slowed her pace and checked cautiously behind her; before strategically positioning herself in front of a dusty shop window which allowed her to examine the reflection of each passerby. A few minutes later, evidently satisfied, she resumed her journey; only to pause once again and loiter on the next street corner so she could scrutinise the passing traffic on the busy roadway. Suddenly, she moved with lightning speed; initially retracing her steps for twenty metres and then taking a sharp left and darting up a side alley which led to the back doorway of a large department store. In a matter of seconds she emerged through the front entrance into a bustling shopping complex, where she secreted herself in a shaded alcove, initially choosing to remain completely motionless as she examined the facial expressions of each individual as they emerged from the dark interior into the dazzling sunlight. She stood there for a full ten minutes, looking pensive and biting her lip; periodically changing her position a little, to gain a better vantage point; but all the time never allowing her gaze to falter from the store's doorway for as much as a split second. To a casual observer, she wanted to give the impression of a person dithering over directions; constantly changing their mind as to which path was the correct one to follow. Someone so supremely lacking in confidence they were convinced whatever decision they eventually settled upon would prove to be incorrect.

Finally, seemingly satisfied, she gave a last glance in all directions, let out a deep breath and composed herself. She straightened her skirt, purposefully hoisted her long strapped handbag a little higher on her bronzed shoulder and set off at a brisk pace in the direction of the town's central concourse.

After walking briskly for nearly twenty minutes Greta entered the forecourt of a smart café and selected a secluded seat under a multicoloured awning which offered some small respite from the withering heat. She ordered a triple Espresso and a fresh orange juice with ice and a slice of lemon, crossed her long, bare legs and lit a cigarette. She was dressed in a flimsy cream top and bright red skirt that finished high above the knee; combined with open toed sandals with heels more suited to the Paris boardwalk than the badly maintained Volgarian pavements. Passing men considered her with lust; women with envy. She ignored all glances, calmly sipped her coffee and appeared totally at ease in the elegant surroundings which blended seamlessly with the image she portrayed.

After some minutes a man of medium height with dark curly hair and an olive complexion joined her; stick thin, he wore a smart business suit in a muted stripe, highly polished slip-on leather brogues and smelled strongly of a powerful, musky aftershave. He removed a pair of designer sunglasses revealing surprisingly light hazel brown eyes, smiled broadly and enquired politely if the vacant chair at her table was unoccupied. When she nodded, he clicked his fingers at the waiter and requested a tall glass of lime juice, and in no time the pair were engrossed in deep conversation.

'*You were definitely not followed? Our lives are at stake if you were not vigilant,*' the thin man enquired anxiously.

'*If I was, it is far too late to worry about it now.......no, Masum, I took the necessary precautions and was most definitely not followed.*'

'*You would be stoned to death for dressing like that in the villages of our homeland. Why is it you find it necessary to dress like a whore even when you are not working?*' said the man nervously, in a voice the faltered as it strived to exude authority.

'*I am working. I'm meeting with you. That is work as far as I am concerned; it certainly gives me no pleasure. You have the cheek to make me what I am and then complain at the result!*' Greta answered angrily, shrugging her shoulders in annoyance as she reached for her lighter and another cigarette.

He frowned, lowered his eyes and shook his head slowly. '*You have changed so much since we first met. The life you lead has made you into a person I scarcely recognise.*'

'*I play a role, Masum. You are well aware of that.*' She leaned forward a little and tugged gently at the sleeve of his jacket. '*Let us hope it is God's will that this will very soon be over; then I can make my own decision as to how I dress and who I really want to be.*'

'*Is the butterfly able to change back to a caterpillar? I am not sure you will find that decision as easy as you may think.*' Masum muttered bitterly. He gave a final uneasy glance to left and right, before settling back in his seat and appearing to at last partially relax.

'*Any further news?*' he enquired, reverting immediately to a businesslike manner in an effort to mask his show of nervousness. He straight way withdrew a fountain pen and small leather bound notebook from his inside jacket pocket.

'*Aspadrian troops are still lined up on the border ready to invade,*' she said unemotionally, '*but you are aware of that already. The First Minister continues to skulk in his office and demands no interruptions while he searches for a suitable counter strategy. Again, nothing you do not already know...........why do I read nothing in the newspapers about the coach crash? They must by now be aware the deaths of the foreign workers were caused by an explosion.'*

'Who is better equipped than you to understand the Volgarian mentality?' Masum replied sharply. *'Like the will of God it clearly passes all understanding.'* He hesitated for a moment and collected his thoughts. *'From our viewpoint it has been concluded that we gain more than we lose by keeping our own council and awaiting developments. The Americans are showing an interest but it's apparent they have discovered nothing that has proved of assistance. Each of the three nations that suffered losses is searching for motives that might help them identify who was responsible. None appear to have made a great degree of progress in that endeavour. There is currently a deep air of distrust amongst our enemies which is best left to fester. Later when the advantages of this strategy are exhausted we might find it is in our interest to engage with the media.'*

'What became of the coach driver?' asked Greta softly.

Masum hesitated, as if giving the matter careful consideration.

'We had a man in position to make certain he would never have the opportunity to spill his heart to his interrogators, but no intervention proved necessary. The driver was shot from a great distance with a high powered rifle but our organisation was not responsible. It is suspected our brother might have purposely stood in front of his cell window to welcome a bullet unconcerned at whose finger was on the trigger. Seemingly, he was ready to die but not by his own hand. A man trained to have no fear of losing his life who was repulsed by the prospect of suicide; a paradox indeed. That is as much as I have so far been able to learn.'

'What about the German?' Greta persisted.

'Schuster's capabilities as a planner remained unrivalled to the very end. For many years he had also provided us with information of the highest quality; yet we were always conscious he could never join us as a brother in arms. Naturally he still hated the Jews but that remained our only common ground. As he got older and work dried up he became obliged to take the job opportunities that presented themselves. Over time he totally jettisoned any degree of ideological integrity; and his political sympathies had always been somewhat suspect, even in the early years. By the end he had clearly abandoned any attempt to differentiate between just causes and those that paid his bills. He just acted as a whore to any paymaster who would deliver his price or had the ability to safeguard his personal wellbeing. Once the bomb had been detonated any mutual interests ceased to exist; his loss was of little importance.'

Greta sipped her strong coffee which had now started to cool and tasted considerably less appetising. 'So, what do we do next?'

'For now my lovely Greta we wait and watch. If Aspadria attacks, as seems likely, then there is a possibility America will get dragged into the conflict. If not America, other nations will certainly become embroiled because greed will oblige them to protect their mining interests. There are all manner of possibilities; too many for us to speculate over at this time. Your role remains unaltered; listen to what is said and keep me informed of everything you hear. Information is the most valuable currency these days. Do what is required to earn it, Greta, and I promise you I will spend it wisely to further our aims.'

Greta again reached across the table to pull at Masum's arm and her voice gained a note of urgency.

'Masum, you haven't forgotten your promise? No matter what happens, for me this is the end.'

Masum smiled reassuringly. *'Of course, of course; how could I forget such a promise?* He drank quickly from his glass and wiped his lips with a pristine handkerchief that was clearly being used for the first time.

'Greta, I need you to understand that the next few days will be vitally important. If things go well we can inflict what our American friends refer to as 'major collateral damage'. Anyone from the west is a good target but the Americans and British are still at the top of the list as we owe them so much for their previous duplicity. Be vigilant, Greta; this situation could provide us with the major breakthrough we have long been seeking.'

Masum stood to go; now looking supremely confident and with a gleam burning in his eyes.

'One last thing; I presume you still have the small present I gave you? Keep it close to hand; an opportunity may arise where you can put it to good use.'

Greta waited five minutes for Masum to disappear from sight, checked her watch, touched up her makeup and hastily retraced her steps. She needed to shower and change her clothing before she was collected by the Italian from the international oil company who always tried too hard to impress her when he had been drinking. His inability to control his tongue had already proved extremely useful which meant there was currently no hope of terminating the relationship, so she was obliged make the best of the situation. She had hoped she would have the time to spend a moment at prayer before she embarked on another night of debauchery, but that was now also out of the question.

Tomorrow would be different though. She had already decided she owed this to herself. Tomorrow she could lock herself in her room and do exactly as she pleased. She would perhaps feign a migraine in order to gain a few hours of total peace. Nobody would pay her any attention with the Ministry now in lockdown as the First Minister tried to anticipate the next Aspadrian stratagem. She would ignore the outside world and read to her heart's content; maybe listen to music on the radio. She would shut her eyes and indulge her favourite fantasy of all; the one in which she had enough money to escape this whole sordid business and set herself up somewhere so far away that even Masum would be unable to find her. A place beyond the reach of all the men motivated only by thoughts of hate and revenge.

In her mind she would again review the letter she had written to Masum many months ago and already refined more than a hundred times. The letter in which she explained to him in words he could not fail to understand, that rather than being prepared to die for her beliefs, she now had a burning desire to live for them.

She would also wallow in a hot bath filled with scented bubbles and for a short time at least, escape the harsh realities of her current life. But even while doing this she would not forget the need to bleach her hair and shave her legs; so the next day she would again be ready to perform the hateful role she acted out so effectively.

CHAPTER TWENTY FIVE

Thomas Farlowe was in need of a place where he could quietly contemplate his next move. This ruled out any thought of a return to the mining camp where community living meant you were never short of company whether you wanted it or not. After some discussion he and Kefira agreed to book in at a small guesthouse on the outskirts of town which boasted some car parking space and rooms that were fully air conditioned.

The hotel was modest but clean and had both a small restaurant boasting a menu of local produce and a very tiny bar. Farlowe dumped his meagre possessions in his room and immediately slipped out to investigate a local parade of shops, where, with a major degree of difficulty, he eventually succeeded in purchasing a change of clothing and some items of stationery. Then, after taking a shower, made more difficult by the need to keep his bandaged head clear of the inconsistent jet spray, he dried himself with a face flannel that might have doubled as a cleaning rag and propped his body into a comfortable position on the bed. He then set about the difficult task of assembling his thoughts.

What did he need to consider; an appeal by an old man he had never previously met, for help he wasn't qualified to give. An old man, let it be said, who was so angered by the prospect of losing his stranglehold on power that he appeared ready to walk out on the country he purported to love rather than accept the prospect of relinquishing his vice like grip. A fantasist who was not prepared to accept the turning of the wheel of time, despite for years having accepted bribes from foreign powers to line his pockets. Was that why the Americans had been hustled out of the country all those years ago? Perhaps they hadn't understood the way things worked in this part of the world.

There was also an awful lot more to take into consideration. A hostile army camped at the Volgarian border ready to invade; not to mention a homicidal girl who, he was reluctantly forced to admit, turned his legs to jelly on the rare occasions that she elected to bat an eyelash in his direction. Not that she had given him the slightest encouragement on that score. If he was truthful with himself her reaction had been rather the opposite. In fact, most of the time she didn't seem to notice him at all; looked straight through him like he didn't exist. Why couldn't he just fancy someone nice and normal who showed an inclination to return his feelings? Perhaps it was something they put in the water down here or the fact he had always been a sucker for a difficult challenge.

When you looked at it logically, was the current situation in Volgaria any of his business? No, it most certainly was not; and yet he had to confess he wanted it to be so desperately it set off twinges in his aching ribs whenever he thought about it.

It presented the adventure he had always craved. The dream that had enticed him to remain in this weird country when sound logic would have put him over the border in thirty seconds flat. It was the incident where the bus had crashed onto his campsite, but with far more potential to exploit. He wasn't just intrigued by the challenge, he was totally captivated. It pained him to admit it, but he had loved the adulation his heroics had brought about. It was the first time in his life he had ever felt really special. Wasn't this the inner craving that had caused him to set out on this crazy odyssey in the first place?

It was his wildest dream awaiting fulfilment. It even made sense of the stuff that prat Kevin Cummings had babbled on about that drunken night all those years before; wild adventure in the raw. Living on the edge of a knife. The sort of thing that would keep you warm in bed on a freezing winter's night when you were no longer able to bend to tie your shoe laces. Something to tell your wide eyed grandchildren with a certain degree of pride. Save the country and win the girl. That was the sort of fantasy worth gambling everything for. He decided there and then he was going to give it his best shot and that nothing in this world or the next would be permitted to get in his way.

He mopped his brow and forced himself to calm down; pushing aside thoughts that while there was meant to be air conditioning in this room the only evidence of it was the drone from an aged motor located somewhere in the upper section of the wall. Right, he needed to stop dreaming and come up with some sort of plan; approach the problem with some sort of method and see what could be achieved with a little application; complete quiet now, total concentration, no distractions; bugger the heat and the air conditioning, this was far more important.

He scribbled notes on scraps of paper and spread them across the floor. He had read this was the way recording artists often chose to compose their lyrics so it was certainly worth a shot. What was the other thing people always said? '*Evaluate everything, discard nothing*'........ no mention of a prayer for divine inspiration, he noticed. That would probably have been the best place to start because he was forced to admit he didn't have any clue what he was doing.

Over the next three hours he tried everything. He shuffled his thoughts like a pack of playing cards without once finding the lucky lady. He wrote different ideas on pieces of paper and shifted them around in ever decreasing circles but no matter which way he looked at it, there always seemed too many snakes and not enough ladders. He had made no progress whatever when a sharp tap at the door announced the arrival of Kefira, enquiring whether he intended venturing out to eat.

The sun had sunk low in the sky by the time they located a suitable café but it was still hot enough to make the well worn jacket he had draped across his shoulder totally superfluous. Kefira had somehow managed to magic a new dress from somewhere and now wore her hair uncovered, which for some inexplicable reason he found more disconcerting than when it was hidden from view. As usual she looked serenely beautiful; as usual she said virtually nothing.

They ate quickly and Kefira paid the bill with some form of banker's draft that the owner didn't seem overly keen to accept. As they walked back to the hotel Farlowe decided to go for broke.

'It was your perfume,' he said.

'You don't like it?' she enquired with a small show of interest.

'It brings back unhappy memories. I smelled it when I came through the doorway on the night I got my head cracked open. It was very strong; like the person wearing it was very close at hand; possibly hidden behind the door. After that I remember nothing until I woke in a hospital bed feeling like I had been run over by a truck. I'll probably get over the physical injuries but the smell of that perfume will stay with me forever.'

'And on that basis you conclude I was trying to kill you?'

'Weren't you?' asked Farlowe.

'No, I was not and I don't think there is anything to gain by discussing the matter further.'

He decided it was time to take a chance. *'Either tell me what happened or I'm getting on the next bus. Can't you just trust me a little bit for Christ's sake?'*

She considered for a full minute before reaching a decision. Even then she proceeded with extreme reluctance.

'Alright; on this one occasion I will explain what happened; but only because we are in such an unusual situation and you are obviously not yet fully recovered from your injuries. I don't think you would last very long out here without me at your side; but I accept that probably you are too dim-witted to understand that.'

She stopped in mid stride and pointed to a wooden bench by the roadside; walked determinedly in its direction, dusted the slats with a tissue she retrieved from her handbag and, looking vaguely affronted, plonked herself down.

'It was illogical. I knew the man who planned the raids on the Aspadrian criminals; I worked with him. I made it my business to study him closely. He was neither a good nor a kind man but he was an expert in the field in which he worked. He had once been regarded as the very best in the business. He was a meticulous planner.'

'Who was he?' Farlowe enquired. *'I met this man but he never told me his name.'*

'It is of no consequence; he is now dead and of no loss to the world. He did many bad things in his lifetime and is hopefully now receiving his just reward in the after-life. However, for all his considerable shortcomings he had an extraordinary ability to plan and organise, and his methods were always based on pure logic.'

She looked deep into Farlowe's eyes making him feel vaguely unsettled before choosing to totally change tack.

'Thomas Farlowe, you do not strike me as a particularly sophisticated person and from our dealings you appear to completely lack any vestige of subtlety or guile; but in my estimation you should be categorised as a naive man, possibly even a stupid one, but not intentionally evil. You were an idiot to allow yourself to become involved in the proposal the German put to you, though I appreciate you would have been placed under heavy pressure to do so.'

She hesitated for a brief moment as if deep in thought, then without warning again altered course.

'When the bus crashed onto your camp site you showed courage and resourcefulness. I followed the story closely in the newspapers and on television. You were exceptionally brave and your actions saved the lives of many people.'

Farlowe thought of lots of good things to say but none of them seemed quite good enough, so he sat with his hands in his lap and waited.

'I also understand logic,' she said, returning without warning to her original theme. *'If there is no evidence of it, from a man like the German then only a fool would fail to be suspicious. Why would he organise a coach to take your people to socialise after you had already accomplished what you were being paid for? There was no logic to that decision. The men had already served their purpose so what more was there to gain? Surely the last thing a man of logic would have wanted was for a group of drunken morons to be seen cavorting around nightclubs drawing attention to themselves. The sensible course of action would clearly be to get everybody back within the perimeter of their mining camps as quickly as possible.......unless, of course, those men were intended to fulfil some entirely different purpose.'*

'You guessed they were going to be murdered?! You worked out they were going to lose their lives and you coolly sat back and watched it happen without lifting a finger,' Farlowe yelled, causing two old men walking on the opposite pavement to briefly interrupt their conversation to stop and stare.

'Of course not; idiot; how could I know what the crazy German had planned? Do you think I am psychic?' she replied sharply. *'I only knew things didn't make sense; so I took the necessary action to ensure you were unable to rejoin your colleagues and by taking that action I saved your life.'*

'By nearly killing me!' Farlowe exclaimed.

'Don't be ridiculous. I gave you a small tap on the head. It was not my fault that you chose to blunder about like a wounded elephant making your injuries worse,' she said dismissively.

'That still doesn't explain it; how did I end up like this?' Farlowe asked indicating his bandaged head, and multitude of bruises and abrasions.

'I needed to justify my actions as the policemen would undoubtedly make reference to my conduct when they filed their reports. I explained that I struck you because you

were a pervert who had made repeated attempts to rape me. They considered your punishment for this crime was inadequate so when they carried you outside they took the opportunity to kick you in the ribs and bang your head on a kerb stone. Their intention was to drop you down a manhole but I persuaded them that further punishment would not be necessary as I intended to castrate you with a pen knife as we journeyed to the hospital.'

'But why did you pick on me?' Farlowe enquired, not knowing what else to ask.

'I make it a policy never to explain my actions. You should just be happy that you are still living,' she replied sharply, before picking up her handbag and starting to walk briskly in the direction of the hotel.

As Farlowe hurried to catch up he was unsure whether he should feel resentment or gratitude; before he had reached a satisfactory conclusion he realised he had placed his arm around her shoulder; and to his surprise she hadn't chosen to remove it.

They collected their room keys from the reception desk and padded along the silent corridor. Farlowe suddenly turned, lifted her from the floor and squeezed her to his chest, burying his face in her hair; breathing in her perfume. They stood for some minutes in a wordless embrace before he broke the spell by lowering her to the floor and trying to lead her to his door.

She squeezed his arm, reached up on tip toe and kissed him lightly on the cheek.

'Perhaps we would be wise not to make this any more complicated than it already is,' she whispered; and in an instant had pushed him firmly in the chest, turned her back and disappeared into her room.

CHAPTER TWENTY SIX

Kefira stood by the door to her room and strained her ears. After a short time she heard Farlowe's footsteps retreat back down the corridor. She breathed out, not realising she had been holding her breath. That had been a very close call. She had surprised herself by nearly yielding to temptation. It was completely out of character and she could offer no rational explanation as to why she had nearly allowed herself to be compromised. This in itself she found unsettling. Fortunately she had come to her senses in time and taken the correct course of action. In her experience, men had always proved to be totally unreliable and there was no reason to suspect this one would be any different from the rest.

She immediately pushed the matter from her mind and began preparing for bed; she cleaned her teeth, put on a nightdress, then flipped open the small brown suitcase that she always kept ready packed in the boot of her car. No need to worry, she had enough clothes for a week or longer and by then this whole thing would long be over. She jammed the case into a convenient gap between the wardrobe and the far wall and again listened at the door. Hearing nothing she extracted her mobile phone and fed in a long series of numbers.

The phone was answered on the first ring as if the recipient had been poised with a hand over the receiver.

'*Kefira Haber,*' she said quietly.

'*An update, please,*' said a toneless male voice, battling to be heard over short bursts of static interference.

'*First Minister Brastic has assigned me to stay with the Englishman, Farlowe. He has today visited the British Embassy but for what purpose remains unclear. I did not see his contact but from his mood when he returned I don't think the meeting proved in any way satisfactory.*' No need to tell him too much. If she did he would doubtless choose to make suggestions as to how she should proceed and she hated being directed by anyone, least of all him. She would do things her own way for better or worse and that meant, as usual, keeping feedback to a bare minimum.

'*Speculate, please,*' said the dull voice.

She had mouthed the words to herself at the same moment they left his lips. Always the same. He was nothing if not predictable.

'*If Aspadria invades, as seems likely, First Minister Brastic must realise he will very soon lose his life. He would be a fool not to seek an escape route. Logically he can only go north by train or fly out from the new airport. His options are extremely limited and he has few friends who would be willing to offer assistance; he has not endeared himself to many people during his years in office. It is possible he was attempting to enlist Farlowe's help to convey him out of the country.*'

That was the easy part; anybody with half a brain could have worked that out for themselves.

'*Anything further?*' the man enquired.

Did he have the word '*probe*' written on a sheet of paper, she wondered. If he did the paper would be grubby and the word spelt incorrectly.

'*The local media reports that the invasion is imminent. There is of course a general feeling of unease.*'

'*No evidence of outside involvement? No signs of a military presence?*' the man questioned, displaying a degree of concern.

'*Rabble rousers on the streets and a few minor riots; nothing more,*' she replied tersely.

'*And......?*' the male voice persisted.

Might as well get it over with.

'*Farlowe has deduced it was me who assaulted him when we conducted the raid on Anouk Tibor's villa; but I don't think that will present any great problem. He seems to have already recovered from the discovery.*' She had better give him something of no importance to occupy his mind or he might start to look further than the end of his nose.

'*He is presumably aware he was manipulated?*' the man enquired.

No, he thought everything that had happened to him in the last few days was completely natural. What did they pay this idiot for? Steady now, a nice polite reply. Remember, he's the one who is meant to be in charge.

'*He will have guessed that by now. He is not a fool. He will know he was used for a purpose but have no idea of the bigger picture; that is of course unless First Minister Brastic chose to open his heart which in the circumstances seems extremely unlikely.*'

'*Be very careful that each step you take is the correct one, Kefira Haber; if this goes wrong we have much to lose. The Americans have been looking for any excuse to get back into Volgaria for many years. We must make certain none is presented,*' he instructed firmly, using the voice of a kindergarten teacher lecturing a mischievous child.

'*I am always careful, comrade. That is how I manage to stay alive.*'

That was so delicious she wanted to hug herself but it had also been extremely unwise. He would hate hearing those words so much they would burn scorch marks into his flesh. She would now need to be very careful. He would be waiting for the slightest mistake so he could take pleasure in pushing those self same words back down her throat.

CHAPTER TWENTY SEVEN

'*Frank, Frank White? Frank, it's Eugene Graveney; I've got a situation update.*'

'*Fire away, Eugene,*' said Frank White sneezing loudly as someone pulled down a window blind that hadn't been used in months, releasing a cloud of fine dust.

'*The last drone over the Volgar shows the Aspadrian supply column only fifty miles from their assault force. It looks like they will cross the river on both bridges simultaneously. I figure they will start out at dawn the day after tomorrow and plough straight up the main highways. It's the obvious tactic. They can use a pincer movement and shut the back door on any military units that try to stage an organised retreat.*'

'*How long do you think the Volgarian troops can hold them back?*' asked White, still recovering from the dust spray and sounding slightly asthmatic.

'*Unless the weather changes dramatically it will only be a matter of hours. As far as we can see from the drone pictures they have nothing bigger than pea-shooters to defend the roads and the Aspadrian tanks will knock them out in no time. It's an uneven fight; the Volgarians just won't be able to get close enough to inflict any real damage. They are in a no-win situation unless the weather turns in their favour so the tank squadrons aren't able to go off road to bypass any road blocks they might have put in place; and according to our weather expert there's more chance of hell freezing over than Volgaria getting rain in the next few days.*'

'*Long term, what's your best guess on how they will mount their defence?*' White enquired.

'*There's only one strategy open to them as far as we can see; fall back to the hills and the desert and conduct a guerrilla campaign. That's always assuming they don't recognise the inevitable and decide to wave a white flag; but going from the past history of the nations concerned I don't see that as a high probability.'*

'Will the Aspadrian tanks definitely hold together, Eugene? They were damned near useless when we ran them.'

'That's anybody's guess, Frank, but the modifications seem to have worked out pretty well. Remember, the problem centred on the vehicles' manoeuvrability, not firepower. If they stick to tarmac with the odd excursion onto hard dry dirt they could get half way across Europe without running into any real problems,' said Eugene Graveney, sounding quite upbeat about the possibility of that happening.

'There's something strange going on down there,' Eugene, said White sounding concerned. *'The story the Aspadrian Government is selling to the locals should be laughed out of court but that isn't happening. I can see no reason why the media has chosen to get right behind it unless they are somehow in on the act. I swear if I read one more story in their press about 'the plight of our Volgarian brothers' I am going to puke. The two nations have always hated each other's guts and that's never been any sort of secret. It will be carnage if we don't get in there quickly; which is of course exactly what we require........then after we have landed, sorted things out on the ground and set up shop, we have the ideal excuse to hang around for as long as it suits our purpose.'*

'Frank, dial back a notch and listen to this,' said Graveney, in the manner of the first boy with his hand up from a class of forty three.

'My boys have been milking a tame Limey working out of the Brit' Embassy in Volgaria and he says the head honcho down there..... what's his name.....Assdick?'

'First Minister Brastic, Eugene, the man's name is Brastic.' spluttered White, either suppressing a laugh or trying once again to clear his nasal passages from the cloud of dust.

'Whatever......the word from our boy is this guy Brassdick is asking the Brits for a get out of jail card. Obviously figures he will be the first one up against the wall when the tanks hit town so he's aiming to be long gone. Given the chance, would we want him?'

Frank White considered for a moment and then shook his head sorrowfully in the direction of a photograph of the US President standing on a tarmac square inspecting a never ending line of immaculately dressed troops standing to attention like toy soldiers.

'He'd never come, Eugene. He headed up that phoney evaluation committee that got us kicked across the border when the survey deal went pear shaped. The U.S. would be the last place he would want to finish up; too many people with sharp knives and long memories still hanging around on Capitol Hill for that to suit him. What are the Brits intending to do?'

'That's the beauty of it, Frank.......they don't know. The boy we've got down there is fully house trained. He cuts out the home side and comes straight to us.'

'This might have possibilities........are you sure the Brits don't have any idea what's going on?'

'Nope, we've been feeding our boy down there on prime steak and he's developed a taste for the finer things in life. Anything that comes his way, we are right at the front of the queue.'

'What exactly is Brastic angling for?' asked White thoughtfully.

'Brit nationality; Lion on the passport; nice little house in the country I wouldn't wonder. Basically, the whole nine yards.'

'Even if we had the chance we could never provide anything like that, could we, Eugene?' enquired Frank White in a voice that seemed to indicate he had a good idea of the proposition he was about to receive, but didn't want to be the one who actually suggested it.

'We can't; at least legally we can't........but let's be honest, Frank; that never stopped us before. Let's say, we

tell our Limey cousins to throw out a big welcome; give Brassdick all the right bits of paper, kiss him on both cheeks or whatever that bunch of faggots do down there; then break it to him gently that the U.S has a fully functioning extradition treaty in operation with the U.K, and that it's seen so much action in the last couple of years the paper's wearing thin.'

Frank White pondered the suggestion for several seconds. 'I don't know, Eugene, I really don't know.'

'Look at it from the other angle, Frank; by the time he gets to know the Brits aren't waiting to welcome him with open arms what alternative has he got? I don't think he's flavour of the month with anybody else right now. The way I see it, it's a bluff that we can't lose.'

'It's got merit, Eugene. I'll grant you it's got merit but I would rather keep the Brits out of it altogether. The word is the old coot's been trying to hang on to his job at any cost. If we could drag him over here and attach some electrodes to his balls, I'm pretty sure it wouldn't be too long before he invited us over to set up home in his front parlour.'

'So we go for it?'

'Yes, but formulate the plan yourself and make it a C.I.A. house operation. Use the tame Limey as a front but make sure the British Embassy knows nothing about what's going down. You'll have to tell your boy what's happening but if he's as dumb as you think he is it's likely he'll follow orders without asking too many questions. If he doesn't; arrange for an accident and make sure it's fatal.'

'I'll get my team to knock something together and get back in a couple of hours for your O.K. This is getting exciting, Frank, it's more fun than I've had in years.'

Frank White repeatedly stabbed the nib adjuster on his biro as he calculated the odds of pulling off a coup. 'Eugene; a couple of important points. The words you just heard me say never left my lips; right? This all has to come from your end. I can't afford to be involved.

Secondly, if by any chance the brown stuff does hit the fan I assume you can you fix it so everything's deniable.'

'Do bears shit in the woods?' answered Eugene Graveney with utter conviction.

'OK my friend, lets run it; I can't wait to see that bastard Brastic's face when he finds out he's just fixed himself up with an extended vacation with his much loved Uncle Sam.'

CHAPTER TWENTY EIGHT

Thomas Farlowe left the hotel at first light and travelled by a series of overcrowded buses to the mining complex where he was employed. The day was scorching even by Volgarian standards and within minutes his clothes were wringing with sweat. He entered the compound by the main entrance and made his way to the staff canteen which was always the central focus of activity on a working day. There he was subjected to a lot of good natured derision from the incumbents for his absence from work and the unprepossessing nature of his voluminous head bandage. Nobody mention the coach crash; emotions were still too raw. Everybody on the vast site had lost a friend or acquaintance in the crash and nobody wanted to dwell on the subject as it served as a stark reminder of their own vulnerability. Added to this, the impending invasion had served to focus troubled minds in a totally different direction. The Aspadrian border was barely fifteen miles to the south and everybody was aware of their immediate proximity to a potential war zone.

After less than thirty minutes Jock Strachan put in an appearance, alerted, presumably, by the bush telegraph.

'*Still swinging the lead, young Thomas,*' he said, selecting a steel chair to his liking and subjecting it to his vast bulk. '*What's that bunch of rags you've got balanced on your head? See what happens when you go out into the big, wide world without Uncle Jock to keep a watch over your wellbeing?*'

'*What's the latest, Jock,*' said Farlowe ignoring the invitation to get involved in a lengthy discussion about something he still didn't entirely understand.

'*Never the man for small talk were you, Thomas? No wonder nobody fights for the privilege of sitting next to you when we venture out for a little light refreshment.*

Now, if you would care to avail me of a mug of strong tea from that vision of loveliness in the pink overalls and knitted headscarf charcoaling bacon behind the counter over there, I would be more than delighted to make you aware of the events that have come to pass since your untimely departure. I can only hope you weren't relieved of your wallet while you were lying incapacitated in the gutter after your beating. That would be an oversight you would never be likely to experience in the fair city of Glasgow.'

'It's always payment in advance with you, Strachan,' said Farlowe, pushing back his chair and heading for the counter. *'Pity you weren't born prettier; you could have made a small fortune in a different line of work.'*

Farlowe trudged the length of the hut and retrieved two mugs of tea which he placed, none too delicately, on the chipped Formica table top. *'Right, Mr Strachan, what do you know that I don't?'*

'Quite a bit my young friend but in order to get the conversation concluded in the short time available I'll keep the important stuff back until you are a wee bit older and wiser. In short, we are deemed safe where we are now situated unless advised to the contrary. The powers that be have positioned a man with a powerful set of binoculars at the Chake crossing; so, if the Aspadrian army takes it into its head to cross the river at Lobstock, in military parlance, we're totally buggered.

As soon as the lookout claps eyes on the first puff of an exhaust fume he's meant to get on the phone so the whole site can be closed down, allowing everybody of voting age and above to organise an orderly departure to a back street bar or brothel of their choosing, where they can amuse themselves while they await developments. Those of more tender years like your good self can choose to be deposited at the airport or railway station, from where they will be obliged to make their own travel plans to get out of the country. We have all provided contact details. After the dust settles we will be advised of the possibilities

140

of resuming gainful employment by telephone, carrier pigeon or a sheet of paper tied to half a house brick. If we don't hear anything in a month it is recommended we assume the worst and sign on at the nearest dole office.'

'In that case, Jock, seeing as how you are unlikely to be overburdened with work, is there any chance you could do me a small favour?'

'None, my boy, none whatever; you know I have strict principles when it comes to that sort of thing and I wouldn't want to set a precedent that might make me vulnerable in future years.'

'Even if I was prepared to admit in front of witnesses that the only reason Glasgow Celtic have not been allowed to join the English Premier division is that they would be likely to embarrass the teams from south of the border?'

Strachan paused with the cup half way to his mouth as if considering a life defining issue. *'Never let it be said I'm an unreasonable man, Thomas. Keep talking while I enter into a moment's deep reflection on the proposal you have just put before me.'*

Farlowe sensed an opening and was anxious not to lose the initiative.

'And a concession that all major engineering innovations of the last three hundred years were made by Scotsmen.......coupled with an admission that the English stole your oil without offering reasonable compensation.'

Strachan screwed his face as if he had been placed on the horns of a dilemma. He lifted both hands from the table and manipulated them slowly up and down in the manner of tilting scales.

'You are heading in the right direction, Thomas, but I feel a little more is required to tip the balance in your favour.'

Farlowe, without thinking, threw the last of his stake money into the middle of the table.

'And that Robbie Burns should be recognised by any discerning Englishman as a far greater literary figure than William Shakespeare.'

141

'Fair minded of you to at last admit the truth of the matter, Mr Farlowe. It is difficult to understand why it took you so long to come to the obvious conclusion. Now, what exactly is that wee favour you were looking out for?'

CHAPTER TWENTY NINE

First Minister Brastic packed and carefully labelled two identical leather travelling cases. Time was now running short. To date there had been no communication from the idiot Englishman but, more troubling, Kefira Haber had not answered her mobile phone in the last twenty four hours. Surrounded by incompetents, it appeared. Farlowe had of course been something of an unknown quantity but from Kefira he had expected considerably better. He had given plain enough instructions; how difficult could it be to carry them out?

He rammed the lids shut, applied his full weight and with difficulty succeeded in securing the brass catches. Another tick on the list. What else did he need to take into account while there was still time?

It would probably be only a matter of hours before the Aspadrian forces surged across the border crossing. He didn't doubt his troops' courage. They would put up a brave enough fight against the old enemy but would stand little chance with the range of weaponry mounted against them. Little time would elapse before it would become necessary for them to abandon direct confrontation and fall back on the guerrilla tactics that were likely to prove much more to their taste. Any way you looked at it his personal situation was very soon going to become extremely precarious.

He peered out of the window. An unexpected deluge was his only realistic hope but even Volgaria's climate seemed prepared to conspire against him. He had been advised the Aspadrian army might struggle to move their tank squadrons across open country but after weeks of blazing sunshine the ground underfoot was now as hard as granite. God appeared to love the scheming Troveski.

Even the angels were evidently prepared to stand at his side.

He paced his office deep in thought. He was forced to admit he would miss everything connected with this exulted position. In many ways he had shaped it himself; utilised the fresh clay he had clawed with his own finger nails from the river bed of the mighty Volgar to fashion a new type of future in a very different kind of world. One where the country's newly discovered mineral wealth meant that for once in its inglorious history all things could be seen as possible. One where a Volgarian could look any other man in the eye and consider himself an equal if not a better. One that brushed aside the chaos that had existed for countless centuries and replaced it with stability and order; a proper structure which benefitted the whole population while still allowing him to dictate each change of direction with total impunity.

Now it would all be gone; the country presided over by that animal Troveski, with Pasonak quite probably happy to act as his brainless puppet. If that proved the case, Pasonak would definitely not feel another summer's sunlight on his skin. Volgaria would never tolerate the Aspadrian yoke around its neck without a hand reaching out for the sharpened blade; and Pasonak was quite definitely stupid enough to allow himself to become the prime target for an assassination attempt.

Considering that eventuality led him to ponder what would happen to his girls. The elite guard; each member trained to obey his every whim and put his life before their own. He had personally selected and vetted every one of them; even taken an interest in little things like the design of the silver flash on the sleeve of their uniform which informed everybody the wearer was to be paid the ultimate respect because she travelled on the First Minister's personal business. He had been careful that not a single member of his sisterhood was a Volgarian national or had close family connections that might distract her from her calling. Each member of his elite force stood alone and owed their loyalty to him and him alone. He had learned the perils of being vulnerable to assassination in his early days. It had proved remarkably straightforward to arrange the elimination of his predecessor once it became apparent he was surplus to requirements.

Where on earth had Kefira Haber disappeared to? At this moment he needed Kefira most of all. Her sharp little mind and pointed talons always served to reassure him in times of difficulty. He could only imagine something bad had happened, otherwise he felt sure she would never have failed to carry out his bidding.

In these circumstances the only question left to consider was when to make his move; too early would obviously be better that too late but whilst there was still a chance of an eleventh hour reprieve he was reluctant take a final decision. Once he was on the move there could be no turning back; in all probability there would very soon be nothing for him to go back to.

If only he could turn back the clock. A year before he had been offered two aged fighter planes by the French at a heavily discounted price. If he had only sealed that deal he could have taken out the bridges and thumbed his nose at Troveski who would have been impotently marooned on the far bank of the river with little prospect of launching a successful counteroffensive. Hindsight added clarity to this vision and caused him to fume with bitter frustration.

He regained his seat and thumbed through the sheaf of papers on his desk for the hundredth time without noticing any obvious route to salvation. Ah well; what would be, would be. The time had perhaps arrived when he should accept the way the dice had fallen and stop fighting against the inevitable.

He depressed a buzzer under the rim of his desk and one of his girls was immediately at his side.

'Ah Greta, will you store my cases in the safe room? It is only a contingency option, but if things go badly......' He allowed his voice to trail away. She would understand the implications at least as well as he did.

She lifted one with a stifled grunt and wiggled her way slowly towards the door. That is another sight he would sorely miss. The girl was not only an outstanding beauty but seemed totally incapable of finding clothes that properly fitted her. Just watching her walk about the place had bought him untold hours of pleasure over recent years. He wondered idly if he might invite her to accompany him on his unwelcome foray into the unknown but immediately discarded the thought as ridiculous. There was enough money stashed safely in his luggage to purchase a hundred Gretas if the fancy took him; there would be no advantage in carrying more baggage than was strictly necessary, even if it was so attractively packaged.

Greta reappeared and with an even more accentuated wiggle of her shapely bottom the second bag followed its predecessor out of the door and into the hallway. He followed her departure as if mesmerised. Yes, there was no question; it would take much to compensate him for the loss of that quite glorious sight.

CHAPTER THIRTY

Farlowe arrived back at the hotel and immediately spotted Desmond Palfrey lounging in the reception area, reading a newspaper and enjoying what looked suspiciously like a large gin and tonic. Farlowe brushed dust from his trousers and approached warily. God knows what Palfrey would tell him next but whatever it was he doubted that he wanted to hear it.

'Thomas, old thing, the sun's just sinking below the yardarm if I'm not mistaken, so I'll put your arrival down to impeccable timing and banish any thought from my mind that you caught a whiff of the cork being loosened from the neck of the bottle. While you are on your feet, old chap, would you mind checking if the bloke in the kitchen has managed to rustle up any more ice cubes? I did warn him there was a high probability you would soon be beating a path to his door in need of kind words and sustenance.'

Farlowe ignored the request and took a seat. *'How did you know where to find me, Palfrey? Why didn't you just ring my mobile? No, never mind; just tell me, what did they say?'*

'Reference me in future only with the well earned honorific, Desmond Palfrey, miracle worker extraordinaire. As I suspected, the Ambassador was extremely reluctant to get involved in evacuating the First Minister to our shores but after long hours of silver tongued persuasion I succeeded in bending him to my will. I think my British compatriot sensed my steely determination and realised he would ultimately prove no match. I put it down to the resolution passed down through the Palfrey blood line from relatives who fought at Agincourt.'

'The Embassy really said they would take Brastic; you are certain they understood what was involved?'

'Farlowe, I will have you know a Palfrey's word is his bond in delicate matters of this sort. If you have the slightest doubt on the matter I am prepared to swear away my life on a box containing the bones of a saint of your choosing. On my honour, as one of Her Majesty's Government's senior representatives in this part of the world, the Ambassador looked me squarely in the eye this very morning and uttered a resounding affirmation. In fact, he has asked me to take full charge of the exit strategy and I intend collecting the required documentation later this evening. Now, will you please stop poncing about and go and sort out that barman!'

Farlowe wondered if he had misjudged Palfrey; then glanced across the table as him swallowing an enormous swig of gin and decided he probably hadn't. Still, anyway you looked at it, this certainly seemed a positive development.

'O.K. but just the one then I'm going to telephone Brastic and pass on the glad tidings. You want another gin and tonic, I presume?'

Palfrey hesitated in supplying an affirmation to the question for slightly more than half a second.

'That, I feel, would pretty much fit the bill; oh, and instruct the barman not to be too abstemious with the spirit; half measures give me wind and I felt he was a little light handed with his first tilt of the bottle.'

Farlowe entered the hotel bar and immediately noticed a small but animated group of guests crowding round an aged television set. He bundled his way to the front of the huddle and enquired what was happening?

'It's about to start,' said an unshaven man who was drinking a rancid looking local concoction and periodically drawing on a well chewed and extremely smelly cigar. 'The cameras are covering the tanks lined up at Chake; the convoy is loading up supplies.'

Farlowe glanced again at the screen then ran through the bar area and into a back yard crowded with overflowing dustbins and broken items of furniture. He searched out his mobile phone and hopped around impatiently as he awaited an answer. After a dozen rings, he was greeted by a series of expletives in a thick Glaswegian accent.

'Jock, it's happening.'

'I know that ye wee English pillock. We got a call from our man at the bridge thirty minutes ago. I'm busy packing my bags, so if you would do me the great favour of getting off the line I can set about planning my escape while there's still time for me to have one.'

'Did you get it done?' enquired Farlowe breathlessly.

'Not the slightest thought for my welfare, Mr Farlowe. Don't you think it would perhaps be good manners to ask after my health and make a passing enquiry as to whether I've got somewhere safe to go and see this lot out?'

'Jock, just tell me if you managed to get it done,' yelled Farlowe with an air of desperation.

'The job was completed a matter of hours after you set off on your travels. You might be an ungracious, ignorant English pillock but for some reason a few poor misguided souls down here still consider you to be a friend. There will be questions to answer once we are back in business, mind you; so I hope you will find yourself in a position to finance a God almighty piss up, or I won't be held responsible for the state of your health.'

'Jock, I love you. Alright, tell me where you are intending to take your holiday?'

'Mind your own bloody business, Mr Farlowe. If I tell you the answer to that question, you will know where to find me and make my life even more miserable than it already is. Now push off and annoy someone else; I've got things to do and people to see.'

Farlowe retraced his steps and was emerging from the back of the bar area just as Palfrey entered through the main lobby.

'Good idea, Thomas; if service is as slow as that I'm not surprised you decided to jump the queue and serve yourself.'

A natural for the intelligence services, thought Farlowe; how MI6 had allowed him slip through their fingers was difficult to understand.

CHAPTER THIRTY ONE

Kefira Haber parked her car in a back street and made her way on foot down the craggy stone steps at the side of a steep hill and along the bank of the river to the Chake Bridge. She was dressed in military uniform and walked with a confidence that discouraged anyone from attempting to interrupt her journey. As the embankment joined the main thoroughfare she hesitated briefly to inspect a shallow slit trench that had been constructed by Volgarian troops in an attempt to slow up the anticipated incursion. It covered the full width of the road and the loose tarmac and rubble from the excavation had been heaped at the roadside to provide a small degree of shelter for the defending forces. Nearby, a machine gun nest had been positioned half way up one of the shallow banks that ran on either side of an adjoining side road. Barbed wire had been liberally strewn at various points along the roadway and small barricades had been thrown together at the entrances to a number of alleys and passageways.

A hundred yards to the east an old anti-aircraft gun had been hoisted half way up a cliff face and mounted on a rocky outcrop. Once levered into position it had been tilted to point down at the entrance to the bridge. The large gun was now leaning precariously over the canyon edge and there seemed little likelihood that it would be responsible for more than one volley before it overbalanced and crashed into the chasm beneath. The whole defensive strategy smacked of innovation inspired by a degree of desperation.

As she arrived at the final Volgarian checkpoint a guard in a mud splattered uniform materialised at her elbow and her journey was briefly halted. The soldier indicated this was as far as she could proceed without special clearance but she pointed to the insignia on her arm and firmly pushed him aside. Initially he seemed prepared to contest the point but a glance at the glinting silver flash on the sleeve of her uniform appeared to convince him it was better to accede to her wishes, and after a small hesitation he reluctantly stepped back and allowed her to proceed.

Kefira walked down the centre of the massive bridge attempting to appear totally calm. She proceeded straight ahead for a short distance before noticing a short steel ladder to her right. At this point she altered direction and used it to climb up to a companionway that ran along the top of the vast metal structure.

She had completed barely twenty metres on her new course before the next guard interrupted her progress. This one was different; he wore a smart Aspadrian uniform. She saluted, handed him a sealed letter and requested that it be passed to the senior officer at the nearby garrison on the other side of the bridge with all possible urgency. At first he seemed to look on this request as some sort of joke but after an animated debate he reluctantly set off to carry out her instructions; commanding over his shoulder that under no circumstances was she to move from the spot on which she now stood on pain of being shot. In direct contradiction of that instruction she spent the next fifteen minutes kicking pebbles into the gorge below in the hope that sooner or later she would hear one hit the foaming water which gushed urgently past the chiselled rock of the mighty support balustrades, fifty metres beneath.

Eventually a perspiring officer of indeterminate rank arrived and she was invited into a small wooden shed that appeared to serve in more normal times as shelter from the elements for the officials that controlled traffic flow across the vast structure. They talked for some time and she passed him a number of photographs which she had secreted down the front of her skirt. He studied the images with profound interest for a considerable amount of time before laying them out in a line along the top of a wooden shelving unit attached to the wall of the hut. After that he made a number of telephone calls to colleagues in Aspadria and in due course two officers in peaked caps, each wearing a uniform decorated with an array of multi-coloured ribbons, arrived and joined the gathering.

An hour later Kefira shook all three men by the hand, saluted and retraced her steps back across the bridge into Volgarian territory, fully aware that her journey home was bound to be interrupted and in consequence she would be unlikely to reach her next destination before the clock was indicating the dawning of a new day.

CHAPTER THIRTY TWO

First Minister Brastic looked down from his window at the deserted courtyard below, feeling considerably more at ease than he had for a number of days. Despite his earlier misgivings, it had proved a good decision to delay his departure. Kefira Haber and the Englishman, Farlowe, had succeeded in satisfactorily fulfilling their assignment, even if it had taken them an age to do so. Better still, the British Ambassador had speedily provided a senior emissary to confer his new diplomatic status. The man Palfrey brought to mind distant times when the British had been a main player on the international stage. He quite regretted their current demise; for all their faults they still exuded some degree of class. A charge that could never be levelled against the Americans, and similarly the Russians.

This was adequately demonstrated by Palfrey's notification that a private jet would be made available to fly him out of the country that very day. This was a luxury he had never previously experienced and one he hoped provided an auspicious omen to a future where luxuries of this sort might soon be taken for granted.

His hand strayed unconsciously to his inside pocket and he was reassured to feel the new passport dig hard into his chest. It was strange that one small document could throw open the gates to such a variety of interesting possibilities. Perhaps his enforced retirement from politics would after all prove to be a happy occurrence. He had possibly been a little slow to accept the passing of the years and step back a little from the grave responsibilities of such an active and demanding role. He certainly had enough money at his disposal and because of that the potential to exploit his new won freedom from responsibility was seemingly infinite. It still grated, though; having to steal out of the country, whose destiny he had personally guided with such care, like a thief in the night, and to suffer that ignominy after having served the national interest so faithfully for such a large proportion of his life. There should at the very least be a monument to his tenure; gold topped to glister in the bright Volgarian sunlight. It would be a minimal accolade to his years of dedicated service to his country's development. Things would be so very different if there was any justice in the world but clearly any form of recognition was now a fleeting hope.

He resumed concentration; the clock was ticking and there were still final details to iron out. He had signed across a number of development concessions to the British as a gesture of thanks for offering him shelter in his hour of need. He didn't see why they imagined the invading Aspadrians would choose to honour the contract but that would no longer be a matter for his concern. He had thanked the Englishman, Farlowe, for his efforts and assured him his Volgarian documentation was now in order. That was a lie but not one that would be likely to inconvenience the young man for any great period of time if his latest instructions were efficiently put into practice.

What he needed now was to run one final diligent check to reassure himself the worry of the last few days had not caused him to overlook any minor detail. It was imperative that he left nothing that might prove a future embarrassment and he had no intention of doing so. The international courts were getting far too enthusiastic with their extradition warrants of late; and for anybody who had occupied a position of power in a developing nation like Volgaria it was essential that nothing was left behind that could come back to haunt him a few short years down the line.

Some of those idiots in the Netherlands seemed to genuinely imagine it was possible to make omelettes without cracking eggs. They would have run from the room screaming if they had been obliged to shoulder the responsibilities that he had needed to cope with on a daily basis. Those sanctimonious idiots sitting in The Hague could make even the most minor indiscretion appear like genocide when it served their purpose. Well, they would be unlucky. There would be no smoking gun with his finger prints on the handle left behind for them to find.

Palfrey, who was to provide the honour guard to the airport and iron out any unforeseen technical difficulties, was beginning to become an annoyance. The man was loitering on the threshold of his doorway jabbering inanely into a mobile phone. He felt an enormous desire to hurl a heavy object in his direction; that would encourage the imbecile to take his stupid conversation further out into the hallway where it would be less intrusive to people who had no wish to listen to the stream of vacuous prattle that poured from his lips. He controlled his rage; opting instead for subtle diplomacy by requesting the inconsiderate oaf to make himself useful by checking his cases were in order for the flight to England and then conveying them from the safe room to the waiting car.

As soon as Palfrey had disappeared down the stairway he rang for Kefira who had been waiting in an ante-room along the corridor. He thought she looked tired as she entered the office and hurriedly approached his desk. There was no question the last weeks had taken their toll. He embraced her warmly and explained his departure was imminent. He placed his hands on her cheeks like a much loved daughter and looked her in the eye.

'You have been a good and clever girl, Kefira; you know you were always my favourite. There is one last task for your old master; can you take care of the Englishman, Farlowe, in the appropriate manner? I believe you are already in possession of everything you will be likely to need.'

She made eye contact and gently nodded her head to indicate she understood his meaning; before taking a step back to watch the man who had been Volgaria's heartbeat for her entire term of service march to the door with his usual purposeful stride. He looked back over his shoulder and raised his hand in a final gesture of farewell before donning a pair of sunglasses and quickly looking away. She suspected there might have been a tear in his eye but there was no way to be sure; in an instant he had turned the corner and was tackling the broad staircase that led directly to the main entrance hall, exuding a confidence that appeared to indicate he had come to terms with his rapid change of fortune and was already preparing to embrace his new future. She walked hurriedly to the window and forced it open so she could witness him leaving the massive concrete edifice for the very last time. She forced a wry smile. She was aware she was witnessing the end of an era; something that would be talked about in Volgarian cafés and bars for decades to come. The complete abandonment of political responsibility by the one person the population had imagined they could rely upon at this most difficult hour.

Greta Fakhri ran up the stairs as quickly a she could without drawing unwanted attention to herself; by the time the car containing First Minister Brastic and the pompous Englishman, Palfrey, had passed the massive front gates, she had collected her belongings and was heading for the dark underground car park where she always garaged her reliable little car. She was working to a tight schedule and realised she had very little time to spare.

After driving for less than three miles at break neck speed she slowed, seeking out the corner shop that sold second hand furniture and sundry bric-a-brac. On the pavement she immediately spotted Masum sitting serenely on an upturned suitcase reading a newspaper. She lightly beeped the horn and in a second he was seated beside her in the car.

'Is it done?' he immediately questioned.

She must not let him see any doubt in her eyes. At this stage he would believe anything she told him providing she kept the mask firmly in position.

She nodded confidently. *'It is done. It is done and now I want to say goodbye to all of this as we discussed. I have kept my side of the bargain and now I expect you to keep yours.'*

Masum turned in the seat to face her and smiled gently.

'At this time it is still a little difficult, Greta; surely you must realise that? You have always proved so useful to the cause. It sometimes seems your skills are truly limitless. I have tickets for the evening train going north. Where is your bag? I think maybe we should share. This will give a strong impression that we travel as man and wife. It will be good for us to spend some time together, like in the old days.'

She should have known better than to think he would keep his word even though he had sworn on his mother's life.

'Masum, you gave me a solemn promise that when this was over I would be free to walk away and resume my life.'

'Times have changed, Greta; things are no longer as simple as they once seemed; please don't be difficult and make me angry. The situation could be different in a month or two. It is clear with the passing of each day that we are gaining in strength and it can only be a matter of a short time before we achieve our final destiny. Now pull over there in the side street and let us combine our luggage; small details like this may prove important if we are searched at the customs check point.'

Greta took a deep breath. That at least had made the decision for her. She flicked the indicator and swung the car into a left hand turn. While doing this she simultaneously glanced in both directions and wound up her window. She stopped the car by a row of overflowing dustbins adjacent to a children's play area, reached in her bag, withdrew a small pistol, and in one smooth action flicked off the safety catch and pulled the trigger three times; not allowing herself time to think in case at the last second she lost her nerve.

The sound was deafening within the confines of the vehicle and for a full minute she closed her eyes and sat frozen in her seat, dreading what she felt certain was bound to happen next; but, to her surprise, nobody came to investigate or even cast an interested glance in the direction of the car.

Masum had unintentionally helped the situation by lolling against the window with a look of mild surprise; holding an expression not dissimilar to one he had often chosen to display to the outside world. Blood spewed from his chest and ran in small red rivulets onto the seat of the car, nicely matching the thin scarlet tie he had chosen to wear that day. Greta felt a strange compulsion to poke him with her finger just to be absolutely sure he had breathed his last but managed to resist the impulse. Instead, she stretched across to the passenger seat and with difficulty adjusted his body position, closed his eyes for the final time and propped a couple of cleaning rags and a loose seat cover under the back of his head. She hoped people would think he was taking a late siesta or had arrived too early for an evening appointment and was resting in the car while he waited for the minutes to slowly tick by. She buttoned his jacket to hide as much of the blood as possible, dabbing at a few flecks which had settled on her dark jacket, her legs and the hem of her short dress. She surveyed herself coolly in the rear view mirror, applied a fresh coat of lipstick and combed through her blonde curls with her fingers. It was all a little surreal; how could that woman in the mirror possibly look so normal after what she had just done?

She collected her bag from the back seat, shut Masum's case in the boot, locked the car and dropped the keys onto the pavement; quickly kicking them in the direction of a convenient storm drain. After a moment's thought she did the same with the gun. The airport was still some distance away and she dare not waste a minute. She peered in through the side window to make one final check of the car, smoothed down her skirt with the flat of her hand and started immediately to walk at a brisk pace towards her destination. A weight had suddenly been lifted from her shoulders and she felt the strange inclination to skip over the ragged cobble stones in the way she had done as a small child. Possibly it was just attributable to the adrenalin rush but Greta Fakhri had difficulty in remembering when she had ever felt less troubled.

CHAPTER THIRTY THREE

Kefira Haber ignored the resounding echo of her footfall on the stone steps and descended to the basement of the Ministry building as quickly as possible. This part of the administration block always had a particularly eerie feel. As it was situated tens of metres below ground level, permafrost allowed it to remain cool for the entire duration of the scorching Volgarian summer; whilst in the depths of winter the subterranean cellar could be guaranteed to resemble an arctic wasteland.

She quickly located her personal locker, hurriedly inserted a key in the door and attempted to operate the lock. Stubbornly it refused to turn. Confused, she yanked hard on the handle, only for the opening panel to smoothly release and swing open, causing her to lose her balance and tip backwards onto the floor. Kefira was immediately alert; it was inconceivable that she would have forgotten to secure that door; it was not the sort of mistake she permitted herself to make. She sprang to her feet and looked closer. It was straight away evident the door had been forced open; the metal by the lock was jagged and quite crudely bent inwards; not a professional job by any means; no sophistication; one undertaken in an obvious hurry with not the slightest attempt at concealment. She would have noticed straight away if her mind had been focused on the present instead of wandering forward to consider the matters she would need to confront in the coming hours.

She refocused and examined the locker's upper compartments. None of her possessions appeared to be missing; the winter boots with a scraping of last season's cloying mud; her thick coat wrapped in a bundle, shaggy like a small headless bear; various pieces of dress uniform she almost never had cause to wear these days. On the lower level was a blue rucksack with leather straps. She thought she had seen it before without being able to recollect exactly where. It was good quality, quite stylish in its way, extremely old and well used; but most definitely not hers.

An image of Greta Fakhri wearing something similar many years previously darted across her mind but she dismissed the thought as utterly ridiculous one second after it had succeeded in bringing a smile to her lips. When had she ever seen Greta wear something that wasn't stylish and new? It would have been the talk of the building. Greta looked like a model and always succeeded in dressing like one. If she wanted a rucksack one of her numerous boyfriends would provide the best one to be found inside the Volgarian borders; and ensure it was presented in wrapping paper of silver or burnished gold.

Kefira dismissed all thoughts of Greta and turned her attention to the alarm bells which continued to ring in her head. She withdrew and repositioned herself some distance further back; once better placed she slumped to the ground and turned her mind to the various possibilities that confronted her.

After some minutes she reached a decision and walked quickly to a small adjoining room which was packed tight with equipment used by the cleaning staff who were charged with keeping the building in a pristine condition. She returned with an aged broom; a relic of many years service, dirt encrusted and almost devoid of bristles. Keeping her distance she used this to prod vigorously at the bag and when nothing happened repeated the process with a lot more force. Finally, throwing caution to the wind, she pummelled the piece of luggage with all her strength.

Still nothing; though she was at least a little warmer from the vigorous if unrequested exercise.

She dropped to the floor, lay on her stomach adjacent to the line of lockers and stretched forward to her utmost limit; then, with the very tips of her finger nails teased gingerly at the buckles. They were stiff and difficult to unfasten mainly due to the fact she was working from a ridiculously difficult angle. Nevertheless, she was reluctant to risk manoeuvring the bag into a better position in case it had been wired to some sort of pressure detonator, so there was no alternative but to grit her teeth and persevere.

After several minutes of patient manipulation the buckles were at last free from their fastenings. She grabbed the broom by the wrong end and used the handle to flip back the covering material, before swiftly leaping sideways to take cover. Again nothing. She returned to her previous position and tentatively stretched her hand towards the small leather toggle which was attached by a short bobbled metal chain to the inner zip. This proved even harder to manipulate, but gradually, an inch at a time, it juddered further and further along the track on its small metal teeth until it would move no more. Kefira adjusted to a kneeling position wiped her brow and allowed herself a huge sigh of relief.

Having at last made progress she edged herself carefully forward and taking care to touch nothing peeked warily inside the top of the rucksack. The contents looked like banknotes; wads of them. Hundreds, no thousands, in a variety of denominations and a kaleidoscope of colours.

She abandoned her training, ignored common sense, and pushed her hand firmly past the untied drawstring and deep inside the rim; then realising the danger immediately withdrew it, taking with her a thick wodge of paper she had gripped with her fingers. Banknotes, it was banknotes; who would have believed it? A thick stack of currency collected into a neat pile and secured by a large rubber band.

She flicked through the individual bills with her finger and thumb, smelled them, pulled the top one free and held it to the light; put it to her ear and scrunched the paper. The crackle was unmistakable. The notes were seemingly genuine.

Scolding herself for her impetuosity she started to take more care. Inch by inch she gradually eased the bag free of the metal cabinet until it was standing in a vertical position on the concrete floor. This achieved, she turned her attention back to the locker where she straight away noticed an envelope propped upright against the compartment's back wall. It had doubtless at some stage rested on top of the rucksack but had become dislodged and slid down the back when she had battered it with the broom handle. She grabbed the paper and studied the blurred address. It appeared to be in Aramaic and meant nothing to her. She flipped the envelope over. On the back was a note scribbled in faint pencil:

Kefira, you were hard but fair and I always respected you. Sorry, I took your pistol. I have a bad feeling I may need it. I hope this is acceptable compensation. The note was marked with a small smiling face and signed simply, *Greta Fakhri.*

CHAPTER THIRTY FOUR

Desmond Palfrey made the sort of a small bow that to the less discerning eye might easily have been mistaken for a nod of acknowledgement. He then corrected his error by fully embracing the required protocol and shaking First Minister Brastic firmly by the hand in the manner smiled upon in diplomatic circles. Before, almost as an afterthought, warmly kissing the departing politician on both cheeks so as to be sure he could never be accused of being insufficiently euphoric in his parting greeting.

With something approaching a regal flourish, the representative of Her Majesty's Government then produced from his inside pocket a gold nibbed fountain pen embossed with a lion and unicorn motif; this he duly presented to the confused dignitary as a memento of his final departure from native soil. In conclusion, he offered a string of profuse compliments and his very best personal wishes for an enjoyable journey and a long and happy lifetime; and all of this with a clear eye and a stiff upper lip, taking no cognisance of the fact he was perfectly aware his rosy prognosis had zero chance of materialising into a happy reality.

Palfrey then fixed a cheerful smile to his lips and in fulfilment of his final official duty felt morally obliged, for a moment at least, to loiter attentively at the foot of the steps leading to the aircraft. At this point he experienced a definite tightening of the muscles in his lower stomach; something more severe than wind and more closely approximating a mild palpitation. He was painfully aware the planes take off had already been delayed by nearly an hour and he was now keen to walk away and become consumed by the airport's bustling crowd without further delay. He was also conscious that any minute the Americans on board the aircraft would reveal their true identity and announce the flight's change of destination. There was a full C.I.A. team secreted in the forward baggage hold and he knew for certain they would be only too eager to get started on the lengthy interrogation they would have prepared for their reluctant guest. These were sights he had no desire to see, undertaken by people he had no desire to meet, so he had made a point of not being enticed any nearer the aircraft than was absolutely necessary.

He reluctantly gave it one extra half minute before turning and speedily retracing his steps across the scorching tarmac; waving an arm in the air in a casual salute in the unlikely event the First Minister, having nothing better to occupy his attentions, might choose to view his departure through a convenient porthole.

Palfrey had arranged to meet Thomas Farlowe inside the terminal building as soon as his official duties were concluded and he wished to make that rendezvous with all speed. There was really no good reason why Farlowe should have decided to remain hanging around the airport as he had no role to play in the current subterfuge. In fact, one of small joys of the black comedy now being enacted on the nearby stage, was that Farlowe still remained happily ignorant of the fact that Brastic had in effect been duped and kidnapped......and on that score Palfrey saw absolutely no good reason to act as a conduit to his enlightenment.

Equally, if Farlowe chose to waste his time kicking his heels, then that was entirely his own choice. The man was white, single and marginally over twenty one, so there was nothing to stop him doing exactly what he pleased. It was highly likely that as the lad was temporarily laid off from work he hadn't got anything better to do with his time; and under those circumstances it would surely be less than civil not to enquire if he fancied a short blether over a couple of beers. He hoped Farlowe would take off that infernal bandage though; dress like that gave entirely the wrong impression and soured the atmosphere when you were settling down for a quiet drink or two in convivial surroundings.

Desmond Palfrey caught from the corner of his eye a sign of movement from the American jet and halted mid stride to watch the departing plane complete its taxiing manoeuvre before, after the briefest of pauses, hurtling down the runway at some incredible speed and lofting majestically towards open skies. Palfrey let out a small sigh of relief; they were finally on their way and out of his hair. Any iota of responsibility for the First Minister's well being that might have been considered to rest on his shoulders was now most certainly at an end. Brastic was now at the tender mercies of representatives of the American Government with the only possibilities of protection coming courtesy of the fickle finger of fate.

Palfrey immediately turned about face and recommenced his walk but had barely completed six hurried strides when an enormous explosion lifted him several feet into the air and deposited his large frame on a rock hard grass verge several yards from where he had started his journey. There was a moment's total silence; followed swiftly by total pandemonium. Someone threw open the glass doors to the main terminal building and a crowd spewed out onto the tarmaced parking area adjacent to the runway. The horn of a fire engine sprang into life and set up a discordant accompaniment to the ringing in his ears. As he struggled to regain his equilibrium a large book descended from the skies and smashed into the ground, missing him by no more than a couple of feet. On impact it disgorged charred pages that were quickly picked up by the ensuing turbulence and wafted hither and thither in every conceivable direction.

From nowhere Farlowe materialised, already bathed in sweat from his short run. He dragged Palfrey into a sitting position and held a handkerchief to a gash on his forehead. Palfrey realised he was now suffering partial deafness, but his eyes followed the line of Farlowe's outstretched arm. Several hundred yards away lay a heap of mangled wreckage. The intense fire that engulfed it had taken hold of the parched grassland that surrounded the airfield and the whole countryside looked to be ablaze.

A group of men came into view through the smoke, running hard and stopping occasionally to click cameras. It seemed probable pictures of First Minister Brastic's funeral pyre would very soon be adorning the inside pages of every newspaper in the civilised world.

Well, that should prove interesting, thought Palfrey, dusting himself down and making a laboured effort to regain his feet.

CHAPTER THIRTY FIVE

Several hundred miles from the scene of Volgarian carnage, Greta Fakhri's plane touched down at Istanbul Airport and within minutes she had passed smoothly through customs without attracting any unwanted attention. She hastily beckoned a waiting taxi and instructed the driver to take her to the Old Quarter. Once there, she booked in at a large hotel where she requested a well appointed room with a balcony and a good view across the Bosphorus. If they decided to look for her, she surmised this was likely to be the last place they would choose to begin their search.

She stared unseeingly into the wall mirror, nervously biting her lip as her mind jumped in one direction and then another. The adrenalin surge was long gone and she now felt very alone. She balanced possibilities, favouring one prognosis and then the next. There was an excellent chance the Aspadrian invasion of Volgaria would take place in the next twelve hours; if this was the case, Masum's body would very quickly become one amongst many. There would be utter confusion and it was highly unlikely anyone would give her disappearance a passing thought. Under the present circumstances she was best staying out of sight and this was probably as safe a hiding place as she would be likely to find.

She unpacked a few item of clothing, removed her head scarf and unconsciously ran her fingers through her golden curls. It had been so fortunate that she had managed to locate the gun. She had forced three lockers open, searching for any sort of weapon that might prove of use before she had struck lucky. Who would have thought it of Kefira? She was the one who had always seemed most likely to play by the rules. Who would ever have suspected the First Minister's right hand girl of having her own private arsenal? It proved a point; it was always the quiet ones that you needed to watch most carefully.

She moved to the balcony and positioned a chair so she was facing across the busy waterway towards the new bridge; it was sprinkled with tiny fairy lights, its outline a stark silhouette against a cloudless sky. She kicked off her shoes, lit a cigarette and rested her feet on the metal railing as she stared out across the open water, but saw nothing of the landmarks spread before her as her mind continued to perform contortions.

She had always liked Kefira even if she was a little strange. She was pleased she had decided to stuff some of the banknotes into her locker. What a joy it would have been to see the look of surprise on her face when she opened the bag and was confronted by enough currency to fashion a new future. There had always been a special bond between the two of them; she had sometimes suspected Kefira was the one person who was able to see through her disguise and recognise what lay beneath the mask of powder and lipstick. However, if that was really the case, then clearly she had never chosen to breathe a word to their superiors or any of the other girls.

What an irony that Kefira also appeared to have a secret all of her own; nobody would have suspected her calm exterior was merely a facade. It would be so wonderful if they could sit and talk; just sip coffee, nibble a cream cake and share the truth. She needed a confessor to whom she could unburden her soul; she was sick of the tissue of lies that had become such an integral part of her everyday existence.

She cleared her mind, pulled the balcony doors shut, turned the key in the lock and began to pace the room. She was still too nervous to sit in one spot for more than a minute at a time. Could she allow herself a drink? No, it was far too early; perhaps later. It occurred to her, she had been acting this part for so long she had allowed herself to turn into the character she had been forced to portray.

She felt a shudder of regret; sorry Masum but you really had it coming. The only way I would ever have escaped your attentions was in a body-bag. What was it you always said about getting your revenge in first? You also complained I was slow to learn but as you now see I eventually came to realise what was required to gain my freedom.

She looked back across the room for some form of distraction; would you believe it, she had absolutely nothing to read. She had loved her books. It was strange to consider the probability that the small library she had accumulated in her room was now in transit to the other side of the world. It was a great shame but there had been no real choice; what else could she have substituted for the First Minister's horde of bank notes at such short notice?

She tried to imagine the look on the politicians face as he unzipped the bag and found himself confronting a pile of classic publications. The perfect irony to inflict on a man who appeared to have read nothing but official papers for his entire life. That would indeed have been a moment to savour.

She shook her head in an effort to clear her mind; she was turning into a person as despicable as Masum. No, not quite that bad she hoped, though she could no longer pretend they were very different. What was it he said? 'Do unto others that which they would do unto you; but be certain to do it first'. I learned that as well, Masum; perhaps this time you would even have awarded me a higher mark for the application of your teachings.

God, she desperately needed that drink; just a small one to settle her nerves and enable her to get a few hours sleep. Tomorrow she would feel different; by the morning she would be another person. One who was calm and rational and able to plan the long trip to a new life in a place far, far away. Tonight she was merely in transit. It was a very long journey between one world and the next and perhaps one that she should not force herself to rush. She opened the fridge and selected greedily from the small spirit bottles in the mini bar. The cold feel of the glass container made her tingle a little inside. A lot of decisions needed to be taken but suddenly she realised there was no immediate hurry; a good night's sleep would make all the difference to her ability to arrive at a sensible conclusion. She looked at the glass and it was already empty. How could that be? She had no memory of even putting it to her lips. Just one more then, but that must definitely be the last. Just one more to help her relax and blur the image of the glassy stare from Masum's sightless eyes as his head lolled against the window of her dear little car.

CHAPTER THIRTY SIX

Desmond Palfrey, dressed in a suit recently besmirched by its brief encounter with Volgarian soil, sat opposite Thomas Farlowe. The older man had a large wodge of lint attached to his forehead by a series of plasters while Farlowe was still wreathed in his decidedly grubby head bandage. The bar, situated barely a stone's throw from the main entrance to the Airport, was now packed to the rafters with bewildered travellers seeking sanctuary from the carnage they had just witnessed; while the bar staff scurried in all directions, making a credible effort to fulfil a role for which they were plainly ill prepared.

Unsatisfactory though the situation was, neither Farlowe nor Palfrey voiced any desire to move to somewhere more accommodating. Palfrey's hearing was still impaired, so their conversation was stilted and intermittent as they tipped back bottles of locally brewed lager, while their fellow patrons voiced loud and vivid accounts of the tragic accident which they all seemed to have witnessed firsthand.

Every few minutes an ambulance, a fire engine or a police car would speed past on the road outside and the bar's customers would crane their necks towards the nearest window in case they were missing a significant development. The wall mounted television had started to show news flashes of the disaster and periodically a deathly hush descended on the room as details were randomly updated.

On a positive note, the pair looked sufficiently disreputable that nobody had attempted to engage them in conversation, let alone broach the subject of sharing their table. It was also evident that customers heading for the toilets or the small garden area at the back of the building were careful to look straight ahead and avoid eye contact.

From what little they had been able to glean from the disjointed television reports, the fires at the airport had now been brought under control and some sort of investigation team had been detailed to comb the wreckage for clues as soon as it was deemed safe to approach the wreckage. The reason why the aircraft had suddenly fallen from the skies remained a mystery. No details of the aeroplane had been released beyond stating it was an American Jet and registered as privately owned. It also seemed apparent nobody as yet had any clear idea of the passenger count or the illustrious personage that was the star fare.

There had been a succession of eye witness reports that all seemed to say roughly the same thing. The plane had been ascending normally when suddenly it had exploded into a sheet of flame and dropped dramatically back onto the periphery of the main runway. The television reporter alluded to suspicions of foul play, without providing any evidence as to how this conclusion had been reached. He also repeatedly pointed out that one near neighbour boasted an armoury that included a comprehensive range of ground to air missiles. Even without being specifically directed, it was evident most people had drawn the same unspoken conclusion.

'One for the road?' asked Palfrey. Farlowe, who was too shell shocked to consider a better alternative, nodded his assent.

As Palfrey disappeared from sight there was a sudden buzz of activity. The television reporter was back on the screen talking loudly and waving his arms like a windmill. His enthusiasm was infectious; everywhere people abandoned their conversations and turned to stare up at the television. A man in a long striped apron emerged from behind the bar, shouldered his way through the milling throng and climbed on a barstool to adjust the television's volume control up by several notches. There was now a hushed silence; everybody stared in a single direction; nobody spoke in as much as a whisper.

Suddenly the place erupted. People jumped up and down punching their fists to the sky. There were a series of mighty whoops followed closely by a mass embrace. Everywhere you looked men, women and children were dancing, singing and shouting. Tables were overturned, drinks spilled and cigarettes abandoned to burn small black holes in anything that proved to be vaguely combustible.

Farlowe struggled to his feet at the precise moment Palfrey emerged from the scrum balancing a pair of glasses half full of amber fluid.

'Apologies, old Chap; got severely jostled.'

'What the hell is happening?' asked Farlowe.

'Couldn't you make it out? That twat of a Presenter just announced that the Aspadrian forces are in full retreat. Nobody seems to understand exactly why they suddenly decided to abandon their attack but that hasn't stopped that idiot on the television screen from proclaiming it as a momentous victory for the Volgarian military. Shall we knock this one back and get out of here? From the way things are going this celebration could go on for days.'

They exited the bar and unsteadily crossed the main road in order to retrieve Palfrey's car. The airport had cancelled all flights but there was still a small crowd gathered at the perimeter fence; watching the smouldering embers of the plane with total concentration as though they suspected that at any minute a survivor would mysteriously emerge and solicit their opinion on what had happened. News of the Aspadrian retreat appeared to have already filtered through to the watchers and the atmosphere was slightly strange. It suggested the gathering would be only too pleased to celebrate the Volgarian victory but were reluctant to do so at a scene that had so recently played host to a monumental catastrophe.

As they said their goodbyes, Palfrey shoved a crinkled envelope into Farlowe's top pocket. *'Give that a squint when you get a spare moment; you never know, it might prove of interest.'* And with that they disappeared off in their separate directions, each sweating profusely in the airless Volgarian night.

CHAPTER THIRTY SEVEN

It was not a Thursday but the inner Cabinet of the Aspadrian Parliament had nevertheless felt obliged to ignore precedent and immediately convene an emergency session.

'It's a total disaster,' said Hartz of the Yellow party. *'We have no option but to immediately tender our resignations and go to the polls. There is, after all, a moral dimension to this complete humiliation.'*

'Is there no other way?' said Schtool of the Red party, conscious that he was nursing an extremely slim majority and the unfortunate incident with the night club hostess and the gram of amphetamines was likely to still be fresh in the memory of his constituents.

'At least there's no prospect of a military coup,' said Spanzetti of the Blue party sarcastically. *'After this debacle there won't be anyone above the rank of Corporal prepared to show their face on the streets for weeks to come. It's a national disgrace, Troveski; a national disgrace of the first order.'*

'We badly need a scapegoat,' said Schtool, his eyes circling the room in predatory fashion, before appearing to be magnetically drawn in the direction of Premier Troveski, *'and we need this person to be exposed as the root cause of this entire debacle with the least possible delay if there is to be the slightest hope of any of us saving our jobs.'*

Attention immediately became focused on the Aspadrian Premier, Igor Troveski, who was seated quietly at the top of the long table, cleaning dirt from under his fingernails with a silver plated letter opener. The room instantly descended into a deathly hush.

'What you perceive as a problem,' Troveski said in a voice barely above a whisper, *'is in fact no problem at all.*

Please permit me to share my thoughts.' He rose from his seat, walked slowly to a drawing board attached to the far wall which displayed nothing but a blank sheet of paper and poked if meaningfully with the blunt end of a pencil which had magically appeared in his hand. *'Nobody will have a word to say against us,'* he continued in a light, melodic tone, *'because we achieved each one of our stated goals.'*

'We what?' yelled Hartz incredulously.

'Firstly, we undertook an extended trial of our new armaments to confirm the recent modifications we commissioned had proved successful,' continued Troveski, as if Hartz had never opened his mouth, *'and to our positive delight they surpassed all expectations.'*

'Secondly, as we had been informed a degree of political unrest was fomenting to the north of our borders, we took the opportunity to conduct our training exercise in an area where we could offer assistance to our highly respected Volgarian neighbour, should such a need arise. Some,' Troveski's eyes flashed and his voice rose to a roar of bitter condemnation, *'suspected that we intended to use this opportunity to further our own interests; but we proved to them we are a country with true integrity. As all around this table will be fully aware, violence has never been the Aspadrian way.'*

'But I thought......' began Hartz.

'Please don't,' cut in Troveski, his face screwed into a pained expression. *'I assure you it is in no one's best interests.'*

'The media will never swallow it,' interjected Spanzetti, always the first to follow a line of reasoning and assess its possible chances of success.

'I think perhaps they might,' replied Troveski, thoughtfully. *'There are extreme punishments for both slander and libel in this country and a deliberate misinterpretation of a politician's stated objectives could very easily be construed as treasonable conduct with unrest prevalent on our northern border; and for this*

heinous crime alone the sentence would quite naturally be flagellation followed by a public execution.'

'But you circulated a pamphlet; I saw it with my own eyes,' said Schtool, sounding completely bewildered.

'Indeed I did, Schtool, and you will be happy to know I would be the last to deny the fact. However, it appears our friends in the media neglected to properly study the text. If you refer to the document in question, a copy of which is attached to the back of today's emergency agenda, you will see it outlines the exact course of action which I have just described. It might be argued that the wording is oblique and that the summing up on page eleven, paragraphs three and four, did not struggle to catch the eye; but I am assured by our team of legal advisers that the point was nonetheless adequately articulated. I am also advised that ignorance of the stated fact would serve as no defence if the full might of Volgarian justice was brought to bear........ and let me assure you, Schtool, in a case like this I would find it impossible to suggest a more appropriate course of action.'

Troveski broke into a warm smile as every person in the room spontaneously leapt to their feet and broke into a thunderous standing ovation that continued uninterrupted for several minutes. He cordially acknowledged each of his colleagues with a nod, a wave or even a sly wink; even shook the occasional hand as he slowly sauntered the entire length of the room to regain his seat. He seemed totally untroubled by the outcome from recent events, as indeed was the case.

True, he had failed to achieve his immediate objective of establishing his ground troops on Volgarian soil; and for the time being at least was obliged to recognise that the accursed Brastic had succeeded in evading detection; but he was ready to accept losing those two minor battles if it ultimately laid the path for him to triumph in the undeclared war.

There was a strong rumour that his old enemy had fled the country; another that he had been so depressed by the prospect of Aspadrian troops crossing his country's borders that he had taken the honourable course of action and committed suicide. Troveski considered both of those possibilities as highly unlikely; yet took solace that Brastic's disappearance had flung wide a far larger window of opportunity.

The opening for decisive action had been seized upon by Brastic's deputy, Pasonak, who had swooped down like a hungry vulture from the skies. It was Pasonak who now wore the purple mantle of office; and he who was already firmly ensconced in the Volgarian Ministerial suite of offices. Pasonak who now represented the voice of authority in Volgaria affairs; and from the bureaucratic and military legions that might possibly have chosen to oppose him, there had come no dissenting voice.

And Troveski viewed this as wonderful news; the best news he had heard in decades; news that made him want to throw his arms in the air; to dance and sing. For, not only was Pasonak a man of little intellect, but more importantly, he was an immeasurably less seasoned campaigner than his illustrious predecessor. In terms of diplomatic prowess he was in fact unfit to lace Brastic's boots.

As a consequence, Troveski felt unexpectedly elated at the result of his endeavours; and fully confident that with Pasonak's lack of experience in guiding his country's destiny further opportunities to achieve his dreams would not be long in coming.

So, as he reclined comfortably in his chair at the top of the table, it was with serene indulgence that he looked about the room at the two dozen grinning idiots excitedly celebrating having retained their minor positions on the great ladder of power; for one further thing appeared equally certain. While this bunch of clowns acted as a buffer between him and the voting public, there was little doubt who would be taking the big decisions when the next opportunity to humble the accursed Volgarian neighbour chose to present itself; and next time round he would ensure the Volgarian nation was unceremoniously trampled into the dust.

CHAPTER THIRTY EIGHT

Frank White eased himself from his seat, moved smartly around his desk and warmly extended his hand in the direction of his visitor. *'Welcome to the White House, Eugene; was the traffic on the freeway any better than last time we dragged you over here?'*

Eugene Graveney walked slowly through the doorway. His face was expressionless and he pointedly avoided making eye contact. Although his shoes still shone and the crease in his trousers would have severed a hawser cable, his shoulders were slumped forward and his tie was not precisely centred. An event totally unheard of at C.I.A. headquarters, Langley. Even his hand shake was soft and flabby; completely lacking in its usual degree of vigour. He looked totally demoralised; like a man whose worst dream had just come true; and at a time when that event had least been anticipated. He dragged a chair into position, fixed White with a cold stare and came straight to the point.

'Don't bother with the bullshit, Frank. Word came through on the grapevine you've been told to clear your desk and I guess that makes me the next in line to do the same thing.'

Graveney, having poured himself languidly into a chair, immediately jumped up again and started pacing back and forth; seemingly holding an argument with some unseen adversary who existed only in his head; an argument he appeared to be losing.

He seemed to be heavily involved in a mental battle to remain rigidly under control while at the same time desperately wishing to vent his frustrations on someone or something. He eventually ceased his march up and down the office and adopted a strange leaning position, with his arms gripping the back of the chair on which he should have been sitting; his body stretched forward at an unusually oblique angle; his knuckles shining white, standing out vividly from ham like fists. He fixed Frank White with a hard stare.

'While I was driving over I spent the whole time searching for the positives I could take from this situation. The only one I came up with was that maybe I could apply for a reduction in my alimony payments. Thirty five years of loyal service, Frank, and that's all I could think to have as my epitaph.'

'I'm afraid whatever decision they reach is now completely out of my hands, Eugene,' said Frank White hurriedly, his brain calculating how quickly he could get across the office and out of the door if the need arose. 'As you observed, I'm out of here myself as soon as they can find someone with big muscles and half a brain to collect my pass card and escort me down the front steps.'

There was a moments uncomfortable quiet as White calculated how best to develop the conversation. He realised he was walking on egg shells and needed to proceed with the utmost care. He decided on the most suitable course of action and pushed ahead.

'After the unfortunate way things panned out, the President has taken the unusual decision to go hands on with the enquiry. I can't say anyone in the building is entirely happy with that decision but who are we to argue with the President of the most powerful nation in the world? He asked me to finalise my term in office by helping you along with your deposition. In honesty, I think he feels a little embarrassed by the need to drag you over here. It's just, in the current circumstances, he considers he has no alternative but to meet with you face to face and hear the whole story straight from the horse's mouth. Obviously he will very soon be obliged to stand up and make some sort of statement about what happened and he doesn't want to take a chance that anything has passed him by. He said to tell you he is just looking for the plain God's honest truth; nothing more, nothing less......

something that he can repeat back to the American people hand on heart with a clear conscience......and he wants to hear it no matter how painful it is to tell or how bad it makes this country look in the eyes of the outside world.'

Eugene Graveney shuddered, almost convulsed, then slid slowly forward until he had resumed a seated position. He breathed out heavily while looking imploringly across the office.

'Oh fuck; just pass me a sharp knife and I'll save him the trouble; I'm dead in the water whatever I say!'

'Don't look at it that way, Eugene,' said Frank White injecting an immediate note of optimism. *'There's absolutely no reason to throw in the towel just yet.'*

White, straightway rolled up his sleeves and gave the impression of a man ready to go into battle.

'For starters, let's run through all aspects of the story you intend to put across. Treat me like a sounding board. Talk to me like I have never heard a single detail of this operation; pretend I've been in the Betty Ford clinic for the last three months nursing a drink problem and have only just got out of the door. That will be excellent practice for reporting to the President, because, as you can imagine, he never had a lot of idea what was happening down there and, as we are both aware, he's no stranger to the sight of an empty whiskey bottle.

As you run through I'll give you some pointers on the presentation and we can work it up from there. It's nothing to me either way, Eugene. I finish up as soon as they can draft in a replacement and between you and me, that isn't going to cause me to lose too much sleep. I've had a better run than most and it will give me a chance to spend more time with Betty May and the kids. I've hardly got to see them over the last couple of years, the way things have been piling up down here.

Right, let's start at the very beginning and remember, Eugene, do not hold anything back. Just tell it the way it really happened and maybe we can figure out a way for you to scrape out of this without getting hung out to dry.'

'Do you really think there's a chance of me saving my job?' asked Graveney, immediately looking a good deal happier. 'Well, I guess if that's the way you want to play it we should probably start with the German, Schuster; Heindrich Schuster had been on our books since........'

'Eugene, excuse me interrupting but I think it's probably important that you have no knowledge of a German called Schuster. I certainly made a point of never referencing Schuster when I talked to the President and in consequence the President has no knowledge of Schuster's existence. If you take my advice, you will forget Herr Schuster ever existed because the man spelled trouble with a capital T. We might think we have a good idea of what Schuster did or what he didn't do but we don't know anything for sure. Things you don't know have a habit of coming back to bite you in the ass; so in my opinion any reference to the German would be a big mistake. Are you reading my lips? Don't open doors that are better left closed and bolted.'

Right, Eugene, if we are now fully agreed it's expedient to omit any reference to our friend Schuster, then let's start afresh. Go right back to the very beginning so you get a feel for the style that you want to put across. Start from the word go. Think of some sort of introduction to lead you in. Hey, I've got an idea; start by explaining the code name you used for the operation.'

'It was called 'Operation Lemon', Frank. It was a sort of in joke, because a lot of the guys thought when we got kicked out of Volgaria it left a sour taste in our mouth.'

'Now, that's very good, Eugene; highly amusing. I'm laughing at it on the inside, right this minute......but I'm not entirely confident the President will pick up on humour of that sort. My suggestion would be to maybe not mention it was intended as a joke; in which case you will be pretty safe in assuming it will pass clean over the President's head. All in all, Eugene, I would advise against using humour when you are talking with the main man. Don't get me wrong, he'll be fine if you fall over a carpet or tread on a nail or something. He's good with the demonstrative sort of stuff. Show him a cartoon and he's like a kid with a stick of candy, but it's wise to avoid anything that could be categorised as 'deep'. He's not what you would call a sophisticated man, Eugene, and if he see's anyone laughing he usually assumes they are laughing at him. He's a bit paranoid in that respect; something to do with his childhood the psychiatrists say. The rest of his family are all highly intelligent, so we've been told, and probably that didn't help. Anyway, all in all, I think it would be best just to avoid humour altogether; unless you feel you have been forced into a corner, that is, and there's no other alternative.'

'Right, I've got that noted.....no humour. Frank, is the President aware of the history of Volgaria; does he know how we got stitched up with the expulsion of our survey team?'

'To be honest, Eugene, the answer to that question is probably, no. Presidents don't like bad news and so they tend to expel it from their memories as quickly as is humanly possible. A bit like they dispense with Senior Aides like me who bring them lots of negative feedback about operations that didn't work out the way they hoped they would. I guess it's a sort of defence mechanism. If you assume the President knows nothing about pretty much anything then you are usually right on the money. I would use that as my standard fallback position during the entire interview if I were in your shoes.'

'So should I start by outlining the history of the place and how that led into what went down?'

'No, I wouldn't do that. The President's not great with geography and a lot of strange names will only serve to confuse him. He threatened to bomb Iraq last year when he got it confused with Iran. It took me a long while to convince him we had already bombed the shit out of Iraq and there wasn't really enough of it left to make it worth us wasting our time going halfway round the world to do the same thing again; especially as the Russians had pretty

186

much beaten us to the punch this time around. No, all in all, I think it is probably best to scout around geography altogether if that is at all possible.'

'OK, Frank I'll try to work it from a different angle......see if this sounds better..........after we got kicked out of Volgaria we kept a close watch on the country, looking for an opening that would enable us to break back in. The head of state down there was a guy called Brastic. A hard nose from the old school who didn't make a lot of mistakes; so we concentrated our efforts on building a strong team with knowledge of the area and its customs, and waited for an opportunity to present itself. We didn't have any specific plan in mind so we cast our net pretty wide and along the way we picked up a minor official from the British Embassy who had a drink problem and a chip on his shoulder half a mile wide. He provided us with the odd news story and bits of gossip and we fed him enough money so he could live the lifestyle he had been looking for, rather than the one he could actually finance from his own pay packet.'

'Let me stop you there, Eugene; it's possible the President will question why we were bribing a bureaucrat who works for one of our closest allies?'

'As you are aware, Frank, in this sort of scenario you are obliged to take pretty much anything that comes along. Having no Embassy over there we were for the most part flying by the seat of our pants; odd bits of data were considered better than no data at all.

Anyway this Brit, Palfrey they called him, worked out that the better the quality of his information, the better he is going to get paid; and pretty soon he takes it upon himself to recruit an engineer working on the mining site itself. Well, from that point the grade of the stuff he brought to the table improved no end. It even got to the stage where we were able to feed in questions concerning specific areas of interest, and start receiving back useful replies.'

'Why didn't we approach the engineer direct and cut out the middle man.'

'Palfrey isn't an idiot, Frank. He kept the identity of the golden goose very close to his chest......and there was another problem. The contact was never made aware there was any U.S. involvement; he thought the stuff he was feeding back to Palfrey was going exclusively to his own side.'

'I'm not sure the President is going to like that, Eugene. He's very big on telling the truth and shaming the Devil. Something to do with his Quaker upbringing I think. Scares the shit out of us on the fourth floor, I can tell you, though we try not to let it show. I think it might be a good idea for you to dispense with the Brit altogether; or maybe you could change his nationality. The President wouldn't be so bothered if he was a Commie or an Islamist......or maybe a transvestite or some sort of deviant like that. Hey, perhaps you could say he was a Chink and while you were telling him that bit of the story you could point at the country on a map; sort of casually, like you were just indicating the place out of politeness even though you knew he would be already aware where it was situated.'

'I'm not trying to tie this up in bows, Frank; I'm just telling you the way it really happened,' said Eugene Graveney, reacting angrily and beginning to sound a bit more like his old self.

'How to present it is something only you can decide, Eugene,' replied Frank White, defensively. 'I'm just a blank sheet of paper; you are the guy who's doing the writing. I can only offer you what I consider to be sound advice and from that you have to make the decision as to what you consider to be the most suitable course of action. I'm just saying, if I were in your shoes I definitely wouldn't go with a Brit. The President has a good idea where England is and that is never a good way to get the party started.'

'Can we come back to that point a bit later Frank; I'm beginning to lose my way with all these interruptions.......well a couple of months back we get word, via this guy Palfrey, that his contact had been asked by the local militia to help with a plan to arrest a bunch of Aspadrians. Aspadria is a country......'

'Eugene, it is best not to go there. Just give the impression that everybody in the room knows where Aspadria is and most likely the President won't ask about it, in case it makes him look stupid. As I have tried to make clear, Geography is not the President's strong point. He views world issues in terms of 'should we consider nuking them or are they just looking for another hand out.' He's a simple man and he makes simple decisions based almost entirely on gut instinct; but given his vast limitations that's probably the most appropriate way for him to go. It's far too easy to overcomplicate this type of issue; having too deep an understanding of the facts would only serve to loosen his grip on what he already finds a very greasy stick.'

'Right, O.K.......I'm afraid from here it gets a little complicated, so bear with me. As far as we were able to gather, the operation was originally devised to act as a final notch on First Minister Brastic's bedpost, before he disappeared off into retirement. He ordered the Volgarian Militia to hit gangs of Aspadrians, while pretending to be commanded by C.I.A. Agents. The participants in this charade were mainly Canadian and U.S. Nationals working at the mining sites who were looking to earn a few extra bucks on the side. The idea was, Aspadria wouldn't kick up a fuss over their citizens being targeted if they thought the C.I.A. was directing the operation. This concept proved fatally flawed. They did just the opposite. The question we should be asking ourselves is why did that happen, but I'm beginning to wonder if we will ever find the time to get interested in doing something that might finish up proving productive.'

'Just a point here, Eugene; the President takes a very dim view of sarcasm so you might want to rethink the last part of your statement. To be honest it's doubtful if he will understand what you mean but in your shoes I wouldn't be the one to take that chance.

Which leads me on rather neatly to something else you should keep to the back of your mind while you are speaking; were you aware the President suffers from Concentration Deficit syndrome? In that last couple of sentences you mentioned a number of things that a highly intelligent man would struggle to comprehend. Please focus on the fact this is the President of the United States you are addressing. I'm afraid you will have to pitch the ball a lot nearer the bat if you want him to have any understanding at all of what you are talking about. Also, with a condition like the President's you need to remain constantly aware his concentration span is unlikely to last longer than fifteen minutes; and it's quite probable you could lose meaningful contact after as little as ten if he's having one of his bad day or there's something he wants to watch on one of the daytime television channels.'

'Got that, I'll make a note to simplify things down, as far as they will go. Right, this was the point in the story where the coach carrying the men from the mining plant was bombed and disappeared over the cliff. As you will remember, there was a total loss of life apart from the driver and he died subsequently, in suspicious circumstances, while under interrogation by the Volgarian authorities.'

'Let me stop you there, Eugene. I think it's extremely important that you edit out ancillary information that will only serve to confuse matters rather than help to clarify them. I can see no good reason to mention the bomb. The men simply died in a coach wreck. Whether their deaths were due to unforeseen negligence or they were victims of an appalling atrocity isn't really our concern; either way, nothing is going to bring them back. Also, as the driver ended up dead fairly shortly afterwards, it seems pointless *to me to treat him as a separate issue. Why don't we just have the driver dying in the coach crash as well and keep things nice and tidy? This will have the additional advantage that it will make it completely unnecessary to address the fact there could possibly have been an Al Qaeda or ISIS involvement. We worked that out for ourselves in case you were wondering, Eugene. You haven't got all the brains locked away in your C.I.A. building up at Langley, you know.'*

'OK, Frank, point conceded. I'll make a note to alter my version of what happened. Now can we just get back to my story while I can still remember what the hell it is I'm trying to say?

Well, the next thing we know, Palfrey tells us that Brastic wants to be lifted out of the country and has put out feelers to the British. By now the Aspadrians are pissed as hell and have a tank squadron stationed at the border so the old bastard probably figured it was now or never if he wanted to get clear of the country in one piece. Of course, Brastic would never voluntarily come to America but we tell Palfrey to try to work it in such a way that he thinks he's going to the U.K. and then we dump him on a secure plane, by which time he'd be in no position to argue.'

'Sounds a bit confusing to me. I can't see the President being able to follow anything as complicated as that and I'm still concerned about the British angle. I can't help thinking it would carry a lot more weight if we could somehow build in a Chink or a Ruskie.'

'Frank, will you please let me get this finished? Thank you!

We forged British papers which were presented to First Minister Brastic by our man Palfrey; he then escorted Brastic to the Airport and handed him over to my team who were operating out of a privately registered Agency jet plane........and a couple of minutes after handover the aircraft blew to bits.'

'Right, if that's it, a couple of questions, then you'll need to take some tough decisions about what goes in the final draft. I have to admit I'm still not comfortable with a number of aspects. Firstly, where's this guy Palfrey? He seems to be the spider in the middle of the web for most of this operation. We can easily extradite him if you think that might help; the Brits are pussies when it comes to that sort of thing.'

'He's gone off the radar, Frank; completely disappeared; we can't find any trace of him. We know he returned to his rooms drunk as a skunk the night the plane exploded but there was no sign of him the following morning. We gave it a couple of days and then made discreet enquiries at the Brit Embassy and they claimed they had nobody on their books who answered to the name. They did however confirm that a 'Desmond Palfrey' had come over a couple of years back with a trade mission and ended up staying in the country. They said he was a bit of a joke and nobody took him seriously. He lived in town with the locals; went completely native except for the way he dressed and spoke. He was also reckoned to be drunk half the time, and they said he only called into the Embassy on odd occasions to use their photocopier and try to get a date with the woman who topped up the vending machines in the Gentlemen's toilets.'

'Perhaps it would be best to pass over Palfrey for a moment. I presume I'm right in assuming the bomb was loaded onto the plane in Brastic's luggage? How long is the list of people with the required access to have made that happen?'

'It proved impossible, Frank; even if we had been working with full cooperation from the natives it's unlikely we would have made much progress. It could have been pretty much anybody who wandered into the Volgarian Ministry. The only thing that came to our attention that was even vaguely interesting was the fact his travel bag was full of books. Looks like our friend Brastic had a real *taste for literature. There was nothing about that in our files.'*

'OK, Eugene, we don't seem to be making a lot of progress, do we? Let's cut to the chase and try to knock out some sort of coherent transcript. Before we start let me again repeat it's important that what we give the President is the complete truth; or if that is absolutely impossible, something nobody would be able to prove is totally untrue.'

Eugene Graveney flopped back in his chair, placed his hands across his stomach and focussed his eyes on the ceiling.

'Frank, I've tried my level best to be totally honest but I'm struggling with this big time. You appear to be asking me to pitch a truthful version of a highly complex operation to a President, who is, to put it politely, intellectually challenged. I am required not to include references in my submission to countries with which he is unfamiliar as they will confuse him. I can't present him with information about how we ignored our special relationship with the British as this will offend his sensitivities; and the detail I can feed him back needs to be included in a concise presentation that doesn't last more than ten minutes to avoid him losing concentration. In reality, Schuster was in all probability heavily involved with everything that went down; the complete drama took place in countries that do exist despite the fact the President has apparently never heard of them; and to our shame we did ride rough shod over British interests. Anyone who can get complex information of this type across to a man with the intellect of the President in a ten minute time slot should be awarded the congressional medal of honour, or maybe even a Nobel prize.'

'Excellent, Eugene, I'm glad you have grasped the basic concept. I did mention it was likely to be something of a challenge, didn't I? O.K, let's clear our minds for a moment and come at this from a completely different perspective; perhaps we are looking down the telescope

from the wrong end; maybe our first task should have been to define the parameters within which we are working. Truth is the President's main requirement, right; but what sort of truth is he really seeking? A man in such high office has limited time and we must work with what little of that commodity he has at his disposal. In order to do this we must edit out peripheral truth because there is no room for it in the equation. This leaves us with core truth which we must cut to size and manipulate into the accessible time slot.'

'Frank, that is total bullshit; if you are saying I need to lie then come right out and say it.'

'No, Eugene, to lie to the President would be totally indefensible. God damn it, this is the leader of our country and probably the most important man on the world stage! The only circumstance in which manipulating the truth could be in any way appropriate would be if it was being done for the President's own good. Even then it could never be condoned let alone justified; though personally I would hold the deepest respect and admiration for any man who was prepared to put the interests of his President and country in front of saving his own neck.'

'Right, Frank, now I'm on message. Just tell me, what the hell it is you want me to say and I'll deliver the speech. By the way, I can't help noticing you manage to remain pretty much invisible in all of this; and you seem surprisingly chipper for a man who will be out of work by this time next week.'

'Between these four walls, Eugene, they wanted a resignation and I offered to take the hit. It's only temporary; I have the President's personal assurance I'll be back in business as soon as there's another student massacre and the media go back to arguing about gun control. He was extremely understanding; said 'I was the sort of man his administration needed in these difficult days' and that 'he would find it impossible to manage without me with an election just around the corner'.

'A safe pair of hands', he said; 'a man of moral stature who he could trust to tell him the things he might not want to hear'. It humbled me, Eugene, I can tell you; and it also gave me a warm glow inside, just knowing I was doing my small part to make this country the greatest nation in the world.

Right my friend, here's a draft of what you need to say; use your own words so it comes over relaxed and natural. Oh, I think I forgot to mention, we discovered that contributions to your pension fund had been understated by $500,000. That error has now been corrected and as for the alimony......well I can promise you that as soon as we sort out a draft of your statement that will get Congress off our backs you will find that the alimony situation will cease to be a concern.'

CHAPTER THIRTY NINE

Kefira listened at the door and checked the hallway before she reached for the phone and punched in a string of numbers. As usual her call was immediately answered by a monotone grunt devoid of any degree of warmth.

'Kefira Haber,' she said.

'Report, please,' came the brisk reply.

She took a deep breath. He always did this; made her feel like a first year student sitting an appraisal. *'The operation is satisfactorily concluded. I am requesting a new directive.'*

'Let us take one step at a time, Miss Haber. First a brief report of your actions.'

'I have already coded and mailed a full report; has it not been received?' she replied impatiently.

'And now I am requesting you to give me brief details so I don't have to wait for it to find its way through the bureaucratic jungle. You know how these things work; it could be days before it finds its way through the system and arrives on my desk. Don't worry about security; that is my concern, not yours. Just do as I am instructing.'

'Yes, Comrade. On the morning following my last debriefing, the Englishman, Farlowe, vacated his room at an early hour without leaving details of where he intended to visit.'

'Would it not have been sensible to sleep with him, then you might have remained better informed?'

'It was not necessary.'

'I will be the judge of that; continue.'

'When he was discharged from hospital I re-bandaged his head. I used the opportunity to place a directional chip and a conventional listening device in his dressing so it would be a straightforward matter to monitor his location and overhear at least part of his conversations,'

she said, endeavouring to keep the slightest hint of satisfaction out of her voice.

'Farlowe travelled by bus and after a short time it became clear his destination was the mineral mine where he was employed, so I used the Ministry car I am allocated and got to the location before he arrived and took up a suitable position near the perimeter fence. I observed him arrive and make his way to an outbuilding where he was eventually joined by a colleague from whom he requested assistance. The device was imperfect due to the range and the fact it was muffled by the head bandage. There was also considerable noise from the heavy machinery operating at the site. However, I was able to hear enough to understand Farlowe's request and anticipate what might follow. I therefore withdrew, moved my vehicle further along the road and secreted it in a lay-by two kilometres south of my original location.'

'This is perhaps a little too much detail, Haber; a little briefer please. I am a busy man.'

She smiled; it hadn't taken long to irritate the miserable old bastard; it was easy as long as you knew the right strings to pull.

'I returned to the site and took up a position from which I had a good view of both the workings and the main Chake highway. Thirty minutes after Farlowe's departure from the mining site there was evidence of large scale activity. A red bearded man who appeared to have some degree of seniority directed a number of large extraction machines towards the roadway at the perimeter of the camp. They proceeded to demolish the fencing and dug deep into the embankment and deposited the loose earth and rubble onto the tarmac. They worked for about ninety minutes by which time there was no banking running along the road for a distance of about forty metres and an enormous barricade of earth and rock blocking the roadway.'

'Did nobody enquire what they were doing?'

'*Yes, a man in a suit appeared to request that they cease their activities immediately and explain their actions.*'

'*Well?*'

'*The men turned off their machinery and entered into a heated discussion which culminated in the bearded man shouting, 'so if you know what's good for you, you'll just fuck off and mind your own business.' After that the man in the suit went back into a cabin and the drivers returned to their machines and recommenced work.*'

'*Then what happened?*'

A slow pace and a lot of detail she decided. He favoured short sharp reports so he could complain they were not thorough enough.

'*I waited until the work was finished and then made a call to a colleague at the militia and requested that she drive to the Lobstock road on the east side of the site to check if it was still operational.*

I collected a digital camera from my car and photographed the scene on the Chake road from all angles. I then drove to the Chake Bridge, on the way receiving confirmation that the road from Lobstock had indeed been sealed in the same way as the one from Chake. When I arrived at my destination I was escorted to the centre of the bridge and entered into a discussion with the Aspadrian forces stationed there. After a short delay I persuaded them that I was not insane and was merely trying to avoid any unnecessary loss of life. I showed him copies of the images I had downloaded and explained where they were taken. In due course some senior officers were summoned and with the aid of the images, I explained how the Volgarian defences had been constructed and how it was now impossible to pass the enormous barricade as the road was completely blocked, with a sheer cliff on one side of the road and a twenty five metre drop on the other; and that whilst I didn't have photographs to substantiate it I was aware a similar situation existed on the Lobstock road. The officer considered the matter for some minutes and then conceded I was probably telling the truth. I made my return journey by car and later by bus. My car is stranded on the wrong side of the barricade and will remain there until the road in reopened.'

'Yes, yes....and your reasoning?'

Surely even someone of his limited intelligence would be capable of working that out for themselves.

'That the Aspadrian forces would not choose to venture across the bridges as there was no possibility of them advancing further than the barricades; and if there was no invasion from Aspadria, there would be no possibility for other countries to engage in an occupation of Volgaria in the guise of an humanitarian relief mission. This action avoided any possibility of the Americans or any other major power having an excuse to become involved.'

'Satisfactory, Haber; I concede your actions appear to have produced the necessary result.'

It must have cost him to say that. She would bet each word was forced out of his mouth through gritted teeth.

'Returning to your original question,' the toneless voice continued with a slight hint of pleasure. *'As a small reward for the success of your mission I have decided you will now be withdrawn from the field in order to undertake a new deployment in the Motherland. I will discuss this matter in greater depth when we next speak but I would suggest you make preparations for an early departure from Volgaria.'*

Kefira bristled, *'But I am prepared to stay. I am now well positioned to further advance my career. It has taken me years to work my way into this position in the Volgarian hierarchy.'*

'You are not required to question the orders of your superiors; merely obey them,' the man continued. *'Have you not considered that you may now be vulnerable? Surely you must concede your relationship with Brastic can only serve to make you a less appealing assistant to his successor, Pasonak?'*

199

'*I think it is more likely he will see me as an ally with the ability to help him feel his way into his new position,*' said Kefira Haber with conviction.

'*Enough, I will hear no more; the matter is decided. We will discuss travel arrangements when next we speak,*' the voice said with an air of finality.

Yes, and one day you will be walking alone a dark street when you will hear footsteps getting closer; then suddenly you will feel an agonising pain in the small of your back, and after you have writhed in the dirt for what will seem like many hours you will consider it a blessed relief when eventually you hear nothing at all. Pleasing though that thought was, it went no way towards solving her current dilemma.

CHAPTER FORTY

The large man in the dark glasses and sweat stained light weight suit walked purposefully down the steps of the plane that had just touched down after completing an uneventful flight from Egypt. He looked up as the thick clouds spewed a smattering of rain onto the shimmering tarmac and smiled broadly. This was exactly as he had hoped it would be. After years of suffering extreme temperature fluctuations a mild overcast day accompanied by intermittent outbreaks of drizzle was exactly what he would have requested from the weather gods that took responsibility for the climatic conditions at Heathrow Airport.

He waited patiently to collect his luggage from the concourse and, that done, headed in the direction of passport control; only to be immediately intercepted by a tall brunette in an anonymous grey uniform who separated him from his fellow travellers and, placing a hand loosely on his arm, gently guided him into a small room with a metal table and two very worn chairs. The room lacked any vestige of character; three walls were totally blank apart from out of date travel posters, whilst the fourth boasted only an elongated, non-opening window with one way mirrored glass. It was reminiscent of an interviewing facility at a central police station, except in this case the glass was reflective on the exterior, and he was the one who had been blessed with something to look at other than himself.

The man was next provided with a large espresso with no milk or sugar and a copy of that morning's Daily Telegraph which he proceeded to casually peruse; occasionally casting a glance at the queues of holiday makers who habitually preened themselves in what was effectively his sole window onto the outside world.

After some minutes he was joined by a thin middle aged man wearing a pin striped jacket and plum coloured slacks, the legs of which were losing a hard fought battle to reach the top of a pair of excessively pointed silver-grey Chelsea boots. The man's wardrobe was completed by a green, designer brand T- shirt featuring a large ostrich with a startled expression; this, quite understandably, appeared to be doing its best to bury its head in shame.

'Good Morning, Mr Cummings,' said Desmond Palfrey, smiling warmly at the new arrival, 'good to see you; and looking as dashing as ever, if I might make so bold. Tell me, do the London fashion houses still pay you a retainer not to loiter outside their better class retail outlets?'

'Hello Des, you appear to have put on a bit of weight since we last met! I thought you told me the food over there was inedible?'

Kevin Cummings glanced hard at his wrist watch, frowned and paused for some moments; giving the impression he should perhaps have been somewhere else at this precise moment in time, but wasn't entirely sure where that somewhere else might have been. He looked at Palfrey again, seeming to slowly adjust to the fact they were indeed in the same room instead of talking on the telephone; before resuming his narrative as if there had been no interruption. 'I'll need to shoot off fairly sharpish, Des. Don't be offended; it's a summons from our lords and masters; God alone knows what it's about. We'll just have time for a quick run through if we can avoid getting bogged down with too much detail. Just to keep you in the loop, you are being officially debriefed by young Goater on the South Bank at three; then I've booked a table at my club for eight where we can relax and cover any......any matters arising from the earlier discussion. Go easy on Goater; he's not done a lot of these and is still feeling his way. We lost Blanchard in the last round of purges; didn't stay unemployed for long mind you; lucky bugger got *himself fixed up almost immediately with a soft option, coordinating security for one of the minor royals.'*

'Where do you want to start?' enquired Palfrey, taking his cue from Cummings and immediately turning to business.

'For now, just an initial statement so I've got something in the locker if I get cornered by one of those bright young things from the top floor; then I'll get out of your hair and let you grab a couple of hours shut eye. The forehead looks nasty, by the way. You had better get matron to take a quick look just in case it's life threatening. Let's make a start. How did you route your return?'

Kevin Cummings seemed almost immediately to forget any need for urgency. He adopted a vacant expression, settled back into his chair and crossed his legs.

'I reckoned it would be at least twenty four hours before the Yanks started taking any serious interest so I went Madrid, Casablanca and on to Cairo. I used three different passports. If they can pick the bones out of that lot they deserve to have me on toast.'

Cummings gave a quick nervous laugh and wriggled slightly in his seat.

'You realise the need to be extremely careful; ever since the unspeakable Blair signed that Extradition Treaty the Cousins have got carte blanche on helping themselves to anyone and everyone who takes their fancy, so we make it a policy not offering any opportunities.'

'Did you get anything out of the files on the 'Kefira' I enquired about?' asked Palfrey, loosening his food-spotted silk tie as he strove to quickly change the subject.

'As far as we can make out Kefira Haber; not her real name we presumed..... but actually it appears it might be. Ukrainian, Jewish extraction from down by the Russian border; the Reds planted her about five years ago. An orphan, K.G.B. schooled, bright cookie by all accounts; put out in the field extremely early despite a rather hefty psychiatric file so they must think she's something special.

203

Worked her way quickly through the ranks at the Volgarian Ministry and in no time had wormed her way into Brastic's inner circle. Ended up pretty much top dog in what must have been a highly competitive pack of hounds.'

'There might be tricky situation looming;' Thomas Farlowe seems distinctly smitten,' said Palfrey, appearing concerned.

'He would be wise to give her a wide berth. The way the story goes, she lost her complete family in a house fire when she was about ten; both parents, two brothers and an Aunt. Pretty horrific, apparently; she was found wandering the streets on the red side of the border shortly afterwards; God alone knows how she got there. I gather questions were asked at the time but they still took her in and enrolled her in a State programme. Why is it we all choose to recruit head cases? Possibly, because they adequately fulfil the needs of the job. Sorry, my mind's wandering. On the subject of Farlowe, what did you make of him?'

Palfrey appeared to have been anticipating this question and answered immediately.

'He's raw but he's good; gullible as hell but he'll soon grow out of that. The roadblocks were his idea; he set the whole thing up from start to finish; nothing to do with me. He didn't confide in me much towards the end. I was still playing the jovial nincompoop so that wasn't altogether surprising. He did well. It's hard to believe he never had the slightest idea what was going on. If you can entice him on board he might prove to be a decent acquisition. How did you pick up on him in the first place?'

'A boring story, and as we are short on time I'll give you the extremely edited version. I was working on a trawl list of third and fourth year University students. Every spring the Recruitment Section present me with details of about fifty names that appear to tick most of the boxes; these I whittle down to a dozen or so that look interesting enough to make it worth popping over for a

chat. In a usual year ten give me the finger because they can't wait to start earning shed loads in the City...........at which point I find myself stuck with the two who I didn't really fancy.'

Farlowe's case was a bit different because I rejected him as soon as I clapped eyes. Firstly he was blind drunk, secondly he was still coming to terms with having lost both his parents in a car accident......which was of course one of the reasons he had been flagged up to us in the first place.....and thirdly, he had already fixed himself up with gainful employment elsewhere, so it seemed highly unlikely he would be even vaguely interested.

Anyway, Farlowe was the last name on that day's listing so I was stuck there with nothing constructive to say to the lad but nowhere else to go. I can only presume that out of habit I waxed lyrical about the wonders of travelling the world with wild adventure waiting round every corner. To be honest I can't remember because I'd already been at it for most of the day. I certainly wouldn't have mentioned Volgaria, though, because I'd never been near the place. At the end of the night I passed him my business card purely out of politeness, waved a fond farewell and as far as I was concerned, that was it; end of story.

The best part of two years later I received a letter with underpaid postage that had travelled three times round the globe, saying the conversation we had that night had changed his life. Apparently on the strength of the rubbish I had been spouting, he had sold up, bought a motorbike and drove the breadth of Europe, before coming to grief courtesy of a Volgarian pothole.

The rest you know; when he was discharged from hospital he walked up the road and got himself fixed up with a job. When I received his letter I couldn't see a lot harm in passing him on to you on the off chance he might prove in some way useful; glad it all worked out for the best.'

'Weird the way things come to pass; sometimes it seems like it's all preordained,' said Palfrey whimsically. *'What*

are the Americans up to apart from trying to find out where the hell I've got to?'

'To be honest, the last day or so things have gone terribly quiet. When an operation goes tits up that side of the water they like to have a moment's reflection before they appoint somebody to carry the can. It doesn't actually matter if it's the right person or not; just as long as someone is prepared to bend over and take six across the rear end. I hear Frank White's been appointed to go down the tubes for this one and there's a strong rumour Eugene Graveney from the C.I.A. won't be far behind him. It's a cultural thing I suppose; well as long as it makes them happy.........look I'll need to get moving in a minute, so we had better get back to business; tell me about Brastic and the bomb.'

Palfrey refused to be hurried; *'rush the Agent and see if he manages to trip himself up'* was in the later pages of the Ministry's debriefing handout, and he had attended ten days out of a two week course covering that and a variety of other conjoined subjects several years previously. In consequence, he made a point of deliberately pausing to compose himself before beginning to speak.

'Brastic only took two cases when he went for the plane. One full of clothes and the other packed with a library of bloody books!'

'Books?' enquired Cummings in disbelief.

Palfrey nodded in confirmation. *'Everything but the Encyclopaedia Britannica; sadly, no sign of the loose change he must have accumulated under his bed. I assume that had already found its way to a Swiss bank or an offshore like the Bahamas.'*

Cummings shook his head as if still unable to believe what he had been told. *'Books? Did you check if they were first editions?'*

Palfrey ignored his inquisitor's enquiry and pushed on.

'Brastic asked me to help with loading his gear into the car and I had a brief opportunity to check his bags. I found the bomb in about two seconds flat. It was packed in with

his clothes; appeared to be triggered by an extremely unsophisticated timer and set to go bang about an hour and a half after take-off; by which time, one assumes, the plane would have been flying somewhere over the mid Atlantic. I wasn't sure what to do. The detonator was obviously Heath Robinson and I was frightened to fiddle with the thing in case it was unstable and blew me to pieces. In the end I just left it where it was; even if I had wanted to draw attention to my discovery it would have been difficult to explain what I was doing rifling through the First Minister's travel luggage.'

'Keep going.' said Cummings, now seeming to be paying marked attention to every word.

Palfrey again took his time before continuing. *'By the time we were ready to leave the Embassy I had thought things through. I explained to Brastic the need for special care in his last hours on Volgarian soil, especially as an invasion was likely to take place any time soon. I then proceeded to spend an age checking the car; feeling under seats and shining a torch into every possible nook and cranny; you know the drill. Once we were on the road I drove as slowly as was humanly possible, selecting the worst lane at every interchange; and by the time we eventually arrived at the Airport we were sufficiently late that the plane had missed its take-off slot.'*

'What the hell was the purpose of that? With a bomb in the car I would have just put my foot to the floor.' said Cummings, once again paying exaggerated attention to his timepiece.

'I had plenty of leeway. I was much more concerned about the bumps in the road that the time factor. It occurred to me, if our Colonial Cousins were going to be inconvenienced, then it would be in our best interests if they were inconvenienced rather a lot. An aircraft going down over the Atlantic could easily be put down to engine failure, pilot error or whatever took their fancy on the day in question; but an aircraft blowing up in Volgarian

airspace, which with any luck would come to earth on Volgarian soil, would be an entirely different matter.'

'*Fair point,*' conceded Cummings.

Farlowe was now in full flow and speeded up his delivery of his own volition. '*And allowing that the wreckage came to rest on dry land, it would be impossible not to deduce that the crash was caused by an explosion, rather than engine failure or whatever else our friends across the water chose to dream up; and in those circumstances there would certainly be all manner of questions, which would only gain momentum when it was found the plane was crammed full with American citizens of dubious pedigree.....and had as a passenger the outgoing Volgarian First Minister!'*

Cummings pursed his lips then for the first time in some minutes allowed himself a broad smile.

'*Yes, I'm afraid that came to light fairly quickly; we leaked it to the press over there as soon as we knew you had crossed the border. You used to be such a fine upstanding citizen, Desmond Palfrey; whatever happened to you? I suspect our friends from across the water will now find it hard to buy their way back into Volgaria at any price.'*

'*As it happens, Kevin, I was nearly too clever for my own good. Because of the volume of traffic caused by people trying to avoid the impending invasion the plane finished up taking off nearly an hour late......added to which the timer detonated prematurely. As things transpired, it had barely cleared the runway before it blew to bits and I only just escaped with my life.'*

'*Which brings us rather neatly to the question of who planted the bomb?*' queried Kevin Cummings, skipping lightly over Palfrey's near death experience.

'*There are plenty of possibilities but I'm not sure it's a question that will ever be answered. If I was compiling a list of suspects one name near the top of the roll would probably be mine. I wasn't short of opportunity or motive. I hope you've got a very deep burrow available for early*

208

occupation because I suspect our pals from Langley will get a tad over overexcited when I don't turn up in one of their early trawls.'

'It might be safer to poison you, Des. Don't worry if you feel a little queasy over dinner; I made a point of booking the table in the darkest corner; and it's also the one with best access to the service elevator.'

After Kevin Cummings had looked at his watch for the tenth time in as many minutes he waved a brisk farewell and speedily disappeared out of the door. Palfrey remained in his seat for a few minutes more, considering their conversation. That appeared to be the hard bit over. He didn't think Goater was likely to prove too much of a problem. As he was new in the job, it was likely he would be slightly overawed by being given the honour of debriefing a senior fieldworker and end up treating the whole business as a box ticking exercise rather than anything deeper. Stroke of luck Blanchard had moved on. Bit of a stickler for getting to the bottom of every aspect was old Blanchard and a first rate interrogator who had a nose for anything that didn't seem to add up. There was every chance he would have proved a good deal more demanding.

Naturally, friend Kevin would continue to probe a little over dinner but he had known the Operations Controller since their early days in training and he judged it wouldn't prove too difficult to keep him at bay. The trouble with desk jockeys was they wanted the results but didn't appreciate that to get them it was sometimes necessary to get your hands dirty. A crash on the runway had been the ideal scenario and a little extra work to make sure it happened had proved worthwhile, even if he couldn't take the credit he so justly deserved. Being slightly injured in the blast was the nuance of which he was particularly proud. Now, that was what you called impeccable timing. There had been no way he could have known Blanchard had moved on to preside over the travel arrangements for a family of chinless wonders. Questions could quite possibly have been asked, and if they were it was important he was in a position to provide the answers his interviewer would need to hear in order to be fully satisfied. When the pressure was on, a get out of jail card like a badly cut forehead was far more important than collecting £200 pounds for passing go.

As long as the Volgarian inspection team failed to publicise that the explosion had actually been triggered by an altitude detonator secreted in a fountain pen and not a timing device hidden in a suitcase then he should remain in the clear. Even if the news leaked out he would have no great difficulty in constructing a suitably adjusted subterfuge. It would come as second nature. He was a true professional; lying was, after all, what he did for a living.

He had also done as much as he could for Thomas Farlowe. He had slipped him an envelope with contact details for Kevin Cummings and it was now up to him whether or not he chose to use them to his advantage. Strange lad, Farlowe, but bags of promise if he was properly handled; still, that was no longer his problem.

He now looked forward to a very long rest. It would be nice to have a bit of peace and quiet after the turmoil of the last couple of years; and as long as the Americans failed to track him down there was no reason to think his extended vacation had a great chance of being interrupted. Pity he couldn't contemplate getting involved in a bit of stage work while he had the leisure time at his disposal but that would perhaps involve pushing his luck a little too far. The local amateur dramatic society had always welcomed him with open arms when he had offered his services and his performances had invariably been extremely well received. Acting was a great way of distracting yourself from a horribly stressful occupation; and lying was what he did best. Whether it was in an amateur capacity or as a means of earning a living, made little difference to Desmond Palfrey.

CHAPTER FORTY ONE

Kefira Haber made a last, thorough check before vacating her office at the Ministry for the final time. It was a sad parting but sometimes it was necessary to recognise when a big decision needed to be taken and acted upon. She had always accepted that chance would have its part to play in any outcome to the current situation; she equally recognised the role it chose might be perverse in the extreme. On this occasion fortune had allowed some useful cards to fall on both sides of the table; yet somehow her hand had never felt like an outright winner.

She knew she should consider herself blessed that Pasonak was newly installed in Brastic's old suite of offices at the far end of the hall. A more experienced First Minister would undoubtedly have made it his business to ensure a full inquiry into the plane crash was treated as a number one priority. A more seasoned campaigner would also have brought down the shutters and secured the bolts to make certain nobody the investigators wanted to interview were allowed to slip across the border before they had been thoroughly interrogated.

None the less, she still felt fortune had proved less than kind. If Stanislav Brastic's aircraft had taken off on schedule there would have been no problem because the debris would have fallen from the skies far out to sea; its demise inconveniencing only a couple of passing seagulls and the odd shoal of highly confused fish. But because of the unexpected delay the accursed plane had barely cleared the runway before it had disintegrated into a thousand pieces; and this fact alone meant the odds on her continued survival had immediately become drastically reduced.

It was no secret Investigating officers had been seen clambering all over the mangled wreckage combing for clues even before the fire from the exploded fuel tanks had been fully extinguished. Kefira was aware a piece of bomb casing the size of a finger nail could reveal the country of origin, the manufacturer, the date the explosive device was produced.......and quite probably the name of the line worker who had tucked it gently into a Styrofoam filled box before waving it goodbye as it was shunted off in the direction of the despatch bay.

If things had gone according to plan this would have been no great cause for concern; but the fact that pieces of the incendiary device may have been blown clear of the main wreckage meant there was a distinct possibility that D.N.A. sampling and finger printing techniques could implicate her as a person who had come into contact with the warped metal fragments.

Quite naturally, this would have proved no problem if the crash had taken place over the ocean where the plane's wreckage would have been strewn over a wide area; thereafter speedily disappearing deep into its waters murky depths. It would merely have left the investigating team the none too arduous task of balancing a probable verdict of engine failure against an unlikely one of pilot error. However, under current circumstances it bore all the hallmarks of a freshly issued death warrant; lacking nothing but the requisite signature and a suitably authorative official stamp to give it the necessary endorsement of true legitimacy.

Another problem added to the ever mounting pile was the fact there was no obvious sanctuary to which she could speedily retreat. Plainly, she could not remain in Volgaria while there was a strong possibility she would be implicated in the First Minister's demise; but equally, a return to Russia would present its own set of insurmountable difficulties. Alive it was possible she could prove a major embarrassment to the State; dead she would be no embarrassment at all. It wasn't difficult to guess which option would seem most attractive to the people experienced in taking this sort of decision. What should have proved her hour of supreme triumph had quickly transformed into a nightmare from which she found it impossible to wake.

She closed the office door without a sound and walked speedily down the stairs, glancing guardedly to right and left to be certain she had not attracted any unwanted attention. Two lorries were on the forecourt delivering tea chests containing the new First Minister's possessions. Men huffed and puffed as they wearily unloaded a mountain of boxes. Nobody gave her a second glance.

As she headed in the direction of the bus stop her mind was racing. Had her Soviet controller perhaps suspected her involvement in Brastic's death? She might as well face the facts. She could expect no assistance from her Moscow handler regardless of what he may have deduced. The way things stood she was totally deniable and that was the way they would want it to stay. It was even possible they would leak her psychiatric file onto the open market to provide a further nail to batter into her coffin lid. She was fully aware, if the circumstances dictated, Moscow central was capable of almost anything.

In the process of losing a night of sleep, she had reached the sorry conclusion there was no alternative but to be philosophical about the predicament in which she now found herself; perhaps this end would ultimately prove more merciful than allowing the charade to drag on for month after month. It wasn't difficult to see her adopted country was controlled by brainless idiots. She would never have been able to abandon the life she had so carefully constructed and return to live in the midst of those self same lunatics, sharing their food and water, breathing the same air and being obliged to pay lip service to the ridiculous directives that governed their hollow little lives. She had been obliged to do that before her foreign posting and her life had been a pure living hell.

Absorbed in her troubles, she turned her heel in the gutter and cursed under her breath as she struggled to regain her balance. A broken ankle was the last thing she needed. Now was the time to remain totally calm and rely on the icy logic that had always enabled her to brush aside any barrier that had been put in her path. Yet, despite her best efforts her brain still continued to regurgitate images of the past.

She was painfully aware she had never been good at complying with illogical dictates or blindly following nonsensical decrees. She had managed to ignore them in the orphanage and had allowed them to wash over her in her years of training but the current situation was completely different. For years she had been very much her own master; years when she had made her own decisions, conscious that she would live or die by their consequences. There could be no going back even in the unlikely event her view of the future was overly pessimistic. She knew in her heart if she was forced to return to her adopted homeland she would quickly wither away, strangled by the turgid bureaucracy and stifled by the constant need to conform to nonsensical doctrines.

She forced that morbid train of thought from her head and focused her attention back onto the present. She needed to pull herself together and get organised; settle the hotel bill, collect the remainder of her possessions then get out of the country as quickly as possible. She wasn't dead yet and she certainly had no intention of going down without a fight. There were positives to the situation in which she now found herself; she would have a head start on any pursuers and plenty of currency at her disposal. She said a silent prayer for Greta Fakhri as she boarded the bus, but still found herself unable to shake off the feeling of despondency that covered her like a funeral shroud; and in consequence remained totally consumed by dark thoughts for the entire duration of her hot and dusty journey.

When she eventually arrived at the hotel the Englishman, Farlowe, was sitting on the porch with his eyes closed. A meeting with him was the last thing she needed. She contemplated trying to sneak past into the hotel but her pride would not allow it; instead she chose to approach him without making a sound, lashing out at his foot with unnecessary force to gain his attention. He awoke immediately, sprung from the chair and blinked repeatedly as he emerged from the shade into the bright sunlight.

'*I was just thinking about you,*' he babbled, rubbing his knuckles into his eyes as he attempted to regather his wits. '*Did you see the papers? Brastic was on the plane that crashed at the airport and a new First Minister is being appointed. Looks like things could be crazy down here for a while. What do you think about us getting out of the country until the situation becomes a bit more settled?*'

Inexplicably she found herself consumed by a ferocious rage. She had not had a good day and now found herself confronted with this idiot, babbling rubbish into her ear. Perhaps this was a good opportunity to explain a few things she would quite enjoy getting off her chest. It would certainly make her feel better and it wasn't her concern whether he liked it or not. Hopefully it would prove successful in encouraging him to go away and leave her alone to get on with her life.

'*You don't have the slightest idea what you are talking about,*' she scoffed. *You don't understand anything. I suspect you haven't even worked out I lied to you from the first minute we met.*'

'*Actually, I did,*' Farlowe replied in a calm voice that only served to make her feel worse. She noticed he had trailing in one hand a length of dirty bandage and in the other the two red plastic capsules that had performed such excellent service in enabling her to keep a track of his whereabouts.

Right, that was it; if he insisted on providing more unwarranted provocation; she abandoned any attempt to contain her growing frustrations.

'*Listen carefully, you idiot, and I'll explain exactly why you are still drawing breath. The German who planned the arrests was a top class planner; possibly one of the best there had ever been. When this man met his death I was warned not to make any alterations to the way he had constructed his strategy in case even the smallest of changes affected the ultimate outcome. I wanted the whole thing to go wrong so I did the direct opposite. I made minor revisions to nearly all of the German's directives in the hope that what I had been told would prove to be correct. One of the least significant changes was to remove you from the equation........but it was, this tiny alteration served to turn everything on its head. Please don't ask me to explain why, because to me it makes no degree of sense. Yet, undeniably, the fact that you remained living when you should have been lying at the bottom of a gorge somehow affected the complete course of everything that followed.'*

She paused to regain her breath before continuing with a further salvo. She could feel her cheeks burning and rivulets of perspiration forming in her hairline and beginning to make their way down her forehead.

'The planner obviously intended for this country to be invaded and because of your intervention that didn't happen. Does this make any sense to you; because it makes none at all to me? You were a tiny piece in a very big jigsaw. A throw of the dice that it seemed hardly worth the bother to take......and yet for some inexplicable reason what happened was all due to the fact you lived when you should have died. One final thing; just so you are under no illusions as to how things stand; I never had the slightest personal interest in whether you lived or died and despite what you now seem to think, that situation hasn't changed.'

She actually felt a good deal better after saying that, though the revelation appeared to have little effect on her unwelcome audience. He just smiled reassuringly, moved a little closer and rubbed a finger lovingly against the side of her cheek.

'None of that matters. The past isn't important. We now have the chance of a future together. How quickly can you collect your luggage and check out?'

She took a forward step and closely examined his eyes. Under her breath she whispered, 'a future together!' and wondered if it was possible he was dumb enough to have really spoken those words. She tried to think rationally. It seemed only logical to deduce he must be suffering from some form of delayed concussion. That was the only explanation that would make any degree of sense. It was beyond belief that he could have been born this stupid and yet still survived into adulthood. His current condition had to be solely attributable to the recent bang on his head.

Why was it that she found this man so irritating? Quite clearly he was merely suffering from some severe medical condition that the hospital had somehow managed to overlook. In all probability the ridiculous words flowing from his mouth were not his fault. In time, he would possibly return to something approaching normality if he was fortunate enough to receive extensive medical treatment coupled with the transplant of a fully functioning brain.

Yet, despite her in depth analysis she still felt strangely troubled. If she could just hit him with something blunt and very heavy she felt certain it would make her feel a good deal better. That sort of action had always proved the most effective remedy to this type of situation in the past.

Why was it she found this man so utterly annoying? He somehow induced in her strange emotions she had no desire to experience. She hadn't felt as unsettled as this in as long as she could remember. She despised histrionic behaviour and had never permitted herself the luxury of indulging in it. Something was badly wrong and the warning voice from the back of her head that she had learned she could trust was telling her to proceed with the greatest of caution. The solution was obviously to kill him but something was succeeding in holding her back. She consoled herself that it could only be the recognition that this clearly wasn't the ideal time.

She decided it would be only sensible to give reasoning one last try. Taking into account his current condition, perhaps her approach had been too subtle for him to fully understand. She moved into his direct eye-line, stood on tip toe and screamed loudly into his face.

'You cannot be that much of an idiot. Surly you can see there is no possibility we could ever be together. I'm not normal. I kill people.'

Farlowe accepted this news with calm resignation. He had suspected as much and this was the conformation he had been seeking; he reached for her hand and gently rubbed the back of it with the tips of his fingers as he looked deep into her eyes. He hoped this would prove effective as a gesture of reassurance because that was plainly what this woman desperately required. It was quite obvious she was suffering some sort of mental meltdown. Was it in anyway surprising considering the pressure she had recently been operating under? It was now important that he took charge of the situation and put her mind at rest.

Before she could launch into a further tirade he rose to his feet. It would seem sensible to now to involve her in the decision making process. It would give her confidence and in no time she would be back to her normal self. He checked his watch, lifted a hand to his brow to shield his eyes from the bright sunlight; then casting a loving glance in her direction he paused to carefully scan up and down the nearby highway.

'Right, now it's time we got ourselves organised; have you thought of where you would most like to go?'

What did he just say? She stood there looking him up and down, in utter disbelief. On the one hand he was obviously mentally unbalanced. On the other he seemed now to have totally lost the power to comprehend the meaning of anything she was saying. She had gone to great lengths to make him understand there was no possibility of them remaining together, but somehow her words had become lost in translation. There would evidently be no point in repeating the exercise; it would be like trying to teach algebra to a dead hedgehog that was floating upside down in a stagnant pond.

She grasped for some sort of viable alternative; there was plainly no way she could allow him to accompany her on a single step of her journey. It wasn't as if he would be of any use as a travelling companion. Rather the opposite, she suspected. In his present condition he would be little more than a walking liability. Perhaps out of pity for the dim witted it would be kindest to give rationality one final try; she breathed deeply, took her emotions in check and changed her voice to one over-brimming with kindness and understanding.

'Look, I do like you as a person and I understand you are doing your very best to be of help but there's really nothing you can do that will make a difference. I've got myself into deep trouble and I need to find a place to go where I will be safe.....and I need to go to this place completely alone. If I don't it is very likely that in a short time I will be tracked down by my past employers and put to death.'

Farlowe adopted a serious expression. It would be best if she was under the impression he was taking her concerns with the utmost seriousness. He sensed there were already small signs of an improvement. For a start, her voice had returned to something approaching a normal volume and she had stopped screaming in his face. How best to handle it from here? O.K. he knew what was required. It wasn't the ideal solution but he could see no reason why it would not be totally effective. Once she felt she was safe she would relax and all her fears would immediately disappear. It was obvious the first thing he had to do was to get her away from here.......and he knew precisely the best way to make that happen. All it needed was for her to place her complete trust in him. In her current troubled condition maybe that was something of a

219

big ask; but what the hell. He was, after all, the man who had single handedly repulsed the complete Aspadrian army. Sounding confident would obviously be the key. He hastily rummaged in his pocket and came out with a tattered piece of notepaper.

'*Kefira, I need you to catch a plane to France; Paris ideally. When you get there ring this number. Tell the person who answers the telephone your full name, that Desmond Palfrey will vouch for you and that you need picking up as soon as possible. Mention me as well. The people who answer will recognise my name. Now, better get going as quickly as possible. Do you need money?*'

Was there no end to this lunacy? It was apparent she had missed a clear opportunity. While he was distracted she could quite easily have located something weighty with which to club him over the head; with any luck she might even have fractured his skull. What was the matter with her? She no longer appeared to be thinking clearly. Just by standing near her he seemed to have some uncanny ability to scramble her thought process. Now he was looking at her expecting a reply. She had better say something to show she had been paying attention; anything would do. In his current condition he probably wouldn't understand its meaning anyway.

'*And then what happens?*'

Farlowe thought it best to avoid going into too much detail. Just keep her moving along in the right direction one step at a time. Get her on a plane to England and everything would work out just fine. Ideally, it would be better if he hung back and completed his contract, anyway. It only had six months to run and there was a substantial terminal bonus which would come in handy if they were going to contemplate a whole lifetime together. He had contact details for Des Palfrey and Mr Palfrey owed him a whole heap of favours. He had been spying for the British Government for over a year and hadn't even claimed expenses. He would telephone and ask Palfrey to sort this matter out. It was the very least the man could do......either him or that strange bloke Cummings he hadn't seen since that weird night all those years ago when he was still a student. It looked like the pair of them worked together though he would never have guessed it. They certainly didn't go to the same tailor! He cleared his mind and concentrated his full attention on grasping Kefira's hands and dragging her to her feet.

'The man on the phone will tell you what to do. He'll make arrangements for you to be allowed into Britain. I don't know how it will work; just trust me. I know how to fix this sort of thing.'

What in God's name was the imbecile suggesting now? As if things weren't bad enough, he now seemed to be suffering from delusions of grandeur. It went from worse to worse. Perhaps he had a drink problem the hospital had failed to diagnose. She struggled to summon up the right degree of sarcasm but even before opening her mouth had a distinct feeling it would prove to be a complete waste of effort.

'And what will you be doing while I'm escaping to my new life overseas?'

'I'll go back to work at the mining site; resume my job and wait for things to settle down. If I'm back working the people looking for you will assume we have just gone our separate ways and it is unlikely England will feature in their search plans. Then I'll follow you over in maybe six months and we can be together; forever if we decide we like each other enough.'

He was quite pleased with that. It offered a sensible solution and alluded to their future together, while still making it clear he was taking full cognisance of her imaginary fears.

She listened, uncertain what type of expression it would be most sensible to adopt. He made it sound so idiotically simple. There were obviously major advantages to being totally deluded. Maybe it would be best just to smile and agree with him in the hope he would eventually lose interest and leave her alone. At this point in time what she needed most was the opportunity to properly concentrate on her predicament without any unwanted distractions; but the biggest one was standing right in front of her and gave the impression of going nowhere in a hurry.

She frowned at the floor and pretended to be considering his proposal, before glancing up to see what exactly he was now doing; trying her very best to avoid making any sort of direct eye contact. He was sitting in the same position looking extremely pleased with himself; as if having solved the problem he had been set he was expecting her to be happy as well; maybe, throw her arms around him and express some words of gratitude. She shuddered at the very thought. She had no idea what might happen if he got his hands on her and she had no intention of finding out. Why hadn't she just taken the opportunity to club him over the head when she had the chance? All this would now be over.

She concluded the best solution would be to find some method of killing him and have done with it. If she only had the means at her disposal it would be over in a minute. She felt around in her pocket for something sharp but nothing came to hand. She was now in a situation she had never imagined in her wildest dreams; stranded in the middle of nowhere, in the company of a deluded maniac, with no obvious means of escaping his attentions. It wasn't even as if she was in a position to call for help. She swallowed a large gulp of air and resolved that no matter what he did next she would remain perfectly calm.

In order to give herself time to think she got to her feet and paced a little, using the opportunity to peek at the writing on the scrap of paper he had pushed into her hand. Out of habit she memorised the name, *Kevin Cummings*, as well as the British phone number. She noted the signatory as someone called *Des Palfrey*. Whoever either of these people might be, she had not the faintest idea. The message appeared to have been scrawled by a child or a drunkard. She stuffed it back in her pocket and immediately dismissed it from her thoughts.

He still hadn't moved but as she approached he looked up expectantly. She smiled at him reassuringly, before immediately realising she had made a fatal error. He would take that facial expression as an indication of acquiescence. Then what would he do next?

Surprisingly, that smile proved the salvation to her predicament. He immediately relaxed, glanced meaningfully at his wrist and repeated that they should both set off in their separate directions without delay.

Thank God; she was saved. Her ordeal was nearly over. He picked her up like a teddy bear he had won at a fairground, crushed her to his chest and then twirled her joyously in the air before kissing her long and hard. Her head went dizzy and a strange emotion washed over her; one that she didn't chose to trust. She had been anticipating this happening but surprisingly it wasn't nearly as unpleasant as she had expected. It seemed even certifiable lunatics had the ability to do this sort of thing to an acceptable standard.

She squinted through half closed eyes and for a moment tried to see him in a different light. He really was quite handsome and smelled a lot better most of the men with whom she had come into contact. Perhaps if her life had not been in imminent danger she could have taken a chance; she had to concede this strange man had at least proved himself vaguely interesting. She had always wanted a pet without ever having the opportunity. She could perhaps have nursed him back to health and looked after him, taken him for walks and that sort of thing. There would always have been the option to cut his throat and bury him in the woods if he ever became an undue burden.

She quickly dismissed the thought from her mind; in the current circumstances it was undoubtedly the best idea to get as far away from him as was humanly possible. He was unsettling; it was almost as if he was being directed by some controlling hand; like he felt obliged to fulfil some sort of vital, life enhancing obligation and would refuse to be thwarted from this quest no matter what barriers were erected in his path. Either that or possibly it was just down to him having a reliable supplier of extremely high quality narcotics.

She appreciated the way he now acted was probably attributable to a symptom of his condition; but no one could question the fact he was mentally unstable even if that wasn't exactly his fault. Then, as she considered these implications further, a troubling thought elbowed its way to the front of a very long queue. Was it conceivable he was even less stable than her? Now, that presented a truly worrying possibility on which to conclude a thoroughly depressing day and she immediately forced it from of her mind.

Instead she collected her luggage, paid the hotel bill and watched as the lunatic that was Thomas Farlowe walked in a determined fashion towards the dusty Volgarian highway; turning back on several occasions to check she was still following his progress so he could blow a windborne kiss. She had managed to convince him she was capable of finding her own way to the airport which obviously pleased him; probably because it offered him an excuse to kiss her enthusiastically one more time. At least she could truthfully say she had left him looking happy as he waved for the final time before drifting round a bend in the road and out of sight; and now he was gone she inexplicably felt very alone. It was like handing back a large dog that had delighted in wrecking your house the minute your back was turned. It was an enormous relief to return it to its owner but for some strange reason you missed the chaos that it had caused once it was finally gone. She consoled herself with the thought that during their final embrace she had managed to steal his wristwatch; and that at last she had managed to wave a fond farewell to the irrational and disquieting Mr Thomas Farlowe for the very last time. That at least was one tremendous weight off her mind.

CHAPTER FORTY TWO

Alright, blessed with twenty twenty hindsight it was easy to see it had been a very big mistake; but how could anyone have been expected to know that at the time. If she had been even vaguely aware Thomas Farlowe wasn't totally deranged, then of course she would have acted differently. Anyone would under those circumstances, presuming they were fully conversant with the facts. But she hadn't been and that should have brought an end to the matter. So why was it she continuing to beat herself up over something she could never had done very much about?

Perhaps it wouldn't hurt for her to run through one last examination of the circumstances; working slowly and methodically, probing for clues; being sure to miss nothing out. Thomas Farlowe was meant to be a mining engineer, and a junior one at that; not someone with knowledge of how to spirit renegade east European malcontents halfway across the globe when they had eventually succeeded in being a little too clever for their own good. She still couldn't satisfactorily explain how he could possibly have come into possession of this store of knowledge if he wasn't employed as some sort of super international spy; but he didn't look the least like one of those and he certainly hadn't ever acted like one.

However, if he wasn't in that field of work how he could possibly have come to gain the information he clearly had at his disposal was completely beyond her. Had his hesitant manner served merely as a front? Nobody in England had been prepared to enlighten her, so it seemed there was only one way she was ever going to find out. Why in God's name hadn't he just chosen to tell her right out? It would have made everything so much simpler for both of them!

When she considered the matter she was forced to concede that maybe he had.......well sort of; and that she, assuming he was totally insane, had chosen to ignore him. Well, in the circumstances wouldn't any rational person have done the same thing?

It wasn't as if he had categorically stated that he had the power to transport people through well guarded national boundaries with seeming impunity; well maybe he had said that as well, but to be honest when you think somebody is a raving lunatic how much notice are you likely to take of anything they say?

Anyway, hadn't she ended up following his escape plan in the exact way it had been presented? Be it that there had been a brief delay while she exhausted every other possible alternative before she had chosen to do so; and while she was being perfectly honest with herself, only then, when she was down to clutching at straws, with her pursuers closing in from all sides.

This over analysing was not helping things at all. She was useless at arguing with herself. She lost every time. She would have stood a much better chance if Thomas Farlowe had been here in person. There was no possibility he would have represented his case nearly as well as she did.

Nobody could have been more shocked when having eventually trundled her way to Paris and made the telephone call in exactly the manner proscribed, she had been advised by a man with a clipped English accent that a car would arrive for her in thirty minutes precisely and could she make sure she was ready and packed. Even then she had fully expected something to go horribly wrong, right up until the moment her vehicle had been regally summoned to the very front of the queue so it would be the first to disembark from the Dover ferry; before gaily breezing through immigration control as if that sort of thing was only for other people, and certainly not murderous Soviet spies escaping retribution from their erstwhile employers.

And so it began. The first rung on the long ladder to total reinvention; the first of many small steps that would ultimately lead her to a different life and a startling transformation into a different person altogether. The only problem was, she still wasn't entirely sure who this new person really was or what exactly she was seeking from the very different situation in which she now found herself.

It was now a full six months since she had caught her first sight of the white cliffs and vowed to put the disruption of her troubled past firmly behind her and settle comfortably into a new way of being.

Now, she was of course no longer Kefira Haber. Rachael Singer was a different sort of person; one still learning where she was going, while clearly having no idea what she would do when she actually got there.

It hadn't been easy but she had gradually won them over; the men in the sharp suits and well pressed uniforms with the never ending questions and infinite variety of suspicious frowns. But eventually she had got her way and they had reluctantly accepted the version of events that she had so carefully constructed. And that was good, because now she was allowed a degree of freedom. Even being permitted to do her own shopping and independently make her way back and forth by tube train from her place of work to the smart little apartment in the Docklands area which she was horrified to find she totally adored.

She harboured a strong suspicion that she was still being followed but whoever covered that detail must be good at their job because she had never been able to identify any obvious stalker no matter how much attention she had devoted to the task.

The first months had of course been pure hell. Mr Thomas Farlowe had not chosen to mention that she would be debriefed quite so vigorously. If he had not been aware of what would await her unexpected arrival she most certainly should have anticipated the type of welcoming committee she was likely to receive. The man Cummings, who for some inexplicable reason chose to dress like a circus clown, had been nothing if not painstaking in extracting every tiny detail. It was a relief that the daily inquisition was now firmly behind her because on a number of occasions she had come very close to telling them the complete truth; and if that had happened she would not have been unable to look herself in the eye ever again.

Happily that was now all behind her and could, for the time being at least, be forgotten; and that was also good, because it had enabled her to move on in the process and take up her own little job. Nothing fancy; Russia Desk of course; interesting to a degree, largely unsupervised and in its way quietly satisfying.

For the first time in her life she found herself to be financially secure. In addition to her monthly salary, the currency she had bought into the country had been placed in a bank account under her new name and she had free access to withdraw whatever funds she decided she required for her day to day expenses. Doubtless they would have imposed some sort of limit on the withdrawals and quite obviously each transaction would later be monitored by a pair of unseen eyes, but this didn't greatly trouble her. It was even possible that as they were perfectly aware she now had nowhere to go, they might have decided there was little point in being over vigilant; and on that count she suspected they were perfectly correct.

She had even made a marked effort to adapt to her new surroundings; developed a taste for fish and chips and the habit of drinking at least four cups of tea every day; spoiling her newly honed image only by still preferring a slice of lemon to the mandatory slurp of milk. All in all she was forced to admit she was now perfectly content.

From Thomas Farlowe she had heard absolutely nothing. He was either sticking religiously to his improvised plan or maybe he had just forgotten about her and met someone else. If that was the case who could blame him; she had hardly offered him any great degree of encouragement to hasten to her side. However, if he had chosen to abandon her it would now prove highly inconvenient as she had reached the conclusion that not only was he not totally insane but seemingly not even an idiot. In fact, if she was being perfectly honest, when she now thought of him she got a small pain in her stomach; a bit like unearned indigestion. The pain without the pleasure; for a woman in her circumstances it came as no great surprise.

It was necessary that this man should very soon knock at her door to avoid her being tempted into to doing something stupid. Her mind kept thinking of possibilities some of which were extremely enticing. She knew in the long run she would regret it if she stepped out of line but she had always been impulsive; it was something in her blood.

Moscow would of course fall over themselves for an agent in her position. They would be extremely lenient over any past indiscretions when dealing with a person who had so much valuable information to trade. It was such a pity that when she had considered the possibilities with care she had reached the conclusion they had nothing to offer that could tempt her into re-crossing that sharp divide.

She found the current situation horribly unsettling. Thomas Farlowe needed to come now; it would be better for both their sakes. Was it possible he had understood exactly what would happen when they had their last conversation six months previously? It seemed inconceivably but she could not come up with a better explanation. She hated the thought she needed any man, let alone one she appeared to have so totally misunderstood, but the fact remained there were things she needed to know for her peace of mind.......and if she was being brutally honest she was beginning to worry that he might never arrive. She now went to sleep at night remembering his gentle humour and the way he always wanted to hold her in his arms. She kept his watch on her bedside table and mourned his absence by watching the small luminous hands incessantly rotate as she lay snuggled alone beneath a duvet cover that was easily big enough for two. She found the situation infuriating. Things like this didn't happen to a woman like her.

Had she heard right at their last meeting? Did he really not care about her past? Would she start a new life with no baggage carried forward from the old? A clean slate to be kept pristine or besmirch as was her whim. She had so many questions to ask him; he needed to come now. She needed the answers to those questions and many others for the sake of her sanity; and he was going to provide them whether he liked it or not.

However, already her mind was turning to a greater concern. If she felt this way about the stupid Englishman when his promise to join her might never become a reality, how terrible would she feel if he proved to be a disappointment? There was no point in pretending; in those circumstances the responsibility would lay with her to take the necessary action. It was a situation she couldn't bear to think about but if he failed to correspond to the image she now had firmly constructed in her head it was one she must be prepared to act upon; so in preparation she now kept both a revealing black negligee and a sharpened meat cleaver nestling in the bottom drawer of her bedside table.

She knew this would prove a ridiculous precaution. Nothing bad would happen. She would not allow it. Thomas Farlowe would arrive at her door in a matter of days and they would be blissfully reunited. They would be completely content in each other company. She was determined that would be the outcome; nothing else would prove acceptable.

He would have forgotten the way she had treated him and be consumed only with thoughts of tenderness. They would be blissfully happy together. He had said he would arrive at her side after six months and he was a person who could be trusted to keep his word. A crazy man; crazy beyond belief; a person who would always want her regardless of the consequences.

Lightning Source UK Ltd.
Milton Keynes UK
UKOW03f1108040617

302606UK00001B/47/P